V

M

Bones in High Places

Also by Suzette A. Hill

A Load of Old Bones
Bones in the Belfry
Bone Idle

Bones in High Places

The Case of the Vicar and the Casket of Crumbling Bones

Suzette A. Hill

SOHO
CONSTABLE

Constable • London

Constable & Robinson Ltd
3 The Lanchesters
162 Fulham Palace Road
London W6 9ER
www.constablerobinson.com

First published in the UK by Constable,
an imprint of Constable & Robinson, 2010

First US edition published by SohoConstable,
an imprint of Soho Press, 2010

Soho Press, Inc.
853 Broadway
New York, NY 10003
www.sohopress.com

A copy of the British Library Cataloguing in Publication
Data is available from the British Library

UK ISBN: 978-1-84901-124-2

US ISBN: 978-1-56947-655-0
US Library of Congress number: 2010004131

Printed and bound in the EU

1 3 5 7 9 10 8 6 4 2

Mixed Sources
Product group from well-managed
forests and other controlled sources
www.fsc.org Cert no. SA-COC-1565
© 1996 Forest Stewardship Council
FSC

To my dear friends Julian and Mary Smith
in gratitude for years of mirth and encouragement

1

The Dog's Diary

It's all very well the vicar Francis Oughterard (or F.O. to me and Maurice) being pleased because that goof Crumplehorn has been slung into jug – but *I* know that things won't last. They never do. Not with our master: he's what you might call accident-prone. Or at any rate that's what Florence the wolfhound says. (But then she's a very nice lady and makes excuses for everyone – unlike Maurice of course.) Speaking for myself, I just think he's plain daft. Mind you, I don't mean barking daft like the organist's aunt who's short of a biscuit or two, but what you might call normally so like a lot of humans are, especially here in Molehill. Though in F.O.'s case it's perhaps a bit extra. Still, it quite suits me him being like that, because it means there's always something going on so I don't get fed up. There are a lot of dogs who lead very BORING lives simply because their masters or mistresses are BORING. Take my friend O'Shaughnessy the Irish setter for instance. His mistress is dull as a day without bones, which is why he is always slipping his collar and wanting to play with me in the graveyard. When we race around the tombs or get up to no good in the Veaseys' garden or with the dustbins, the setter says it is like having a shot in the rump with the vet's special tonic. I like the games too of course – but having a murderer for an owner and not someone who does

1

nothing except go to the hairdresser and play whist all day, I don't have *quite* the same need.

And besides, there is the cat Maurice to keep me company. He's a one, all right! What you might call a real sniffy basket. But somehow, despite all those airs and graces, I can't help liking him. Which is probably just as well, because we have been sharing the vicar's home for nearly three years (at least, that's what Maurice tells me – not too good on sums myself) and if I didn't get on with him things might be a bit OFF. But on the whole it works pretty well, i.e. he tells me to bugger off, and I take no notice. It suits us both. And frankly without him – or F.O. messing around – don't know what I would do with myself: BORING!

Anyway, after all that stuff with Crumplehorn and the knife, and F.O. doing a stint in hospital and everyone saying how brave he had been (as a matter of fact it was me who savaged that fat slug – but I know when to be modest), he has been fairly calm. But something is starting to rattle him all the same. You can always tell – begins crunching those gobstoppers nineteen to the dozen, and the fag smoke over the piano gets thicker and thicker. But the real clue is when he starts missing the notes. I've got a pretty good ear, you know – unlike the cat who's got a F-O-B-Y-A about music (fobya about most things, come to think of it), and sometimes just to wind him up I remind him what they use for fiddle strings, and he goes berserk! That's fun, but sometimes he just goes into one of his sulks and sits under the holly bush for hours on end, which is when I get restless and look for O'Shaughnessy or go down to the crypt and listen to the ghosts gurgling.

The vicar ought to do that – he would find it really soothing when he's having one of his frets. And like I said, I think he's about to have one soon. There's an awful lot of dud notes being played (he's normally spot on), and I heard him on the blower the other day talking to that Gaza person – the Type from Brighton. He was getting very red in the face and jabbing the blotting pad with his pen nib. I don't always get the hang of human words but Maurice does, and he explained it was something to do with going to France and digging up some stuff in a crumbling house that once belonged to the old girl he did in. I said I thought that sounded pretty interesting as I like to do a spot of digging myself. But the cat only smiled his superior smile and said that as it was gold and not bones they were after, my own particular skills would be OTEEOSE – at least that's what it *sounded* like, but half of Maurice's words I don't understand anyway. When I asked him what it meant, he thought for a while and then said that the oteeose thing was a bit like me. He seemed to think that was very funny, but I don't suppose it was – the cat's jokes are not known for their humour. Not like mine, which are JOLLY GOOD!

2

The Cat's Memoir

I suppose there *are* other cats who are martyrs to fortune, but for those who have not yet achieved that status I issue a word of warning: at all costs avoid vicars. Humans by nature are peculiar, but vicars more so. I have lived with only one in my lifetime but he is more than enough and I feel I can generalize from that particular. My master's asinine attempts to keep his head above water while juggling with forces even more neurotic than himself are a trial indeed, although not without interest.

A further trial is the dog. But as long as one takes a firm paw he can be managed. As a matter of fact, having the creature as a companion is not without its benefits. One can, for example, chew over with him the details of the day, expounding and honing one's viewpoint. The dog of course invariably insists on putting his own viewpoint (generally at variance with my own and *never* honed), but I can ignore that, and broadly speaking our alliance is congenial.

Occasionally his observations are pertinent, although naturally one is careful not to acknowledge this too overtly as it goes to his head and he becomes insufferable. Nevertheless, he had a point about the vicar ... he was indeed getting het up, and on the whole I am not surprised. After all, with that dubious specimen from Brighton at his coat tails yet again even the most self-possessed might get windy. And the vicar (canon actually – bizarre though that may seem) is far from self-possessed. In fact, one less fitted to eliminate one of his own kind it would be hard to imagine. However, he did it, and we reap the consequences – which are considerable.

Bouncer tells me he finds it all 'jolly good'. It strikes me as neither jolly nor good: the dog himself generates enough drama as it is, without F.O. adding to the theatricals. That being said, our master and his absurd criminal pursuits do provide a certain frisson to life, which, after residing with his victim Mrs Elizabeth Fotherington for quite long enough, I find refreshing. The vicar's injudicious action in the wood rescued me from her stifling clutches, and thus, insane though he is, I owe him a debt of gratitude – which, when appropriate, I show.

Admittedly Bouncer is tiresome; but fundamentally he has a good heart, and I have tried my best to inculcate in him an element of decorum – though it appears but rarely. However, as my Great Uncle Marmaduke was given to remarking, 'Nothing feline is ever lost' . . . I am not *entirely* clear what he meant by that, but doubtless it is of great wisdom and I am sure that by continuing my association with Bouncer the dog can only benefit.

Whether the vicar can benefit from anything at all is a moot point, but we do what we can to monitor his trials and to contain the grosser blunders. However, despite the settling of the Crumplehorn débâcle, both Bouncer and I could foresee just such another blunder looming, and coping with its developments has been fraught with peril. But things seem moderately resolved now . . . although, to quote the dog's inelegant phrase, it was 'a damned near thing'.

It all started with the wretched Brighton Type, Nicholas Ingaza, who had got it into his crooked head that he could exploit the vicar's title to that battered French property which had been left to him by Mrs Fotherington. This gift was far from appreciated, for the last thing F.O. wanted was to be linked in the public mind with his victim – let alone as her principal heir. As detailed in my previous memoir, the embarrassment of the cash legacy had been bad enough, but despite the inquisitiveness of the police he had dealt with it fairly well. And then just as he thought that all financial connection was severed, out of the blue came the bombshell: his entitlement to her château in France with its rumoured Nazi gold.

As I explained to the dog, left to his own devices F.O. would simply have destroyed the deeds, and the tiresome building would have eventually sunk into the ground with none being the wiser as to its intended owner. The problem is that with the Type from Brighton breathing down his neck our master rarely is left to his own devices . . . And thus Ingaza smartly pocketed the deeds, forged the vicar's signature, and fired by the prospect of unearthing gold (or at the very least getting his hands on some profitable real estate) persuaded the vicar that it was in everyone's interests (i.e. his own) to make an investigative trip to the Auvergne for an assessment of the domain – or, as Bouncer would say, 'to case the joint'.

This is a matter I shall return to, but meanwhile there are things to be attended to here in the graveyard: the pursuit of pigeons, mangling those grotesque plastic flowers beneath the Browns' headstone, stern words with the hedgehog and some light badinage with the belfry bats. I think too that the new sexton's spadework needs inspection. I don't know the vicar's view, but personally I think he is cutting corners. It won't do!

3

The Vicar's Version

Elizabeth was at the root of it: Mrs Elizabeth Fotherington, my victim and my persecutor. Persecutor? The word carries overtones of menace and malevolence, and in all honesty I cannot think that either term applied to Elizabeth. Rather the reverse in fact, for she was a woman of nauseating, albeit steely, sweetness. But persecuted I felt nonetheless. It was the blandishments, the patronage, the coyly romantic effusions, the merciless smothering pursuit, which appalled – terrified – and in the end snapped my nerve and pushed me into that fatal act, only yards from my vicarage, in the summer of 1956.

The date and circumstances are embedded in my memory: her outlandish overture on that peaceful shaded path, my eardrums and the wood's silence rent by the unctuous babbling, the insistent pawing at my elbow, a feeling of sudden revulsion followed by numbed detachment ... Then suddenly, with a few brief tugs at her conveniently draped scarf – it didn't take much – the thing was done: noise stopped, the wood returned to its sylvan calm. And I had become a murderer. What Nicholas Ingaza would doubtless describe as being 'overcome by events, dear boy'.

In fact, come to think of it, I believe that is exactly what he *did* say at some point, when later, in a spasm of intemperate revelation, I spilt the whole can of beans. It happened in a moment of weakness (a state not unfamiliar to me), and while the confession was possibly of some psychological value at the time, in various ways I have been paying for it ever since. 'As so he should!' I hear you say sternly. Yes, you are perfectly right – and I mention it less as a defence than as a means of explaining some of the ramifications my act has induced. Murder, like its close companion deception, spins a tangled web. And sitting at the centre of mine is Nicholas – charming, chummy, and preposterously relentless.

If one is rash enough to confide in a disgraced seminarian – high jinks in a Turkish bath – turned entrepreneur of sharkish bent and shady dealings, trouble is bound to ensue. But that, as I have discovered, is the nature of murder: burden becomes heaped upon burden, and things that seem initially expedient sooner or later backfire. In my case generally sooner.

However, it is not simply Ingaza's knowledge of the business that puts me in his power, but also the debt that I owe: for in a moment of crisis during the original police enquiries I had asked him to substantiate a fiction I had been forced to concoct. Without then knowing the full details (my 'confession' came later), he did this with brisk efficiency . . . and with genial good humour has been exacting the toll ever since. Any protest from me is met with the pained, 'But my dear chap, don't you see, it has made my position very delicate. After all, there's a hefty penalty for confounding Her Majesty's law enforcers . . . bad for business, you know.' Invariably he will murmur something about a *quid pro quo,* and with conspiratorial wink sleek his hair and offer me a Russian Sobranie which I accept in silence.

The problem is that the single *quid* multiplies alarmingly. True, I had myself elected the role of assassin (no, not elected – blundered into), but since then Ingaza has cast me as chief protagonist in a variety of his dubious schemes, and most recently as stooge in his search for buried gold in a godforsaken French ruin left me by my victim. This last has been a particularly taxing experience from which I have barely recovered. However, to be away from the crags and vicissitudes of the Auvergne, and back in the staid safety of Molehill, my Surrey parish, and the comforting flagstones of St Botolph's church is a massive relief which even my bishop, Horace Clinker, fails to unsettle (for the time being at any rate).

Although Nicholas had made it more than clear that he proposed we should investigate the Fotherington Folly (as it had come to be known), there was fortunately an interval between the edict and the date of our setting out. Apparently Brighton's art-dealing fraternity was undergoing a lucrative phase and he was engaged in a number of 'delicate transactions' which required his full attention.

I was relieved at that as I had a number of things to deal with myself, one of which was at least as delicate as anything Ingaza might be connected with – i.e. my forthcoming Canonical Installation and Inaugural Address, a nerve-racking event which haunts the lives of all recently promoted canons, stipendiary or otherwise. Fortunately my post was of the latter sort: an honorary one attracting no fee – but thankfully also few duties. Much to my bishop's displeasure, it had been conferred upon me some months previously in tacit gratitude for scuppering the chances of a universally disliked cleric hell-bent on securing the then vacant post of archdeacon. Since the candidate in question had happened to be Bishop Clinker's protégé, my superior had taken a dim view of my elevation. But there was nothing he could do, and in any case, the bishop's own affairs were sometimes what you might call a shade delicate as well, and there had been more than one occasion when I had helped smooth the episcopal path.

For example, his passion for playing tiddlywinks with Mrs Carruthers is something he chooses to keep well under wraps. However, like much that is clandestine, it can lead to moments of acute embarrassment (that appalling business in the allotment shed being a painful case in point*). Thus, irked by my knowledge but reliant on my assistance, Clinker views me with a mixture of pique and resentful tolerance. And as a respite from the awful Gladys, I suspect I represent a half-decent port in an exhausting storm.

The bishop's problems are, of course, less acute than mine, and do not have the threat of the noose hanging over them – though some would say that living with Gladys was a comparable fate. However, all is relative, and in moments of benignity I experience twinges of a wary loyalty . . . But few such twinges were felt when I encountered him in Guildford a few days prior to the inaugural ceremony.

I had nipped over to remind myself of the layout of the pro-cathedral's chancel and choir stalls. The ceremony is an elaborate and tortuous affair and it doesn't do to be seen taking a wrong turn in the prescribed perambulations. I was familiar with the general protocol but thought it wouldn't hurt to 'walk the course' before the day itself. Once I get the hang of things I am all right, but I recall only too well being a raw recruit at Aldershot during the war, and the sergeant-major's apoplectic despair as he tried to cajole me into turning left rather than right on its parade ground. It had been a time of mutual trauma. And thus, still smarting from the memory and not wishing to relive it, I took the necessary precaution.

As it was a Friday afternoon there were few people about, and I was just ambling thoughtfully up the central aisle and eyeing the pulpit from which I would deliver the Canon's Address, when there was a brisk tap on my shoulder.

'Ah, Oughterard,' Clinker's voice boomed. 'Having a little rehearsal, are we?'

I jumped, inwardly cursed, and then assuming an air of casual ease agreed that that was exactly what I was doing.

* See *Bone Idle*

'Good, good,' said Clinker. 'Sensible thinking. I've seen many a new canon make a hash of things. Amazing really. Wouldn't want that, would we?' There was a note of hopeful challenge in his voice.

'Absolutely not, sir, not at all!' I smiled wanly.

We chatted for a while about the ceremony and other related matters, and he pointed out the new hassocks which I dutifully admired. And then, clearing his throat, he said, 'I think, Oughterard, I might say that congratulations are in order.'

I was surprised and could not think what on earth I had done to merit such recognition. However, composing my features into a modest smile, I replied appropriately: 'Goodness, is that so, sir?'

'Yes, it is rather. You see, I have won my half-blue.'

Disappointment and amazement jostled for position, the latter outstripping the former by a good length. A *half-blue*? At his age! And in what, for heaven's sake? I stared blankly.

'Yes, thought you would be impressed. It was the Bracknell Cup that did it, made my mark there all right. The judges were most complimentary.'

Daylight dawned. My God, he was talking about *tiddlywinks*.

'Remarkable, sir. I had simply no idea that they awarded blues for board games.'

His expression soured somewhat. 'Of course they don't, Oughterard, but tiddlywinks is in a league of its own and has long been regarded as one of the more civilized sports – not, I may say, a mere *game*. However, you lead a sheltered life and I suppose can be forgiven for not knowing.'

A sheltered life? That was rich! Nothing sheltered about cultural larceny, let alone the Foxford Wood nightmare. However, anxious to reap the bishop's 'forgiveness', I said brightly that I was sure his partner Mrs Carruthers would be most gratified. To this he replied that Mrs Carruthers was but Gladys wasn't, and on no account

11

should I mention it to her: 'Mrs Clinker has limited knowledge of the sport and even less of its value.'

Since I am punctilious in ensuring that my encounters with the bishop's wife are minimal, I thought the likelihood of my conversing with her on the subject distinctly remote. Thus assuring him of my discretion, I said soothingly that doubtless true aficionados would recognize the honour and that it had surely been admirably earned.

He looked pleased and thanked me, adding a trifle wistfully, 'Yes, it is nice to be appreciated in such matters.' I felt a rare stirring of sympathy and was about to make further assurances, but was numbed by his next words.

'Anyway, one thing at least will please Gladys: we are taking our holiday next month. There is of course the initial hurdle of Belgium and my sister-in-law, but after that we shall be motoring through the . . . uhm, never can think of the name . . .'

'The Ardennes?' I asked helpfully. 'So easy from Brussels and I believe it is beautiful countryside.'

'No, not the Ardennes,' he exclaimed impatiently. 'Myrtle is always dragging us off there; after all these years I know it like the back of my hand! No, we are going well south – to the Auvergne, *much* more interesting.'

I had discovered from the atlas that the Auvergne is a very large area, and thus the chances of our encountering Clinker and Gladys were about a million to one. And besides, despite being in the same month, it was unlikely their sojourn would coincide with the dates of our own brief foray. But despite such rationalizing, the news struck like a blow to the solar plexus, and not for the first time I wondered why Fate had selected me for such persecution.

'Fascinating,' I murmured. And then gingerly, and with winded words, enquired what dates he expected to be there.

'Mid-October. Rather a nice little place by all accounts, a village called Berceau-Lamont – quite high up, I believe. Myrtle has friends there.' She would, I thought. She just frigging would!

Berceau-Lamont – the nearest village to La Folie de Fotherington. According to Ingaza it was a small hamlet set on the lower slopes of a precipitous mountain about a mile to the north of the château, boasting a church and, apart from a pond and some rambling goats, not much else. His description had been uncomplimentary, although if the bishop's sister-in-law had friends living there presumably it must have had something to commend it. However, its qualities or otherwise were now entirely irrelevant: what mattered was that it was in the immediate vicinity of La Folie and that Clinker and Co. would evidently be visiting at the same time as ourselves. Did Fate know no bounds to its cruelty?

I listened to him describing the fishing he hoped to do and Gladys's determination to take her painting paraphernalia. A blanket of gloom descended as I envisaged the likely complications and embarrassment should we have the misfortune to encounter them. Questions would be asked. What was I *doing* there? What was my connection with the ruined château? How *extraordinary* that it should have belonged to the poor lady murdered in my parish! *Who* were my companions? . . . I thought of the boisterous Eric, Ingaza's domestic sidekick with his cockney slang and raucous guffaws; and (with a shudder) of that egregious curé from Taupinière, Henri Martineau, their seedy Gallic accomplice roped in to 'help with the lingo, dear boy'. I could see only too vividly the raised quizzical eyebrows, Myrtle's pursed lips, and the lowering scowl from Gladys . . . and mentally cringed at the prospect.

And then with a flash of horror I thought of Ingaza himself. Bad enough having to explain the other two, but how on earth after all these years was I to explain to the bishop the sudden emergence of Brighton's sharpest and shadiest art dealer? Nicholas Ingaza: ejected from St Bede's (then under Clinker's own administration) for matters of gross misconduct, ex-jailbird . . . and long, long ago at Oxford, the bishop's one-night standing folly. To a man such as Clinker, governed by status and Gladys, such entanglements are best forgotten or at least kept veiled. A sudden encounter with Nicholas and his satellites on a remote foreign mountain top would hardly be good for him. But more to the point, it would hardly be good for me. The fallout would be dire: I should be blamed for everything and doubtless banished to the frozen wastes of the north or packed off to administer some obscure Home for Indigent Clergy – or worse still, to manage a Temperance Mission in Peckham. And it would all be Nicholas's fault! Wretchedly I tugged at my collar and contemplated the Auvergne in all its looming menace . . .

'I say,' said Clinker, 'you're looking a bit tense, Oughterard. Hope you haven't been overdoing things. Nerves probably – I've noticed it before with the new canons: it's the prospect of the ceremony. Gets them down. And then there's the special Address of course, always a fraught business. Still, I dare say yours will be all right . . . more or less.' And with those words of comfort and inspiration, he rattled his car keys and sauntered off to the main door.

I drove home, fed the dog, and with lacklustre energy attacked the piano and the whisky.

The next day the post brought two books for me to review for the parish magazine – *Tips for Vergers* by one Cliff Underdown and *Best Baking for Bazaars* by a Lady Doworthy. Neither excited my imagination, and I dispensed with them quickly in favour of a frantic telephone call to Nicholas.

Just as feared, it was not Nicholas but Eric who answered. 'Oh, it's you, Frankie,' was the cheery response. 'Might have known – there's nobody else what calls us before ten o'clock in the morning. What can I do for you?'

Wincing at his term of address – a recent adoption which I feared I was stuck with – I apologized for my ridiculously early call (9.50 a.m.) and explained that I had some rather bad news for Nicholas. 'You see, Eric, I have just learned that Bishop Clinker and some of his family will be in the French village at the same time as ourselves. It could all be a bit tricky . . . Uhm, in the circumstances I fear he may feel we ought to cancel.' (I tried not to sound too hopeful.)

There was a pause, and then Eric said doubtfully, 'Well, I shouldn't think so – bought the three ferry tickets, he has, and got the documents and all. There's a hefty fee for cancelling, and you know what Nick's like wiv the old spondulicks.' I did know. 'Still,' he went on, 'you'd better speak to him later – after he's had his gasper and coffee. He won't make no sense at the moment.' And he gave a throaty chuckle.

I agreed that that would be best, and was about to put the phone down when a thought struck me. 'Eric, did you say three tickets? But there are four of us – you, me, Nicholas and Primrose.'

'Oh no, old son – just you and yer sister. You don't catch me going orf to Frogland and eatin' bleedin' snails and such – no fear! Besides, somebody's got to stay behind and mind the shop – there's a couple of deals going on here what needs *rahver* careful handling, as yer might say. And if His Nibs wants to go gadding orf to foreign parts, then he's welcome, but I'*m* staying here.'

Well, that was a relief at any rate. But I envied him his resolution, and thought wistfully how pleasant it would be to remain in Brighton with nothing to do but 'mind the shop'.

I sighed and turned my thoughts back to *Baking for Vergers* and *Tips for the Bizarre*.

A little later, bogged down by vergers and bazaars and wondering if it was too early to knock off for a restorative, I was disturbed by a loud thump at the door. It was the telegraph boy, an increasingly rare species, and I knew it could mean only one thing: Primrose.

In her youth my sister had been a rabid sender of telegrams – usually requesting money of our parents or announcing some firm purpose unlooked for by the recipient. In middle age, and a successful artist earning a lucrative living churning out scenes of sheep and churches for the popular market, she has considerably less monetary need. However, though now comparatively sparse, her telegrams still have the power to bemuse and unsettle. And thus it was with some reluctance that I took the yellow envelope from the boy, read it quickly and assured him it needed no reply.

BLOWER KAPUT, it read, KINDLY INFORM RE FRANCE STOP WHOSE CAR WHAT LUGGAGE QUESTION MARK IMPERATIVE THAT I KNOW STOP YOUR SISTER.

I sighed and shoved it on the mantelpiece. Since the French trip was more than two weeks away I failed to see the urgency; but women tend to fuss over these matters and I knew that a delayed reply would only provoke further demands. The need for an early restorative grew more pressing and so I poured a small gin and lit a cigarette.

I was just reflecting what details I should put in my letter, when the telephone rang. Assuming it would be a parish matter at that hour in the morning, I was surprised to hear Primrose's own voice.

'I thought your phone was up the spout,' I said.

'Well, it's better now,' she said briskly, 'some little man came to fix it and he actually got it right. Now Francis, I have a lot of preparations to make and need your full attention. I hope you are listening.' I assured her I was hanging on every word.

'Oh yes? That'll be the day! Now look here, what about the travel arrangements? I assume that we shan't be expected to cripple ourselves stuffed into your Singer. Presumably Nicholas will bring that old Citroën of his. Can't say I like the look of it, always reminds me of the sort of thing the SS used to favour in the war. Still, at least it's bigger than your rabbit hutch.'

I was stung by that, having particular affection for my battered but trusty roadster. However, I assured her we would indeed be travelling in Ingaza's car, and that since Eric had elected not to come there should be plenty of room.

'Well, that's a mercy,' she said, echoing my own thoughts, 'he makes such a *noise* on the telephone! Doubtless he is the soul of charm and wit, but I don't wish to be deafened before my time.'

Primrose had only recently become acquainted with Eric – or rather his disembodied voice at the end of Ingaza's phone line. Indeed, she had only recently become acquainted with Ingaza, to my considerable disquiet having allowed herself to be bamboozled into joining forces with him in a project of joint benefit and dubious good: namely supplying the Ontario art market with fake eighteenth-century pastorals. At the time I had objected strongly and warned her of the dangers of such an undertaking, especially with someone like Nicholas. But my words had fallen on deaf ears and I was gently reminded by both of them that, being a murderer, I wasn't exactly in the best position to give advice on such matters. Which of course was true – but it did not stop me worrying, nor for that matter feeling distinct pangs of moral unease. Old habits and values die hard, and it went against the grain to see my sister in collusion with someone as tortuous as Ingaza.

Was perhaps Primrose herself crooked? No – that's the irony. In many ways she is a model of propriety. Her student days at the Courtauld had, admittedly, been wildly wayward, but she possesses an inherent sense of justice and fair play and is a stalwart, if bossy, ally in times of crisis. She is, however, incorrigibly mercenary; and I think it is this, coupled with an acute pride in her artistic ability, that made her susceptible to Ingaza's overtures. The painting of those fakes was a challenge to her ingenuity, and the thrill of a financial coup a draw she could not resist. Fundamentally honest, she had, I think, persuaded herself that the whole venture was simply a test of artistic endeavour and entrepreneurial skill. In this of course she was pandered to and encouraged by Ingaza ... However, it is not my intention to ruminate upon Primrose and her moral ambiguities. I write simply to record as best I can how the three of us (four if you count the impossible Henri) fared on that questionable trip to Berceau-Lamont and La Folie de Fotherington.

4

The Cat's Memoir

All I can say is that if the vicar and his sister assumed they could swan off to France without my being involved, then they could certainly think again! I am a cat of agile brain and probing curiosity and had no intention of being left behind by F.O. while he embarked on so questionable an enterprise with the Type from Brighton. Admittedly, when Bouncer and I first sniffed it in the wind I had thought the plan was bound to abort, being too absurd to get further than F.O.'s atlas. Indeed, I expressed that opinion to the dog. Bouncer, however, seemed less certain, saying that his bones told him otherwise – his exact words being, 'You just see, the bugger will go and we'll be left.' Naturally I never pay attention to his wretched bones and assured him it would come to nothing.

However, with the Type's telephone calls more frequent and F.O. growing more tense, I began to think that the dog wasn't so far off the mark. It was when the sister started sending her telegrams that my suspicions were really aroused ... and the vicar's frantic purchase of a new French dictionary finally confirmed them.

It was plain that the dog was disturbed by the thought of his master disappearing to foreign parts (having had a bad experience with his original owner decamping to South America*). However, when I told him it would be

* See *A Load of Old Bones*

only for a short time and that I had overheard F.O. arranging to settle him with Florence, he recovered his spirits remarkably well, reminding me incessantly of how admired he was by the wolfhound, and that her nice owners were 'dab hands with the grub'. In fact, as the time drew nearer for the vicar's trip, the more excited Bouncer became at the prospect of his own little holiday – going so far as to ask whether he should apply a spit and polish to his rubber ring. Since the item was ingrained with months of dirt, I said I thought this an excellent idea but it would need a considerable amount of saliva. The ensuing cleaning process was objectionable but useful, for it kept him fully occupied and thus gave me time to consider my own plans. These naturally were both bold and masterly.

Although the odious Crumplehorn was firmly incarcerated in Broadmoor (the lunatic asylum in Berkshire distrusted by humans), I was nevertheless worried that things might yet again prove perilous for the vicar. He is not of a robust ilk, and accompanied by one as slippery as the Brighton Type his chances of being dragged into more dangers seemed distinctly high. There was of course the sister – who might be expected to exert a modicum of control over matters, but having seen her assaulting the sherry and drooling over those dire chinchillas, I could not be too sure. Thus I felt it my inescapable duty to accompany our master on his travels and ensure that he returned, if not hearty (God forbid), then at least hale.

This decision was not such a sacrifice as you might think, for I have to admit that having once been treated to the ramblings of Pierre the Ponce (Bouncer's friend, the toy poodle) re the pleasures of Continental life, I was now tempted to see for myself just how well the other half lived. According to Pierre, the French pilchard was of a quality so rare and exquisite as to make all other varieties pale into watered milk. Of course the poodle is a notorious *blagueur* and such claims are typical of his Gallic showmanship. Nevertheless, I couldn't help wondering . . .

* * *

So, the decision made, I drew up my strategy. Quite a simple one really: I would become a stowaway – both on land and on the high seas! The prospect gave me a frisson of excitement, and despite my usual discretion I could not resist confiding my plans to Bouncer. He stared at me for some time with what I took to be surprised awe. And then he said gravely, 'You'll rue it, Maurice. You'll be as sick as a dog.'

This was not the response I had expected, and for a few moments my buoyant spirits were quite dashed ... so much so that I considered a sulk was in order. But just as I was preparing for such, it occurred to me that with only three days to go before the vicar's departure, time would be better spent in planning tactics. Thus pausing only to tell Bouncer to watch his tongue I made my way briskly to the graveyard, and under the branches of the old yew spent a most profitable hour devising ways and means.

I was interrupted in this by a loud barking, and the next moment the dog appeared tousled and panting. 'I've been thinking,' he announced.

'That's nice,' I murmured. 'What about?'

'Your trip to foreign parts. You had better start practising.'

'Practising what?'

'Mewing in French of course.'

'If you imagine,' I replied, 'that I have any intention of adjusting either my accent or my vocal cords, you are entirely wrong. Foreign soil does not necessitate adopting foreign peculiarities!' He took no notice of course, and hurtled into the shrubbery, rump triumphant and lungs fit to burst. Deafened, I returned to the kitchen; and settling myself by the boiler engaged in some meditative grooming.

This lasted for a lengthy period, but was broken by the arrival of F. O. who, fresh from bell ringing, started to warble and grind peppermints in the most irritating way. However, the interruption was just as well for it reminded me that it was time to reflect further upon my stowaway – i.e. how best to insinuate myself into F.O.'s car and thus to

France. I slipped through the cat flap and returned to the graveyard where, settled comfortably on one of the sunnier tombs, I cogitated.

This went well, and I was on the verge of returning to the vicarage and my pre-prandial milk, when in the distance I saw the dog bounding about. I watched his antics for some moments, and then, just as I was poised to slip into the long grass, he saw me and came cantering over. In some excitement he suggested we should settle ourselves beneath the yew tree as he had something important to say. Travel plans complete and in no hurry for my milk, I said I could spare a few minutes, followed him to the base of the tree and sat down expectantly.

'I know something you don't know, Maurice,' he began smugly.

'Oh yes,' I said indulgently, 'and what is that?'

'It's what I heard some of F.O.'s cronies gassing about. It's to do with London and something they had seen there – something like a story with curtains.'

I pondered. 'Ah, I think you mean a play, it's what humans look at from time to time and pretend they are other people.'

'You mean like us when you pretend to be a giant tiger and I'm the brave wolf?'

'Something like that.'

'Well, this play thing has got a special name, and I thought you would like it because it's to do with catching mice.' He cocked his ears and grinned.

'Catching mice?' I said with interest. 'How do you know?'

'Because it's called ...' He paused dramatically. 'It's called THE MOUSETRAP!'

As it happens I did have a vague recollection of the title. Stem Ginger, the cat down the road, had said his people had seen it – but it sounded disappointing as from what he could make out there were no mice in it at all.

I was about to say as much to Bouncer, but before I had a chance he went rollicking on: 'And what's more, there's a murder in it – just like F.O.'s.'

'Not like F.O.'s,' I observed, 'I gather there are substantial differences. Besides, I cannot quite trace the direction your thought is . . .'

He looked blank and then shook his head impatiently. 'If you mean you can't see what I'm getting at, I'll tell you . . . *I* know whodunit. Heard the piano tuner telling the vicar. And it's a *deadly* secret – has been for ages. But I *know*, you see. So what do you think of that?' He swaggered around wriggling his stern.

'Bouncer,' I exclaimed sharply, 'on no account must you ever divulge that secret. Stem Ginger told me it brings years of bad luck – and there's quite enough of that around as it is, coping with the vicar.' I fixed him with a forbidding glare.

'Hmm,' he muttered, 'we'll have to see about that. I heard F.O. say the thing had gone on far too long and would probably last for a hundred years. I shall be dead by then and won't have told anybody. BORING.'

'Well, you'll just have to be bored,' I snapped. 'I do not propose having my fate put in jeopardy because you cannot keep your mouth shut. So kindly remember!'

It cut little ice. He looked sly, commenced to snuffle at the yew roots and lifted his leg. I gave a disdainful mew and left him to it.

5

The Vicar's Version

As expected, the Canonical Address was mildly nightmarish; but I managed to survive both it and the attendant ceremonial, exhausted but unscathed. And with the whole thing safely behind me I was able to relax somewhat, revert to normal parish life and take stock of things to come, i.e. the Auvergne project.

Despite my dread misgivings, such was the relief at the resolution of the cathedral business, that I began to view this event with a degree of equanimity. Perhaps after all it would prove to be simply no more than a diverting break from pastoral responsibilities. With luck Ingaza's obsession about my entitlement to the Fotherington domain would subside, fizzle out into a whim of no practical consequence. The three of us (four if the questionable Henri ever did materialize) would merely pass an agreeable sojourn in foreign territory not normally explored.

A surfeit of encounters with the cloying Mavis Briggs and the acerbic Edith Hopgarden served to bolster this vagary, and I almost began to relish the prospect of the trip. Mavis had been particularly irksome regarding her wretched *Little Gems of Uplift*. You would have thought that having contrived to get two volumes of those mawkish verses printed she would be content to let things rest. Not a bit of it: enthused by the success of the first two (displays on diocese bookstalls and quavering readings to captive audiences), she was now obsessed with producing a third ... and with me writing its Introduction. This was a burden that began to eclipse all else in its awfulness and made the prospect of the French expedition positively rosy.

Thus it was with moderate resignation that I started to prepare for my departure. This included making arrangements for Bouncer and Maurice to be fed and overseen. The cat, being the more independent and self-contained, needed only scant attention, but I had managed to prevail upon the owners of the giant wolfhound Florence to take Bouncer as a lodger for the duration. They are canny creatures, dogs, and on one or two occasions I had caught him gazing at me with that intent quizzical look which seemed to suggest he knew something was afoot. Fanciful perhaps, but live with a dog long enough and you develop a nose for such things. Maurice of course remained inscrutable on the subject.

Bouncer had not stayed away before on his own and I was a little worried about how he might cope – or behave. The Watkins were a cheery couple and I did not want our relationship to come to grief should the dog cut up rough and be impossible. Thus it was decided that he should be left with them a couple of days prior to my departure to adapt to his new surroundings and get used to my absence. I pinned my hopes on the wolfhound: with luck her placid presence would be a comfort. I also ensured that the guest arrived equipped with his basket and box of trusted toys.

In fact Bouncer took to the move like a duck to water, sniffing around the house, wagging his tail and rolling nonchalantly on the kitchen floor. He then rushed off to cavort with Florence without giving me a backward glance ... which in the circumstances struck me as a trifle cavalier. However, it meant I could now attend to the journey without further qualm.

To my dismay I learnt that our ferry to Dieppe would be leaving Newhaven at crack of dawn. The obvious thing would have been to stay the night with Primrose in Lewes, but the previous evening I was due to chair a meeting of the St Botolph's Historical Society, something which I rather enjoy. Thus there was nothing for it but to get up before first light and drive straight to Newhaven picking up Primrose en route. I had loaded the car the night before, but nevertheless rising at four in the morning is not my idea of fun, and I was not exactly in sparky mood as I set off from Molehill on damp roads and under blustery skies. But I got down to Sussex in good time and collected my sister as arranged.

We drove to Newhaven in silence, at that grey hour neither of us in the mood for chat. But as we approached the dock Primrose exclaimed anxiously, 'I know we've got our passports, but I suppose we *can* rely on Nicholas to bring all the tickets. I don't fancy walking up the gangplank only to have my way barred at the last moment for want of some vital document. It would be most disappointing!'

'Oh, he'll have everything,' I assured her gloomily, 'including the wretched deeds. He's not going to let the chance of gain slip by on account of lost travel tickets – more's the pity.'

'Don't be such a killjoy, Francis. You'll see, you'll probably fall in love with the place when we find it, stake your claim and retire there for life.'

'Oh yes?' I answered. 'If the new police superintendent or that ferret-nosed Samson get to hear of my link with the Fotherington estate I shan't be retiring anywhere except into one of Her Majesty's penitentiaries – or more likely, through Mr Pierrepoint's trap door.'

'Too late to think of that now,' she said briskly, 'and don't be so theatrical. Now, brace up ... and mind that seagull, you nearly ran it over!'

I swerved, and drove into the car park beside the main quay where we were to rendezvous with Ingaza. There was a scattering of vehicles but no sign of the black Citroën, and for a few moments of joyous reverie I had a vision of its owner being confined indefinitely to bed with lumbago or cholera. Naturally, the vision faded, for seconds later we saw his car appear around the side of the Customs shed and drive smartly through the gates into a space close to our own.

He got out and opened up the boot, gesturing to us to bring our bags. I think I had half expected him to be sporting a Breton beret or jaunty Maurice Chevalier boater, and was relieved to see otherwise. As it was, with raincoat collar turned up against the morning dank, and slouch hat pulled well down over his sharp profile, he looked not unlike an effete form of Philip Marlowe. Presumably as a gesture to holiday convention, the customary emaciated tie was replaced by a knotted silk scarf.

It was as well that we had little luggage, for large though the boot was, almost half of it seemed to be allocated to assorted cases of whisky. I recoiled. 'Good God, Nicholas, we can't take that with us. It'll be impounded and so shall we – are you mad? Besides, what on earth do you want that amount for? We can hardly drink it all ourselves.'

'Always handy for oiling palms and wheels,' was the reply. 'Scotch is one of the few British things the French appreciate – it's considered "*très snob*" over there. Now keep your hair on, old chap, it'll be perfectly all right. They never bother at this hour. Besides, we've got the vestments.'

'Vestments! What are you talking about?'

'Camouflage of course. Borrowed them from a mate of mine who's keen on dressing up as a choirboy. They come in quite handy for this sort of thing – a couple of surplices strewn on top of the stuff and they'll think we're a bunch of ecclesiastical outfitters, or parsons off for a sing-song at Taizé. Now, where's your collar?'

'My collar?' I asked faintly.

'The dog collar. You did bring it, didn't you?'

'Yes, but I wasn't expecting to –'

'Well, then, put it on! The boat sails soon and we've got to find the right loading bay. Hurry up.'

I went back to the Singer, shut and locked its boot, fumbled under the dashboard for the collar and clipped it round my neck. As I did so I surveyed the Channel with its bleak skies and sullen waves, and felt slightly sick.

I returned to the other two who were standing in front of the Citroën's bonnet engaged apparently in some sort of dispute. 'But it will spoil my hairdo,' I heard Primrose complaining, 'and besides, I never wear black next to my face, it's so ageing!'

'What on earth's the matter?' I asked.

'It's your sister, she refuses to wear this black headscarf,' explained Nicholas taking it from his pocket.

I stared in bewilderment. 'But why ever should she?'

'Because it will all contribute to the clerical effect. Seeing her with you the Customs will probably think she's a sort of part-time nun. Lot of them about these days. The more sober we look the better.'

I eyed him up and down. 'Nicholas,' I said firmly, 'do not imagine that anyone could ever take you for being sober, either in look or in deed. I think this whole thing is utterly preposterous and I see no reason why my sister should be expected to go around with squashed hair looking like a quasi nun just because you cannot resist filling your car with alcoholic contraband.'

'Exactly!' added Primrose.

He looked at us, slightly taken aback by our joint revolt, and then shrugged his shoulders. 'Oh well, if that's how you feel, we can waive the headscarf, I suppose – but mind you display that collar, Francis, until we're out of Dieppe at least . . . and remember to smile. It makes you look witless.' I scowled, lifted our cases into what space there was, and leaving Nicholas to arrange the 'vestments' clambered into the back seat. I was not looking forward to the voyage . . . In fact I was not looking forward to anything.

6

The Dog's Diary

They've put up a lamp post, you know – at the end of the
road. Only a couple of canters from F.O.'s front gate, and
BRAND new. What do you think of that! I told
O'Shaughnessy, and he said we should have a race to see
who could christen it first. He bet me his leftover bits of
Chum that I couldn't get there before him. Well, that was
a challenge all right. I mean, I wasn't having that setter
sniffing around and shoving his leg all over the place
ahead of me, so I took his bet – and won! They don't call
me Fleetfoot Bouncer for nothing . . . Though as a matter
of fact it's got nothing to do with speed but all to do with
KNOWING the route. Which I do. It's the route that F.O
takes me on his nightly hike around the churchyard, and I
know every inch, corner and paving stone of the way. And
I know about that crumbling kerb in front of Edith
Hopgarden's house that she's always moaning about, and
the way the pavement dips just before you reach the place
where they've put the lamp post, *and* the short-cut by
Tapsell's fence. So for all his long legs, poor old
O'Shaughnessy didn't stand a chance – not a cat's chance
in hell.

And talking of cats, I'm beginning to miss that bastard.
I think he's only been gone a short while – though I'm
not too clued up about time and such things, so can't be
sure. But it's already starting to feel a bit draughty without

29

him ... You get used to all that hissing and spitting and laying down of the law, and somehow without him and the general ballyhoo from F.O. life seems a bit tame. Not that I'm complaining, mind you. Staying with Florence the wolfhound and her owners is jolly good. The grub is first class and everyone is very nice and chummy, and I've been given a new blanket with a really good SMELL. I sneaked over to the church yesterday and dragged it down to the crypt and had a kip among the ghosts. Then I tried to fix some more of those Latin words in my mind so I could tell Maurice when he comes back, but the ghosts were making such a racket it was difficult to concentrate. But I've managed a couple, such as *tua culpa* which means 'It's all your fault, Maurice,' and *canibus gratias* – 'Thanks be to dogs'. Of course the cat will look superior and pretend I've got it all wrong but secretly he'll be quite impressed. After all, no fleas on Bouncer!

Matter of fact, though, I am feeling a bit itchy – but it's nothing to do with fleas. It's my Sixth Sense (the one the cat is so sniffy about): it gets into the bones and doesn't half make me feel funny. Like now for instance. My nose is getting all warm and dry and the fur round my collar has started to prick. That's a sure sign of something odd going on – probably ABROAD where Maurice and F.O. have swanned off to. The cat's all right, more or less (he usually is), but I'm not so sure about the vicar. I think his feet are in it again ... though of course, being with the Brighton Type, I suppose they are bound to be. Only this time I think they're in deeper than usual and things are going to be a bit HAIRY. Mind you, the cat would say I was imagining things. But I know what I know.

Anyway, think I'll trot off now and chew things over with Florence. She is very big and very soothing and talks a lot of sense. I like that. Her owner is taking us both to the park this morning and we shall have a right old romp, and because she's a bit soft will probably buy us some chocolates on the way home – especially if I put on my Orphan Bouncer act.

7

The Vicar's Version

As Nicholas had predicted, the Customs procedures presented no threat and we were waved through without a word – though whether that was to do with my dog collar and 'witless' smile or simply early morning apathy, it was hard to tell. Far more disturbing and painful was the crossing itself: a nightmare journey of churned-up seas and churned-up stomachs.

The principal problem was whether to sit quietly below with a book and steadying brandy or to totter around on deck braced by gale and drenching spray. Neither was congenial: the saloon being hot and full of the wan and whingeing, the deck cold and heaving. In the end I divided my time between both areas, feeling sorry for myself and yearning for sight of the French coast. Of Nicholas there was not a sign. Having boasted on a number of occasions of his impervious sea-legs, he had, I later learnt, procured a space in the purser's cabin where he had remained prostrate and green for the entire voyage. Indeed, it was probably the sight of the driver's jaundiced face and blood-shot eyes that deterred investigation of the Citroën's boot when we finally reached Dieppe.

Of the three of us it was my sister who held up the best. Indeed, to my envy, she seemed to be almost enjoying herself. Chatting gaily to the French barman and exchanging Gauloises and pleasantries with two male passengers standing next to her, she was clearly getting in the holi-day mood.

Returning later to the saloon after a challenging stagger on deck, I saw that the three of them had retired to a table and were playing dominoes. Admittedly, the table was anchored to the floor, but given the circumstances I felt this was no mean feat. Seeing me, Primrose hailed me over and made introductions.

'Francis,' she said, 'do come and meet Mr Climp and Mr Mullion. They live quite near you, over in Berkshire ... Crowthorne, didn't you say?' she asked, turning to the taller of the two.

He nodded. 'That's right – nice little place as long as you like rhododendrons and adders. It's the sandy soil, makes 'em both flourish!'

I smiled politely and asked if they were on holiday.

'You could say so. Got a bit of business to attend to in the south,' said the other, 'but thought we'd combine it with a spot of walking and sightseeing first. I was here in the war, you know. First time back. Be interesting to look at a few old haunts. Though things have changed of course – no more tanks and Jerries getting in the way.' He laughed.

At that moment the boat gave a sudden lurch and the dominoes skidded to the floor but I was checked in pick-ing them up by the sound of a child's excited voice announcing that the town was in sight. I rushed to the porthole, eager as the child to salute dry land. We were indeed approaching the arms of the harbour, and already I could make out the buildings on the quay and in the dis-tance the outline of the cathedral tower.

Disembarkation was what you might call leisurely, and the crawling pace as we edged nose to tail down the vehicle gangway did little to improve Ingaza's recovery from his *mal de mer*. He slumped limply over the steering wheel, mechanically fumbling at the gear stick as might a sort of clockwork cadaver, groaning and muttering oaths at any official who impeded us – or for that matter waved us on.

As we made our slow way down to the quay, my attention was caught by a smart-looking Austin-Healey a couple of vehicles ahead. Sleek and low-slung, its silver-grey chassis made stylish contrast to the more homespun appearance of others in the queue. Of those only our vintage Citroën Avant was in any way distinctive, but whereas that vehicle had about it an aura of subtle menace, the Austin sparkled with breezy elegance.

Primrose too had obviously noticed the car, for she suddenly exclaimed, 'Goodness, look who's in that Austin-Healey. It's the two I was talking to in the bar, Messrs Climp and . . . oh, I can't remember the name, something like a fish or a window . . . Ah, yes, that was it, Mullion. Anyway, fancy them driving a make like that!'

I was also slightly surprised, for they had not struck me as the sort to ride about in high-powered sports cars – though admittedly such judgements are absurdly shallow. Primrose turned to Nicholas who, now that we had negotiated both gangway and officials and were moving more briskly along the quayside, was beginning to look vaguely human.

'What do you think, Nicholas? Isn't it odd that those two should be in a thing like that? They weren't even good dominoes players.'

'Don't know what you're talking about,' was the weary reply. 'You may recall that I have been dying for the last three hours. In the circumstances my fellow passengers are of little account . . . Christ, I could do with a drink!'

'It's only ten o'clock. You'll just have to wait.' And she proceeded to tell him about her companions in the bar, while he manoeuvred us around the cobbled streets of Dieppe having missed the turn for the exit road south.

'Useless signposts,' he muttered, 'give you no warning. We'll have to go all the way round again.' And performing

33

an abrasive three-point turn he shot up the nearest side street.

'Stop! Stop!' I suddenly shouted, gripping his shoulder.

'For God's sake, Francis, you'll have us all in the ditch!'

'Yes, but you must stop, you really must!' He swerved to the side of the road and braked violently, and I started to wrench at the handle.

'Oh really, Francis, you haven't been taken short, have you?' protested Primrose. 'Why on earth didn't you go on the –'

I made no answer, being now out of the car and starting to race back the way we had come. I rounded the corner and stared. The street was empty except for a passing cyclist, crossbar draped with onions; and I felt a fool. Clearly the months of subterfuge were taking their toll and I was having visions . . . And then I saw it in a shop doorway: the dog, lifting its leg against a sack of vegetables.

'Bouncer,' I cried, 'stop that!'

The creature lowered its leg and looked round guiltily, saw me and started to bay.

As always the noise was dire.

'Shut up!' I yelled. He stopped, and with head cocked on one side slowly began to wag his tail. There was no doubt about it, it was him all right – every mark and hairy feature. And even from a distance I could discern bits of the old green collar peeping out from the thicket around his scruff.

I approached cautiously, my mind a whirligig of confusion and disbelief. How? How? How? Why wasn't he with the Watkins and the wolfhound? I had settled him there only three days ago, leaving him safe and smug sucking up to Florence. What on earth had happened, and how on earth did he get *here* of all places? In a daze I called him to heel (an order which for once he instantly obeyed) and together we walked slowly back to the car.

Not unexpectedly we were greeted with consternation and horror.

'How *could* you, Francis!' cried my sister.

'Trust you to foul up the works. That's all we need!' echoed Ingaza.

They seemed to think I was somehow responsible and had engineered the whole thing. It took me some time to convince them otherwise. Then once the fulminating had subsided I suggested I try to ring the Watkins to find out what had happened.

'You had better let me come with you,' said Primrose. 'You'll never cope with the French telephone system on your own.' I was grateful for that and we set off in search of a public phone box, leaving Nicholas to grumble at the dog.

With Primrose's help the mechanics of connection went surprisingly smoothly and I was relieved to hear Diana Watkins' voice at the other end. I was just clearing my throat to make diffident enquiry, when she broke in: 'Oh Canon, I can't tell you how sorry I am, the most dreadful thing has happened. I feel so ashamed. It's, uhm . . . well, I'm afraid it's Bouncer: he's escaped – in a lorry!' And she launched into a long and tearful explanation.

It was a curious tale, but knowing Bouncer's habits I felt a measure of sympathy and could hardly blame his distraught custodian. Apparently she had been exercising the two dogs in the park, and because Bouncer was being so good had let him off the lead to frolic with Florence. All had gone well until she was approached by a fellow dog owner eager to chat. They had been talking for barely a minute, when glancing up she saw a very large pantechnicon parked in a lane adjacent to the park, and into which Bouncer's stern was rapidly disappearing. Before she had a chance to do anything, the driver had walked round to the rear, slammed the doors and driven off. As the thing disappeared down the road all she saw was a foreign number plate, and its doors bearing the slogan: 'Grinders' Dog Biscuits – Only the Best'.

Between tears and gulps Diana made further apologies and said how much Florence was missing her playmate. I calmed her down, said that miraculously the fugitive was safe with me, and assured her there were no hard feelings. I think she went off to have a triple gin. I wished I could do the same, but that would have to come later . . .

Eventually, back in the car with the dog settled next to me and my companions grimly resigned to his presence, we once more traversed the town. This time we managed to find the right route and were soon out on the open road. We had not gone far when a lay-by came up on our right where there were a couple of British cars parked, a battered Humber and, apart from a patched tear in its hood, a pristine silver Austin-Healey. As we drove by I saw one of its occupants hunched over a map spread out on the bonnet. It was the taller of the two Primrose had introduced me to on the boat. The sighting prompted her to resume telling Nicholas of her encounter with them.

When she had finished there was a long silence. And then he said musingly, 'Crowthorne . . . that's a bit of a coincidence, isn't it?' At the time the remark's significance entirely escaped me, but later it became only too clear.

8

The Vicar's Version

Despite the still heavy skies and tiredness from the recent rigours, now that we were actually in France, and un-molested by its Customs inspectors, I began to relax and enjoy the journey. I had not visited the country since a couple of times to Brittany well before the war. Then I was a boy, encumbered by shrimping nets and parents. I recalled that it had been my task to carry the lilo – a gigantic yellow creation which, to my father's fury, I invariably managed to puncture. Pa spoke an ersatz French – loud, ill-pronounced and drawling – a source of cringing embarrassment from which Primrose and I had fled whenever possible. Apart from that and the disputes over the lilo, my principal memory was of the hotelier's two pug dogs, sparky little fellows who answered to the names of Merde and Méchant.

Thus with so brief a memory and experience, it was pleasant to sit back and absorb the wide rolling country-side with its fluttering poplars, grazing dun-coloured cows, lime-washed farmhouses and ubiquitous grey church steeples. Now and again we would pass a wagon of turnips or be waved at by children in navy smocks and ankle boots. At one point I even saw a gaggle of geese being herded by a small girl as if she had stepped straight out of an Impressionist painting ... Yes, I reflected, this was surely better than Mavis Briggs and her elevating

Gems. I stretched, opened a fresh packet of humbugs and wondered if I might now be permitted to remove my collar.

After a while the *paysage* became more hilly and wooded, with a proliferation of narrow lanes and thick hedges, and I realized we were already immersed in the famed bocage. Fleetingly I thought of those lumbering Shermans and the skulking German Panzers ... But before my imagination could take a firmer grip Nicholas exclaimed, 'Oh hell, I've left the maps in my case. Not quite sure about the next bit, I'd better check.'

'Good,' said Primrose, 'I could do with stretching my legs.' He stopped the car and she got out, while he wandered around to the back.

I also got out, released the dog, and leaning against the bonnet lit a cigarette and watched a couple of thrushes as they fought over a worm. I was just taking my second puff when there was an anguished yell from the rear – 'Christ almighty, I don't believe it!' I spun round just in time to see a dark shape streak from the open boot into the roadside undergrowth.

'That's your bloody cat!' he cried. 'Are you mad! What the hell did you bring that for?' I stared dumbfounded at the tussocks of scrub where I knew Maurice to be lurking. There was a suspicious stillness: neither sound nor sign. But he was there all right, watching us, weighing things up, planning his next move.

'I did not bring him,' I hissed. 'He must have jumped in somehow at the last moment.' And turning back to the undergrowth, said in wheedling supplication, 'It's all right, old man, you can come out now. We'll find you some nice haddock.'

Naturally there was no response, and apart from Ingaza's imprecations there continued a fraught silence. I tried further coaxings but to no effect.

'Well, if the little perisher won't come out we'll just have to go without him,' grumbled Nicholas. 'We haven't all day to waste on your peculiar creatures – I suppose that damned wolfhound will appear next.' I cast a nervous glance into the open boot, half expecting to see Florence's shaggy hide, but mercifully it contained only suitcases and the surpliced whisky.

'I think,' I said, 'that if we get back into the car and start the engine he may emerge – you know, sort of pretend we couldn't care less.'

'Some of us don't,' replied Nicholas grimly.

At that moment there was an anguished shriek from behind a tree where Primrose had repaired to answer a call of nature. 'Christ, what's that bloody creature!' She emerged, straightening her skirt and looking distinctly flustered.

'It's all right, Primrose,' I replied soothingly, 'I think it's Maurice.'

'Maurice? You mean your cat? What's he doing here – my God, that's all we need!'

'Precisely,' I said drily. 'Now be quiet and we may be able to catch him.' I dropped to my hands and knees and started to croon his name enticingly.

'Not that way,' Primrose said irritably in a loud stage whisper, 'he was behind that tree.' She stooped down and started to peer into the bushes.

After a few minutes of fruitless searching, there was a call from Nicholas by the roadside. 'Come on. Don't hang about.'

'But we haven't found the cat –' began Primrose.

'You don't need to, the bugger's here.'

We scrambled towards the car. And there he was, sitting squarely on the bonnet grooming his whiskers. He gave us a cursory glance and then continued his task with dedicated attention. Regarding him intently from below, and surprisingly silent, sat Bouncer. I wondered why the dog hadn't set up a hue and cry at the creature's sudden appearance; but there's no accounting for animals and I was in no mood to ponder the matter. Thus I marched up to Maurice, gripped him firmly by the scruff and, shoving the dog in ahead, resumed my position on the back seat. Here, comfortably ensconced on my lap, the stowaway gazed up impassively as I parried the grumbling brickbats from the front.

'Well, that's not going to endear us to any hostelry when we turn up asking for rooms plus a special boudoir for the cat and dog,' said Nicholas testily.

'No need to exaggerate,' I replied. 'There'll be no bother. If necessary I'll leave Bouncer in the car – he's quite good like that, you know. And as for the cat, I shall simply carry him in under my arm with a nonchalant air. No one will say anything.'

'Hmm – fine in theory, unlikely in practice,' said Primrose. 'I remember you trying to appear nonchalant as a boy – you simply succeeded in looking furtive and sinister.'

'Tell you what,' suggested Nicholas, 'we could at least shove the cat into Primrose's handbag, it's big enough!'

'You'll do no such thing,' she cried. 'I'll have you know this bag cost innumerable guineas from Bond Street. It's not silk-lined and initialled just to be a cat-carrier!' Despite her protests, it struck me as quite a good idea and not one to be immediately discounted . . .

There was a silence. And then Nicholas exclaimed, 'But how on earth did he get himself into the boot at all? You *must* have had something to do with it, Francis. He couldn't have hitched a lift in two cars unaided.'

'I've told you,' I protested, 'I know nothing about it. You don't think I'd want to bring him on this joyride, do you? And if we're searched on the way home they will both have to stay in quarantine for months.' I stared down in dismay at the bundle of fur on my lap, and it stared back with unblinking eye.

'That creature moves like greased lightning,' observed Primrose. 'I saw him stalk and ambush a mouse once. Not exactly a pretty sight. But he'd got the whole thing down to a fine art all right. Mouse didn't stand a chance . . . He obviously slept in your motor last night. And then when we were all jawing in the car park with the doors open and messing around with the bags, he must have slipped out, lurked under the chassis, and jumped into the Citroën's boot at the last moment.' She laughed. 'I expect those absurd vestments were a godsend.'

Nicholas gave a whistle. 'Little blighter!'

Conversation lapsed, and worn out by the traumas of the ferry crossing and the animals' charade, I fell into a light doze.

I awoke with a jolt to the sound of a curse from the driving seat and an anguished protest from Maurice. We were on some minor side road overhung with trees and strewn with potholes, one of which the Citroën had clearly encountered.

'Hell's teeth!' exclaimed Nicholas. 'That was near, almost got the back axle.'

'If you went a little slower,' observed Primrose pointedly, 'such hazards might be better avoided.'

There was a pause, and then he said mildly but carefully, 'Unlike your Morris Oxford, this car was not built to be driven at hearse-like speed by octogenarians through the purlieus of Lewes and Eastbourne.'

She didn't like that. 'At least their owners don't harbour delusions of being Fangio,' was the tart response. 'And if you imagine that –'

'I say,' I said brightly, 'the sun's come out over there. You can see it through the branches. Things are looking up – how about stopping for a coffee?'

'Good idea,' said Nicholas, 'and then your sister will have time to check the tyres for punctures.'

I could not see from the back seat, but knew she would be growing pink and formulating some sharp put-down. I leant forward. 'And tell you what, the first one to spot a café gets a *digestif* on me.'

'Good Lord,' exclaimed Nicholas, 'you *are* in the holiday mood. Better make it two while you're about it – we shan't hear that offer pass this way again.' And so saying, he accelerated (smoothly) and passed Primrose a mollifying

Sobranie. For the next twenty minutes there was silence as they scanned the terrain with hawk-eyed intensity.

Eventually we approached a crossroads and a better surface, and taking the route south continued for another couple of kilometres until we reached a small hamlet which at first seemed to have nothing in it at all, not even a filling station. But as we rounded the bend, resigned to pushing on, Primrose suddenly cried out, 'Oh, there's something, look!' On the edge of a tiny square there were a couple of zinc-topped tables, a battered umbrella and a tricolour waving wanly in the breeze. A lurcher lolled under one of the tables, and at the other a girl in pinafore and slacks sat engrossed in a book.

As we got out of the car, I heard Nicholas murmur to Primrose, 'Remember – that's two *digestifs* Francis owes you.'

'Yes,' she replied sweetly, evidently still smarting from his reference to her Morris Oxford, 'one for me and one for him.'

He grimaced good-humouredly, and adjusting his scarf sauntered over to the girl. In fractured but theatrical French he asked for three coffees and a look at the *carte des vins*. The latter was sparse, listing mainly Stella beer and one or two local ciders. The appallingly bitter Cynar featured, as did the French version of Babycham. There were, however, three brands of pastis. Nicholas, with unctuous charm and fulsome gesture, tried to elicit which of the three could be recommended. But torn from her reading, the girl seemed unminded to discourse on their respective merits, remarking with a Gallic shrug that as far as she was concerned they were '*tous la même chose*'. As she ambled off to fetch our order I glanced at the cover of the discarded book: the title read *J.P. Sartre et la Bêtise Anglaise*. I placed it on the other table.

Our order arrived and, despite its chicory addition, we sipped the coffee appreciatively. And then even more appreciatively we diluted the pastis from the water carafe, lit cigarettes and took our ease in the now warm sun.

'Hmm,' said Nicholas, stretching languidly and sniffing the air, 'I can smell the south.'

'You do talk nonsense,' laughed Primrose, 'we're barely out of Normandy!'

'Ah, but it beckons, it beckons . . .'

'So does Maurice,' I said. 'Look.'

They turned towards the car where a furious face glared out from the back window.

'He does look a bit disgruntled,' observed Primrose.

'When doesn't he?' said Nicholas. And then in kinder tone suggested I took 'the poor little toad' out of the car and find him some milk. 'Go on, the girl's bound to have some.'

Diffidently I approached both Maurice and the girl. The cat was unexpectedly compliant and allowed himself to be hoiked from the back seat with little demur. But I was nervous of asking for anything extra from our po-faced waitress. A baby in hand might have seemed more legitimate. However, I pushed through the plastic ribbons of the café entrance and enquired tentatively if there was any chance of some water for the dog and milk for the cat. The girl gestured towards a tap and a cracked bowl, and then to my surprise her impassive face broke into beams of delight, and in the next instant she had wrested Maurice from my clasp and carried him off to some nether region behind the counter, babbling to whoever was within to 'donnez du lait au pauvre petit chat anglais. Il a beaucoup de faim.' I had not thought that Maurice looked particularly hungry (though I suppose he must have been) but was grateful that the girl seemed so concerned for his welfare.

I poured the water for Bouncer and then hung about for some time waiting for Maurice to re-emerge, which he eventually did: still in her arms, and looking placidly satisfied and more than a little sticky around the gills. 'Je lui ai donné aussi des grosses sardines,' she announced happily, 'et maintenant il va dor-dor!' Go 'dor-dor', would he? I thought gloomily. More likely be sick in my lap. However, I thanked her profusely, settled the bill, and retrieving a mellowed Maurice joined the others. It struck me as odd how cat and waitress had so transformed each other's demeanour, and wondered what Sartre would make of it.

We were just preparing to leave, when there was the sound of a low engine and swishing tyres, and moving at absurd speed there flashed past a silver-grey sports car. The dozing lurcher leapt up and started to howl, and from the barber's shop next door came the protest, '*Merde – les foux Anglais!*'

We looked at one another. 'That was that Austin-Healey 100,' announced Nicholas.

'Not the one on the boat again!' I exclaimed.

'Yes, your sister's friends, Climp and Mullion.'

'Or Mullion and Climp,' I giggled, clearly having drunk my Pernod too quickly.

'They weren't my friends,' said Primrose indignantly. 'They merely engaged me in conversation – passing the time of day.'

'Well, at that rate they are certainly passing the time of day all right – they'll be into dusk by now!' replied Nicholas, adding as an afterthought, 'Quite a lot of these Fangio fellows about, it would seem.'

We returned to the car, and I asked helpfully if Nicholas would like me to drive for a while.

'No fear,' he said.

Thus we pushed on. And other than Nicholas treating us to an embarrassingly awful travesty of Charles Trenet singing 'La Mer', all went peaceably. But despite the novelty of the landscape with its changing scenery I was glad when Primrose announced that it was high time we started looking for somewhere to lodge for the night.

'I know it's still only late afternoon but if we leave it much longer our choice will be limited, and I for one do not propose sleeping in some third-rate B&B with dodgy plumbing and cackling geese.'

'Such negative thoughts,' replied Nicholas lightly. 'One's

in France, you know, not England. We're bound to find something perfectly adequate that even you will approve. I've marked a number of places listed in the Michelin, they can't all be full this late in the season. And who knows, we might even bump into the Episcopal Progress.'

'Don't even joke about it,' I said. 'Besides, they left days before us and are bound to be settled in their friends' house by now.' Gloom fell as I had a momentary vision of Clinker with rod and waders suddenly bearing down on me from some mountain tarn in the vicinity of Berceau-Lamont . . .

We had made good progress and were now about fifty miles north of Clermont-Ferrand, and began to look seriously for somewhere to stay. We passed and discounted a couple of nondescript places at the roadside, and were just wondering about a third, equally indifferent, when Nicholas suddenly slammed on the brakes and made a sharp turn into a winding lane. Primrose emitted a shriek of protest and the dog barked reproachfully.

'Sorry,' he said, 'I only just saw the sign.'

'What sign?' she asked indignantly.

'The one to L'Auberge du Cheval Blanc. It's listed in the book and is supposed to be pretty good. Might as well have one night of civilized living at least. Don't think we can expect much from Berceau so we had better make the most of it while we can. It says they do a wonderful *civet de lièvre* for which people travel miles, and the wine list is supposed to be superb.'

'Yes, and probably jolly expensive,' I said grimly.

'Come on, dear boy, you only live once. Besides, just think, when we've taken possession of your property *and* its Nazi treasure, we'll be quids in and can treat ourselves to all manner of fancy places.'

Before I could tell him he inhabited a world of crazed delusion, he had launched once more into a mangled version of 'La Mer'; only this time it was accompanied by growls from Bouncer and a peevish protest from Maurice,

45

who having woken up was intent on making his presence felt.

And thus a few yards further on we made our musical entry into the car park of L'Auberge du Cheval Blanc. It did indeed look expensive, but also very nice; and despite my qualms, the thought of a comfortable bed and lavish dining room was an inviting prospect. I hoped they could accommodate us.

'You two stay here,' directed Nicholas, 'while I make enquiries.' He got out and strolled towards the entrance. While he was gone Primrose and I discussed the question of the animals, i.e. how best to manage them. I thought it unwise to resurrect the possibility of her handbag for the cat, and suggested instead that we left both in the car for the time being and that after dinner I would make a surreptitious retrieval and sneak them up to my room.

'But you'll still have to feed the brutes,' she said.

This time I did mention her bag: 'It's got a very neat outside pocket, just the place for a few scraps from the table. It would be ideal.' I waited for the eruption but none came for her attention was focused elsewhere.

'I say, Francis,' she exclaimed, 'you'll never guess what I've just seen.'

'What?'

'Over there, on the other side of the big Renault – it's that Austin-Healey again. It's just driven in. I'm sure it's the same one that Climp and Mullion were in. What a coincidence!'

I looked in the direction she was pointing and saw the sleek silver bonnet and distinctive headlamps. It was an Austin-Healey 100 all right, but whether theirs one couldn't be sure. The occupants weren't visible and I was about to get out to take a discreet look when Nicholas appeared and signalled a thumbs up. 'No difficulty,' he announced, 'they'll be only too delighted to have us. I've seen the rooms and everything is absolutely *comme il faut*. In fact, a distinctly good find.' He grinned broadly, obviously pleased with himself.

9

The Cat's Memoir

As you may expect from one practised in feline strategy, all went entirely to plan, and it was with little difficulty that I concealed myself in the vicar's car and then subsequently the Type's. I was rather pleased with my handling of this later transference for it required both speed and fine judgement. But it is not for nothing that I am the great nephew of Marmaduke The Houdini, and fine genes will always out.

I cannot say that my sojourn in the boot of the Brighton Type's car was congenial (distinctly cramped and stuffy), but unlike my human companions I found the motion of the waves pleasantly soothing – a fact that I was careful to impress upon Bouncer when next I saw him. Some of my earliest memories are of spending long hours being cat's-cradled in the garden hammock with Uncle Marmaduke, and I think its swaying rhythm must have fitted me for undulation. Anyway, whatever the cause, my time on the boat was agreeable – which is not something that can be said for the first hour or so on land. Squashed, hungry and hot, I was becoming as Bouncer might say distinctly 'ratty'. And added to the physical discomfort there was also a nagging disquiet over something I had happened to over-hear as the boat docked.

Roused from my snooze by thuds and noises, I realized that preparations were afoot to move the cars and rally the passengers. And then there was a light rap on the roof and I heard an alien voice say, 'So you think this is theirs, do you?' Whoever was being addressed must have confirmed, for the voice then added, 'With that type and vintage it shouldn't be too difficult to keep tabs on 'em, even though it is a French one. It's definitely him all right. Just like his picture in the paper – same gangling legs.' There was a pause, and then another voice said, 'Watch it, they're coming!'

A few moments later I heard the driver's door being opened and the Brighton Type groaning, 'For God's sake where are those sodding pills!' He was clearly under the weather and I had no sympathy. Besides, I was too puzzled by what I had just heard to give thought to Ingaza's foolish agues. Unlike Bouncer, I do not possess – or imagine that I possess – a sixth sense. Nevertheless there was something in the air and in the voices that I did not like. I couldn't quite put my paw on it, but it gave me a distinct feeling of unease. However, in my current position there was nothing to be done, so I curled up again and attempted to snooze.

Fat chance of that. After twenty minutes of aimless cruising around, the car suddenly screeched to a halt, and five minutes later there was a violent commotion and I could hear the *hound*, of all creatures, being hauled on to the back seat! Later of course he gave me a rambling explanation as to how he had arrived, but at the time his presence seemed incredible – and I was distinctly put out by the intrusion. Nevertheless, being a cat of philosophical cast, I resigned myself to the new situation with characteristic goodwill and unruffled fortitude . . . But as we drove along I could not help being piqued by the thought of Bouncer lolling in comfort while I was squashed beneath the luggage and whisky. Eventually, of course, I made my presence felt by staging a spectacular escape into bushes at the side of the road. Irritated by the long incarceration, I naturally made the whole episode as difficult as I could for them, and for the rest of the journey ensured that I was comfortably nursed on F.O.'s lap and given all due attention.

10

The Vicar's Version

We trooped in and deposited our cases in the rather plush bedrooms. Primrose suggested we should reassemble in the bar immediately. But as there seemed to be nobody about in the corridor I thought that if I was quick I might be able to sneak the animals in via the fire exit at the end of the passage. Thus I returned to the car but quickly realized that it was more than I could handle to smuggle both cat and dog simultaneously – one pet might pass unobserved, but two? So with Maurice curled on the back seat, I seized Bouncer and we sloped our way back to the side entrance. The cat would just have to wait till later.

After a lightning wash and brush up I joined the others, who were already taking their ease with aperitifs and menus in the lounge. The room was warmly lit and had a large wood-burning stove sizzling in one corner. Thick rugs were strewn on polished flagstones, and a set of stags' heads bearing remarkably imperial antlers adorned the walls. Settling ourselves under their placid gaze we discussed the day's journey and surveyed the other guests.

There weren't many of these: a trio of what I took to be local farmers, scrubbed and shiny-booted and obviously entranced by the host's bill of fare; a well-padded woman in pink, nursing a diminutive poodle which she was fondly feeding with cocktail nuts; and a young couple on a far sofa cocooned in martinis and mutual admiration. Apart from appreciative grunts from the farmers as they scanned the menus, the place was quiet and the mood mellow. I smoked a Gauloise (when in Rome etc.), savouring the moment and glad of the comfort of the armchair after the confines of the Citroën's back seat.

Like the farmers, Nicholas and Primrose had immersed themselves in the menu, discussing earnestly the relative merits of the *civet de lièvre* and *canard pressé*. My own choice already made, I watched with interest the white poodle on its owner's pink satin lap, and was just musing on the little dog's fastidious table manners compared to the chumping chops of Bouncer, when I heard a rather flat English voice at the bar asking for a gin and tonic. I turned my head . . . Mullion stood there. Or Climp.

Clearly Primrose had been right about their arrival in the car park. I felt an ill-defined irritation, which increased when I saw the man's companion enter the room and join him at the bar. I could not explain the irritation but somehow their presence annoyed me. Certainly they had been perfectly civil when Primrose had introduced us on the boat – but that did not necessarily mean that I wanted my journey through France punctuated by their appearances. It was, I suppose, simply xenophobia in reverse: enjoying the novelty of France I did not wish to be dogged by my compatriots, least of all by the same ones.

I averted my head, hoping not to catch their attention; but too late, they had already seen us and were moving across the room. Inwardly grumbling, I composed my features into a smile of surprised welcome.

'Well, see who it is, fancy meeting you again,' began the taller (Mullion, I subsequently learned). 'Thought we had left you at Dieppe! Your sister did mention you were making for this area but it's funny meeting up here, all the same.' He laughed loudly, and nodding towards Nicholas added, 'I must say, your friend looks rather the better for wear than when we last saw him. Thought he wasn't long for this world!' And he laughed again, raising his glass to Nicholas who returned the gesture with a wintry stare.

'Are you staying long?' asked Primrose brightly. 'It's such a comfortable hotel, it almost seems a pity to leave.'

'No, we're pushing on in the morning,' said Climp. 'We've only got a fortnight's leave and I want to get some fishing in, and Ted's keen on revisiting his old wartime haunts – somewhere in the Massif Central, wherever that is. My geography's none too good so I leave the map reading and such to him. Dominoes is more my line and I like a good opponent.' He grinned familiarly at Primrose and looked around – clearly hoping to draw up a chair. Fortunately none was to hand. They hovered vaguely for a few moments, and then Nicholas stood up, waved imperiously to the waiter and announced in impeccable French (which I think he must have been silently practising) that we were ready for our table. Nodding curtly to Climp and Mullion, and with Primrose and myself dutifully following, he moved briskly towards the dining room.

The pink lady was already ensconced and busy with a bowl of mussels which she was attacking with dedicated relish. I noticed the poodle was still on her lap, but now largely obscured by the folds of the enormous napkin cascading from its mistress's throat. A twitching nose would occasionally poke out rather like a hedgehog emerging from hibernation. The sight of the creature being so casually accommodated lessened my anxiety about Maurice and Bouncer and I felt easier about having them up in the bedroom. That at least was a relief. And like the pink lady, and following the French custom, I tucked my napkin into my collar and fell to my steak.

For a short while there was silence as we attacked our food and savoured the burgundy. And then turning to Primrose, Nicholas said, 'Those two – what was it you said they were talking about on the boat?'

She frowned, trying to recall. 'Oh, I don't know – I told you in the car – this and that, nothing in particular ... anything to pass the time really.' Then she smiled complacently: 'But I held my own during the dominoes all right, swept the board with them!' I also smiled for I remembered from old my sister's skill in that particular sphere, and our father's fury when yet again he found himself trounced by her sharper skill.

'Yes,' said Nicholas patiently, 'but what were they *saying*? I mean, did they ask you any questions about where you were going or who you were?'

'Well, they asked the usual questions as travellers do. Wanted to know if we were on holiday and were we visiting any particular area in France, all that sort of thing.'

'I see . . . and did you volunteer any information?'

'*Volunteer* information? You sound like an intelligence officer! I merely said we were going somewhere in the Auvergne to look at an old ruin that Francis was interested in. I certainly didn't say that he was the actual owner or that he had the deeds.'

'Wait a minute,' I interrupted, looking up from my steak, 'I certainly do *not* have the deeds. They were appropriated, as you may remember, by someone else sitting not two feet away.' I glared at Nicholas who naturally took no notice.

'Oh well, as good as,' she replied. 'Though, as a matter of fact, when I mentioned that my brother was a clergyman they did seem very eager to know your parish, and I remember that when I told them what it was, Mullion had laughed and said, "Ah, yes, of course, the Reverend Francis Oughterard of Molehill – that's the name. I remember."' She turned to me: 'Don't know why he should exactly, but I suppose you were in the papers over that frightful Crumpelmeyer rumpus . . . Or only being in the next county perhaps he read it in one of those dreary diocesan magazines they strew in dentists' waiting rooms – though can't say he seems the type to read that sort of thing. On the ferry he kept muttering about how nice it was to be out of "blinking uniform", and it crossed my mind he might be a fireman or one of those cinema commissionaires . . .' She broke off, looking towards the pink lady. 'I say, have you *ever* seen such an enormous gâteau! My goodness, I can't resist it, I shall have to have some.' And picking up the menu she started to peruse the dessert section with avid concentration.

'Hmm,' said Nicholas, frowning slightly, 'think I'll just settle for a smoke and a Scotch – although blowed if I'm paying inflated Frog prices when we've got our own supply in the car. I'll see you two later.' And he got up and strolled towards the door, ignoring Climp and Mullion but flashing the pink one a smile of lavish charm. When this was beamingly reciprocated over the mound of gâteau I was reminded of how adroit he was at handling old ladies. Perhaps if I had possessed the same talent I should now be a free agent and in thrall neither to him nor to nightmares. As it was . . .

After coffee in the lounge I bade goodnight to Primrose, exchanged a few pleasantries with Climp and Mullion, and went out to the car to retrieve Maurice. With a pang of guilt I realized I had completely forgotten to get him any food and felt nervous about my reception. A pinpoint of light glowed near the car and I smelt the familiar scent of a Russian Sobranie. Nicholas was leaning against the bonnet, cigarette in one hand, plastic cup of whisky in the other.

'So there you are, dear boy,' he greeted me. 'Thought you'd forgotten the cat. Not that it matters – little bugger's fast asleep. In fact, you could probably leave him there all night.'

'No fear! He'd make a mess deliberately, just to show who's boss.'

'Ah – well, that's the last thing we want,' he said nervously. 'Better get him out pronto!'

I opened the door and yanked out Maurice while Nicholas rootled for another cup and poured a generous ration of whisky. Given the amount stashed in the boot this seemed an entirely proper offering. We sipped in silence and I kept a straining eye on Maurice as he prowled around the shadowy car park.

And then Nicholas said quietly, 'Your sister hasn't been too bright, has she?'

'Whatever do you mean?'

'Pouring out our business to those two.'

'I would hardly say "pouring it out". Anyway, why worry? The main thing is she didn't reveal that I had been left the deeds by Mrs Fotherington and am thus technically the owner. The last thing I want is for that particular link to be publicized. Otherwise I can't see that it really matters. It's not as if she gave the name of the place – and in any case they're only a couple of rather intrusive chaps on holiday from their work or wives. We shan't see them again – at least I hope not, three times is quite enough!' I laughed, and scanned the car park searching for a feline shape with glittering eyes.

There was a long pause, and then Nicholas said, 'Look, Francis, I know you're not the brightest spark in the box, but hasn't it struck you that there's a rather consistent pattern emerging?'

'What do you mean?'

'For a start they come from Crowthorne. And then, according to Primrose, Mullion seemed unduly curious about your parish and clearly recognized your name. They are also heading roughly in the same direction as we are, i.e. into the Massif Central – a large area admittedly – and just happen to have chosen for their first night the self-same place as ourselves. The odds for that particular coincidence are very long indeed, especially as we had already seen them whizz through that village in Normandy at a hell of a lick ... so by rights you would expect them to be miles ahead of us, and yet they drive in here within minutes of our own arrival.'

'Perhaps they took a long diversion,' I suggested.

'Perhaps – but try looking at the whole picture.'

'The picture would be clearer,' I said irritably, stung by his earlier jibe, 'if I knew why you keep harping on about them coming from Crowthorne. You mentioned it in the car as well.'

He groaned. 'Crowthorne, Francis, is where bloody Broadmoor is and your fat chum Crumpelmeyer! Or had you forgotten?'

As a matter of fact I had forgotten, and apart from being startled by his words, I also felt a fool. Such was the notoriety of that grim establishment that, despite once learning otherwise, my schoolboy imagination invariably placed it vaguely in some desolate mythic outpost far removed from the security of conventional life. That it was situated in the vicinity of a pleasant Home Counties village rarely registered with my consciousness . . . It did now.

I cleared my throat and took another mouthful of whisky. 'Are you saying that they have something to do with the prison and are thus interested in my connection with Victor Crumpelmeyer?'

'Got it in one, old cock.'

'But that's absurd! I grant you it's a coincidence that they come from Crowthorne and also seem to know my name, but there must be hundreds of people living in the neighbourhood who have no connections with the asylum at all.'

'Not if they are "on leave" and glad to get out of their "uniforms".'

'You mean that they are . . .'

'Yes, of course I do. Screws. Bloody screws!'

I stared into the dark, digesting his words. 'So you are saying that these screws know Crumpelmeyer and that it is through him that they have heard of me, and for some reason, having bumped into us on the boat, are keen to cultivate my company and to discover precisely where I am going?'

'Something like that,' he murmured.

I laughed nervously. 'Oh really, Nicholas,' I protested, 'you read too many cheap thrillers. Just because there are one or two rather tenuously linked coincidences you have created a whole scenario in your head!'

'That's just it, old cock, I do *not* have a scenario in my head. Far from it – which is why I need to work things out.'

He sighed. 'However, clearly nothing helpful can be expected from your direction, so I'm off to bed.' And thus saying, he stubbed out his cigarette and ambled off back to the hotel, leaving me to finish the whisky and round up the cat.

11

The Cat's Memoir

It is just as well I am a cat of stoical disposition for, as earlier mentioned, the indignities I had to undergo on that foreign journey were disgraceful! No doubt lesser felines would have collapsed under the strain, but being of fine fortitude and not easily thwarted by the slights and blunders of human beings (even those of the vicar), I naturally persevered. Having made it my mission to protect F.O. from his own ineptitude I had no intention of failing. But I can tell you, the deprivations were considerable.

Take that first night in the hostelry the Brighton Type had chosen ... they forgot to feed me, if you please. Yes, so intent were they on their own food that they entirely overlooked *my* nutritional requirements – wasn't even offered a pre-prandial saucer of milk. When F.O. and the Type later woke me from my nap on the car seat I fully expected to be offered some choice titbits – but all they did was shove me out to stretch my legs while they smoked and guzzled whisky. Not a word about my supper! And then the vicar whisked me off to his room assuming I would be content to sleep the night through. Well, I certainly wasn't having that, oh no!

The moment he was in bed and had started to snore, I quickly moved to the bedroom door which fortunately was only on the latch. After teasing it with a paw I was able to open it a crack and insinuate my way into the corridor.

From thence I padded downstairs towards the kitchens – easily located by the lingering odours – and slipped into a pantry and commenced my midnight forage. Very productive it was too: I liberated a wealth of enticing scraps, threatened a mouse, harried a cockroach, and enjoyed what Bouncer would doubtless describe as 'a right old feast'.

Satiated but by now far from sleepy, I decided to take the air before retiring. No difficulties with this – the pantry window was gaping wide and I easily jumped on to the lawn below. Here I crouched by what seemed to be a ground-floor wing with a number of sash windows, some still lit. Being curious by nature I thought I would practise my skills of reconnaissance. So with a lithe leap to the sill I crept along, peering into the various rooms. Disappointingly there was nothing of note: people stumbling around in pyjamas, cleaning their teeth, arguing, reading books, clambering over each other – the usual nightly antics of human beings.

But just as I was losing interest and about to seek diversion elsewhere I encountered a window that was open; and sitting at a nearby table were two men, still fully dressed, stooped over a large map. Nothing remarkable in that, you might think. Not normally. But when alongside the map there is a folded newspaper with a clear picture of your master squinting up from the page, it does tend to give you pause for thought ... And that is exactly what I did: paused, thought, looked and listened.

As soon as I caught their words I realized they must be the same pair I had heard muttering outside the car on the boat. It is not always easy to grasp what humans say – their vocal cords are defective and they enunciate poorly – but over the years I have developed a fair grasp, and the conversation was roughly as follows:

'Apart from that cock-up earlier, so far so good. Just as well you spotted them when you did otherwise we wouldn't have stood a chance. We'll have to stick pretty close tomorrow ... But my God, that was a stroke of luck bumping into him on the boat like that – obviously "meant"!' There was a coarse guffaw which made me flinch and I backed into the shadows.

'It's only *meant*,' said the other voice, 'if he can be used, i.e. if we can relieve him of that map of the Fotherington place you seem so sure he's got – though I still think you're barking up the wrong tree.'

'Look,' said the larger one slowly, 'our friend Crumpelmeyer may be a blathering loon but there's shrewd cunning there all the same ... he was probably quite bright before he flipped and murdered his wife. If Oughterard is travelling to the Auvergne and looking for some property, as the sister let drop on the boat, ten to one he's on the same trail as ourselves and going to the same place. Crumpelmeyer didn't knife him for nothing, deranged though he is. There's method in that madness and I'm damn sure he knows the vicar's got the plan ... You do realize that according to him the likely positions of that gold are actually marked on it by two dots? We'd be mad not to follow this up!'

'But Crumpelmeyer never had a sighting of those documents. How does he know there are two dots?'

'Apparently the wife was always going on about them. Her mother held the title deeds and had told the daughter all the details. That's why Victor murdered her, stupid sod. When the old girl died he assumed her daughter would automatically inherit the deeds and plans as well as the money – only she didn't. Left it all to the parson instead! Poor old Victor was so incensed he strangled the wife out of spite and then went on to knife the vicar while trying to get hold of the things.' There was another snort of laughter.

'Cor,' replied the other, 'what you might call a fated family. Didn't he do the mother in as well?'

'That's the story and what the authorities reckon, but I'm not convinced of it myself. During the last couple of months I've got to know our friend pretty well – sort of made a study of him. And the odd thing is he freely confesses to murdering the wife and attacking the vicar – one of his most favoured topics of conversation in fact, sort of takes a pride in it – *but* he almost never mentions the mother, shows no interest at all. It's as if she never existed for him. No, I think someone else was responsible for that one.'

There was a chortle from across the table. 'Maybe it was the vicar. That'd be a laugh!' He picked up the newspaper and stared quizzically at F.O.'s photograph. Some laugh, I thought, flinching nervously. This was getting too near the hind leg! 'But I still think it's a long shot,' he continued. 'On the other hand, if Crumpelmeyer's right and the stuff *is* there like you think, I don't see why some poncy parson should get his mitts on it. What about the Workers, I say!'

There was a pause, and then the other said slowly. 'As it happens, you could be right. Crumplelmeyer's bonkers all right, but all the same he's clearer in his mind than when he first came in; and although he barely mentions the mother-in-law, just recently he made an interesting comment on Oughterard.'

'Oh yes, what was that then?'

'It was something like, "I know that sort – cool as they come, and devious as hell. I wouldn't put anything past him. Not anything." Well, at first, of course, I thought it was just old Victor having another of his mad rants, angry about his lost money . . . Except that he wasn't ranting. He was thoughtful, *very* thoughtful. I asked him what he was getting at, but he just smiled that fat smile, muttered something that sounded like "killer clerics", and then clammed up . . . didn't utter another word. But I could see he was still thinking, sort of preoccupied. And you know, I keep remembering that . . . and wondering if he wasn't on to something, something which could prove *exceedingly* useful – what you might call a handy little lever . . . Though, mind you, it's not only the parson we've got to deal with – there's that other one, his minder or whatever. Smarmy bastard. Didn't like the look of him at all – pretty shifty if you ask me. Snooty with it!'

I was just thinking how right he was, when with a gasp and an oath he leapt to his feet. 'There's a bloody cat out there. Get down, you little bugger!' And before I had a chance to retreat I was knocked roughly from the sill, landing heavily on some stony ground below. 'Can't abide cats,' I heard him exclaim. 'Mean slinking creatures.'

Hell hath no fury like a cat maligned, and I made it my mission there and then to get my own back on such a gross specimen. Even the Brighton Type treats me with more respect than that! However, it is not for nothing that I am Great Uncle Marmaduke's nephew. And taking a leaf out of his discerning book I limped valiantly back to F.O.'s room, where, having told Bouncer exactly what I thought of the human species, I spent the entire night under the bed plotting my revenge.

12

The Vicar's Version

My bed was extremely comfortable despite the large bolster favoured by the French, and for the first half of the night I slept soundly. However, I awoke at about four o'clock and, although enjoying the softness of the mattress, had the greatest difficulty in getting off to sleep again. Nicholas's comments in the car park were bothersome, and try as I might I could not rid myself of images of our fellow travellers and their apparent interest in my movements. As in the car park, I kept telling myself that Nicholas was jumping to conclusions and that his suspicion of their being Broadmoor warders and knowing the wretched Crumpelmeyer was wildly off beam. But the more I thought the less I slept, and thus the more I thought . . .

Finally I must have drifted off, for the next thing I saw was the sun shining through the blinds and Maurice's petulant face thrust close to my own. He was clearly impatient to be out, and dutifully I pulled on shirt and trousers and discreetly took him down to the side door into the car park. (Better than tempt fate and risk bedlam, I had left Bouncer snoring and chasing dreamtime rabbits.)

Hoping to snatch a little longer in bed I was about to go upstairs again, when a voice behind me said, 'Well, you're up early, Reverend. Must be like us, making an early start.' Climp stood there grinning amiably. Clutching a raincoat and a large holdall, he was evidently on his way to the car.

'Well, actually,' I began vaguely, 'I was about to check the oil –'

'*And* let your cat out, I dare say.' He must have seen my startled look for he went on. 'Oh yes, I guessed that little geezer was yours. Saw you with him last night. Put him in your room, you did. And then when we heard the dog bark we knew he had a friend in there too. Still, don't worry, your secret's safe with us.' And he leered conspiratorially.

'What secret?' I asked defensively.

'You carrying animal contraband,' he laughed. 'Going to put them in six months' quarantine when you get back to England, are you? Seems a long price for the old mop and mog to pay for such a short trip.'

'Ah . . . well, you see – uhm – extraordinary really, they seem to have jumped into the car at the last moment and it was difficult to know quite what to do.' My voice trailed off. I was annoyed to be put on the spot like that and could hear the confusion in my tone, which annoyed me even more.

'Oh well, you're bound to get them through all right. After all, you being a vicar and on the straight and narrow and all that, I don't suppose Customs will bother. And if that's your only fiddle you can't have much to worry about, can you?' He grinned, opened the door to the car park and added, 'See you at breakfast before we go, I expect. Toodle-oo.'

It was ridiculous, but for some reason I was rattled. In itself the animal business was less than minor, and yet I was irked to think that their concealment had been noted by Climp and Mullion: something to do with loss of face and dignity, I suppose. But there was another thing that nagged. Was that reference to the 'straight and narrow' and my 'only fiddle' merely the crude banter that it seemed, or did it veil a more sinister meaning? The Fotherington affair has coloured my sensitivities, and sometimes the most innocent remarks seem to hold a menace never intended. I tried to persuade myself that I was overreacting, and would doubtless have succeeded had it not been for Nicholas's remarks the previous night. As it was, I climbed the stairs back to my room irritable and disheartened.

Breakfast lifted my mood. In keeping with the excellence of our supper, the Auberge provided a rich assortment of freshly baked croissants, bulbous brioches, a kind of cream cheese, bowls of luscious apricot jam and even additional sticky pastries. I have a sweet tooth, and along with the real coffee such fare more than compensated for the absence of an English 'cooked'.

'Doesn't stint himself, does he?' observed Nicholas to Primrose as I returned from the sideboard to our table with laden plate.

'Never did,' she replied, 'even on Cook's day off when we had to endure Mother's burnt offerings ... disgusting really.'

I took no notice, enjoying the novelty of cakes at breakfast and thinking that at least I might as well reap some small benefit from Ingaza's avarice.

After a brief discussion about our itinerary, the others went off to finish packing and settle the bill, while I poured more coffee and pondered the merits of brioche or a second pastry.

Thus occupied, I did not at first see him. Indeed, when I did he had already seated himself across the table in the chair Primrose had just vacated. I was startled and distinctly peeved by the interruption. The pastry lost its savour.

'Ah,' said Mullion, 'Ken said he thought you were leaving pretty soon. Long journey, I expect.'

'One could say so,' I replied vaguely.

'Oh yes, like ourselves ... very like ourselves.' He paused, smiling but eyeing me intently. 'In fact,' he continued, 'I think we're all set on the same route.'

'Really?' I said with some indifference.

He leaned forward, his elbows on the table. 'Yes,' he said slowly, 'really.' The tone was pleasant enough but the words were pointed, and I began to feel a gnawing discomfort. 'In fact,' he went on, 'according to our Mr Crumpelmeyer, it looks to me as if we might be heading to the same area, somewhere high up in those French mountains.' Discomfort ceased to gnaw and became a ravening wolf.

'Ah,' I said faintly, 'Mr Crumpelmeyer . . . you, er, know him, do you?'

'Oh yes. Well, we would, wouldn't we . . . I mean, us all coming from the one place. We're what you might call his special mates – *look after him*, if you get my meaning.'

'At Crowthorne.'

He nodded. 'At Crowthorne.'

There was a silence. And then I said stiffly, 'Well, I hope Mr Crumpelmeyer is doing well . . . must be rather difficult, I imagine . . .'

'Oh no,' Mullion exclaimed, 'not difficult – more what I'd call *interesting*.' He continued to stare hard.

'Yes, I suppose it is . . . the er, the psychology of it all . . .'

He laughed. 'You could say that – though of course it rather depends on whose psychology we're talking about, doesn't it?' I made no answer, trying to make out where the hell we were going and not liking it one jot. 'You see,' he continued, 'he's very talkative, is Mr Crumpelmeyer. Likes nothing better than a good natter . . . Oh yes, old Victor will talk the hind leg off a donkey once he gets going!' I said nothing and rather pointedly looked at my watch.

It had no effect, for he went on: 'Yes. And do you know, the funny thing is he talks a lot about *you* . . . Odd that, isn't it? About you having got some documents which rightly belong to him.' And he had the nerve to stretch out a hand for one of the croissants. Had I been Primrose doubtless I would have slapped his fingers, but being her brother I merely looked po-faced and tried fruitlessly to cast my mind elsewhere.

He leaned further forward and with a slow wink said, 'I think you know the ones I mean – those papers the old girl had, that old girl found strangled in the wood just near you, the one you were so friendly with. Or at least, that's what the press said at the time ... Of course, Victor's always had that bee in his bonnet about you and his wife's money – it's why he knifed you. But we rather get the impression it's not the only thing on his mind. It's as if he suspects something else, something in the past ... silly really. But then that's Victor, you can never be sure what's fact and what's fiction. It's the madness, makes things difficult to sift ... On the other hand, sometimes he's right on the ball, *right* on it. You'd be surprised.' He relaxed his elbows and sat back, face in repose.

I opened my mouth to utter I knew not what. But at that moment Nicholas appeared in the far doorway impatiently signalling me to hurry up. I don't think I had ever been so pleased to see him and, despite his obvious irritation at my leisurely breakfast, I gave him an eager wave. And with a curt nod to Mullion left the room as fast as dignity would permit.

Once in the haven of the car and clutching the cat on my knees with Bouncer heavy on my feet, I crunched peppermints obsessively.

'For God's sake,' drawled Nicholas, half turning, 'can't you stop that racket? It's like having a wildebeest in the back.'

'Or a gnu,' said Primrose, 'and you've only just breakfasted!'

'So what's a gnu?' enquired Nicholas.

'Much the same, I think,' she replied. And they launched into an earnest debate about the variety and habitat of giant antelopes, while I closed my eyes and tried to digest the import of my recent exchange with Mullion. Later I would recount it to my companions, but at that particular juncture all I wanted was amnesia and a smooth ride.

To begin with, the ride proved smooth enough; but amnesia was less achievable, and despite the muted snoring of Maurice I was only too awake to the memory of my encounters with Climp and Mullion. There was something smooth and knowing about the pair of them, and I was unnerved by Mullion's brazen innuendoes and his pointed surmise that they were travelling to the same area. Ingaza's earlier disquiet had now infected my own imagination, and I felt as if I were being shadowed, taunted . . . targeted.

I eased my foot from under Bouncer's dead weight, and brooded further. At best their close link with Crumpelmeyer was an uncomfortable coincidence – his attack upon me and connection to Mrs Fotherington being something I preferred to forget. But at worst – and I was beginning to fear the worst – there could be something really sinister in their purpose . . . What exactly had mad Crumpelmeyer been saying to them? Clearly that I possessed the wretched deeds to Elizabeth's property – but what *else* might he have alleged in those crazed babblings? Anything and everything!

Such was my agitation that I very nearly asked Nicholas to stop the car and return to Dieppe. The whole enterprise had been absurd from the start, and now, with this latest set of events, it was distinctly alarming. However, even as the impulse came upon me I knew it to be futile. Ingaza was hell-bent on getting something out of that ruin – whether gold or equity – and to believe he might abandon the scheme now was like expecting Canterbury to turn Muslim. Besides, I thought, suddenly riled, why should I permit myself to be intimidated by those two leering jokers? They might be used to browbeating the lunatics in Broadmoor, but the lunatic from Molehill was another case altogether! Thus temporarily emboldened, I ruffled the dog's fur, lit a cigarette, and gave myself up to watching the rolling pleasures of the French countryside.

As we moved further south the terrain became rugged, the road winding, and what had been blurrily distant hills were now rearing craggy peaks. Our valley was green and wooded but up on the heights the vegetation appeared sparser and the early autumn colours were largely veiled in a pall of grey.

'Looks a bit murky up there,' observed Nicholas cheerily. 'Poor old Henri won't like that when he arrives – gets tetchy in bad weather. He's difficult enough at the best of times.'

'Well, if that curé starts getting difficult with me,' observed Primrose tartly, 'he'll soon learn otherwise. There are quite enough fractious clergy as it is.' She turned in her seat and gave me a dazzling smile which I returned with appropriate gestures. 'Anyway,' she went on, 'apart from being useful for his French, I don't really see why he should be with us at all. From what I recall he wasn't exactly a tower of strength over those ridiculous hidden paintings last year.'*

'No, not a tower,' agreed Nicholas, 'just marginally less cack-handed than the other one.'

'Oh, very funny,' I said, and was just about to make a scathing comment about his own part in things, when he continued:

'But you see, Henri is bringing something of essential value.'

'Oh yes?' I said doubtfully. 'So what's that?'

'His contraption.'

'His *what*?' cried Primrose.

'His gold-digging contraption, his metal detector.'

'Oh no,' she groaned. 'Are you really serious? I thought we were just going to have a little potter around – make a general surveillance for future exploration and see if the place was saleable. I didn't really think you intended hacking into the ground at this stage.'

'Grass doesn't grow under Old Nick's feet,' he replied blithely. 'No time like the present. Get in there while the sun shines – before our friend in the back has another turn.'

* See *Bones in the Belfry*

68

'I do not have turns!' I said testily. 'And besides, we don't have any shovels.'

'Ah, but we soon shall, he's bringing those as well.'

There was a silence as we reflected upon the curé replete with shovels and his contraption. And then Primrose said, 'I think I need a large drink – and I dare say the dog could do with one too. Perhaps, Nicholas, you would be so kind as to stop at the next likely place.'

The next likely place proved to be a good ten miles further up the valley on a road of tortuous bends; and by the time we arrived Primrose was not the only one in need of sustenance and a breather.

We parked in the village square, an attractive space with an ornate war memorial at one end and fountain and flower beds at the other. While Nicholas and Primrose went ahead to a café, I introduced the cat to the flowers and exercised Bouncer. Then, fearing he might cut up rough in the car, I shoved Maurice under my arm and joined the others. They were sitting in front of three large Pernods and had ordered bowls of *pommes frites* accompanied by thick, heavily garlicked mayonnaise – a dressing as deliciously different from our native salad cream as Münster cheese from blackboard chalk.

We ate and sipped in appreciative silence. Eventually, clearing my throat, I broached the subject of Climp and Mullion.

'I don't entirely trust them,' I said.

'Hmm,' observed Nicholas drily, 'took you a bit of time to reach that conclusion, didn't it?'

'Yes, well, we're not all au fait with the criminal classes,' I replied irritably.

The moment the words were out of my mouth I began to flush to the roots of my hair, feeling a prize fool; and was grateful that Nicholas merely gave a lop-sided grin and murmured, 'No, of course not, old bean, of course not . . .'

'Look,' broke in Primrose, 'just because that Mullion man was impertinent at breakfast doesn't mean to say that he's harbouring sinister intentions. Doesn't know how to conduct himself, that's all. You're being oversensitive, Francis, always have been ... Besides, even if we do meet them again – which I very much doubt – what on earth do they hope to achieve? Rob you of the gold?' She laughed derisively and turning round tickled Maurice under the chin.

'As a matter of fact, Primrose, I suspect that is exactly what they *are* hoping to do, given half a chance,' said Nicholas quietly. 'Or at any rate, get hold of that plan to the property. You may remember that Mullion was in the Berceau-Lamont area during the war and probably knows the château, and is quite likely to have heard local tales about the legendary Nazi loot.'

'Oh, come on!'

'Just think about it,' he said. 'They made a point of getting into conversation with you on the boat, showed keen interest in where we were going, turned up at the Cheval Blanc just as we also happened to be there and tried to insinuate themselves into our company. It's now confirmed that not only are they warders from Broadmoor where Crumpelmeyer is banged up, but they're his own allotted minders and obviously familiar with the original case and his connection with Francis. But what is even more to the point is what Mullion revealed at breakfast, i.e. that they know all about these deeds and the plan marking the supposed location of the rumoured gold. They also believe – according to the ranting Crumpelmeyer – that Francis deliberately curried favour with Fotherington, overturned Violet Pond's claim to her mother's property, smartly whipped the deeds and is hoping to reap the benefit while keeping it all deadly secret.' He paused, lit a cigarette and turned to me. 'You see, old chap, with you sniffing around in the grounds of that ruin flourishing the vital map they think they're in with a chance; especially as they suspect you're not quite straight, a weakness which of course they hope to fully –'

'But Francis *is* straight,' protested Primrose. 'He never wanted to get his hands on those papers! If anything it was you who –'

Nicholas raised a quizzical eyebrow and coughed discreetly. 'Straight*ish* perhaps. But there is that other little problem which he's not too keen to bruit abroad. And unfortunately that one is *fact* and not merely a supposition . . . Makes you a trifle vulnerable, dear boy.'

Vulnerable, my foot! Ingaza should know! But for a moment my persecutor looked almost sympathetic, while I inwardly quailed to hear him echo my own nagging fears about our fellow travellers.

'Yes,' I murmured faintly, ' but there's more than that. Clearly Mullion is intrigued by Crumpelmeyer's suspicions and thinks the château claim is not the only thing I may have been involved in . . . You're right, Nicholas – they are after the loot. But what's far worse is they're determined to get me anyway – probably banking on a whopping reward. Think of the headlines: "Violent Vicar Brought to Noose by Her Majesty's Bold Prison Officers." Oh my God, it's ghastly!' I leapt from the table, frightening the cat and spilling my drink.

'Francis is not well,' cried Primrose. 'We must go home immediately.'

'Like hell,' muttered Ingaza. 'If you imagine I'm going to be unsettled by this pantomime, you're wrong. Mullion, Climp, poor old Francis – I'm not budging. We shall continue as planned: hunt the treasure – or at the very least lay claim to the château – get back to Blighty and keep our heads down. Damned if I'm going to be buggered about by a pair of thieving mercenary screws from a godforsaken lunatic asylum.' He polished off the dregs of his Pernod, glared at Maurice and told me to sit down. I did as ordered, but this time it was my turn to raise an eyebrow . . .

And thus, quitting the café, we proceeded on our merry way up to Berceau-Lamont: me nervous as a kitten, Ingaza grimly obstinate, Primrose resigned, and the animals snoring their heads off.

13

The Vicar's Version

Eventually we arrived at the village, and drew up outside its only hostelry, La Truite Bleue, a small undistinguished place where Nicholas had somehow managed to make an advance booking. How he had found its reference I had no idea – clearly not from the Michelin Guide, that was for certain! We got out of the car and began to unload the luggage. I was nervous about the reception of Bouncer and Maurice and left them temporarily on the back seat while we went in to announce ourselves. Nobody was in evidence, and we hung around awkwardly in the small shabby foyer, coughing politely in the hope that our presence would eventually be registered. Nothing happened.

'Surely there's a bell or something,' muttered Primrose. 'We can't stand here all day. Absurd! Go and look in the bar, Francis, somebody must be around.' I was about to do her bidding, when from the nether regions came a cacophony of wild violent barking, followed by an ear-splitting blast of the Marseillaise and what sounded like a door being targeted by a battering ram.

'Tais-toi, méchant chien! Tu veux une claque?' shrieked a female voice. The pounding of the door came to a shuddering halt, the barking trailed off; but the music – martial and magisterial – played on. And then that too was abruptly halted.

In the merciful silence we regarded one another with startled eyes. 'Well, something's stirring,' observed Nicholas.

A door at the back finally opened, and down the narrow passage advanced a thin woman in a flowered pinafore and with greying hair pinned in an impressive bun. She greeted us affably enough, announced that she was Madame Vernier the patron's wife, and requested that we sign the hotel register. This was produced from a rickety side table artistically graced by a vase of virulent plastic flowers and a sheaf of faded tourist leaflets.

As we completed the signing ceremony, supplying the usual details and passport numbers, there was a further canine thudding from the rear, and loud snatches of the French national anthem could again be heard. Madame must have seen my look of puzzlement for she embarked on a voluble explanation far too rapid for my untuned ears. The distinguished name of President Clemenceau featured largely in her discourse, as did the words *'pour la patrie'*, *'très musicale'* and *'méchant garçon'*.

Frankly I couldn't make head nor tail of it but, seeing Nicholas grinning to himself, asked him if he could broach the subject of Bouncer and Maurice. He nodded, and in his usual mix of floral French and absurdly flattering English indicated that we had brought two animal companions and would be eternally grateful if Madame could possibly accommodate them. As hint of such gratitude, he said that should anyone be remotely interested, there were a few samples of best Scotch in the car boot taking up valuable space.

I thought she might not understand, but quick as a flash came the response: *'Alors, combien de bouteilles?'* Nicholas said that for the time being there were three. This evidently satisfied her, for to my relief she shrugged indifferently and replied that since the inn already had a dog, horse, two pigs, hens, goat and donkey, additional creatures would be of little account.

That settled, I returned to the car to rally its occupants, while the others went ahead up to the bedrooms. As I opened the door Maurice darted out and shot ahead towards the entrance, clearly intent on making the new place his own. Bouncer and I followed more slowly, the dog sniffing the air and making ruminative growling noises. Presumably he could smell the pigs.

Halfway up the stairs we bumped into Nicholas coming down. 'What was all that about Clemenceau and the dog?' I asked.

'Good question,' he replied, smiling wryly. 'Simple really. The animal is called after Clemenceau because the original owner, Madame's father, was intensely patriotic and an avid admirer of the old statesman. The music emanates from the creature's collar via a batteried security device primed to operate every time he tries to escape – i.e. whenever he moves beyond a hundred yards of the inn's perimeter. Sometimes the thing misfires and goes off at random moments – as we heard just now.'

'But it's an awful racket!' I exclaimed. 'How can they live with it? Can't they change the collar – or the tune?'

'They like it. Reminds them of Madame's late parent. Apparently it took the old boy months to devise the thing and it was his pride and joy. But more to the point, the dog likes it too. Gets moody if he's parted from it for too long – like a sort of musical comfort blanket, I suppose.' Nicholas looked down at Bouncer, and added musingly, 'And I thought your hound was mad enough . . .'

'Did she say what breed it is?'

'Didn't need to. We were introduced when you were out at the car. I'm not good on these things, but I should say he's a sort of cross between an Airedale and one of those giant poodles – a bit like a curly camel really. Actually, I think he's mildly batty.'

He continued on down the stairs while Bouncer and I went in search of our quarters – a small room with garish wallpaper and basic facilities.

*   *   *

Ten minutes later, having unpacked and briefly tested the narrow bed, I joined the others in the hallway.

'I think we should take a walk to get our bearings,' said Primrose briskly, 'and see if we can get a glimpse of the Folie from up here.'

'Good idea,' I agreed. 'But we need to be a bit discreet – it would be awful to bump into Clinker or Gladys. They're staying close by – though with luck may have moved on by now, but somehow I doubt it.'

'Oh, come on, Francis, always the pessimist. We probably shan't get a single sighting of them – and even if we did, would it really matter?'

'Yes,' I said shortly, my mind once more beset with lurid images.

She laughed and turned to Ingaza. 'You're coming, aren't you, Nicholas? It'll do us good to stretch our legs after all that time in the car.'

'Not just now,' he muttered. 'Er . . . got something rather pressing to do first – in the village.' He sounded slightly shifty and I was curious.

'What ever do you want to do in the village? We've only just got here.'

He hesitated. 'Postcards actually – I noticed they had a few on display outside that mangy shop we passed.'

'Postcards? Who on earth are you going to send postcards to? Besides – can't they wait?'

He looked sheepish. 'It's Aunt Lil. Old bat always demands at least two, otherwise there's hell to pay and it'll cost me an extra visit to the bandstand at Eastbourne. Or worse still, the casino at Bournemouth.' He sighed. 'Better get it over with, stop it preying on my mind.'

Surprise gave way to sadistic satisfaction as I recalled the elderly Lil's penchant for bandmasters and gambling dens. It was gratifying to think of my Nemesis in the merciless grip of his incorrigible old aunt. Whether she preyed on Ingaza's mind to the same degree as he preyed on mine, I rather doubted; but there seemed a certain piquancy which satisfied my sense of justice. Thus I grinned cheerfully and said something to the effect that I was sure his fond aunt deserved such an attentive nephew. His response was unprintable, and getting up abruptly he sloped off towards the village.

Left to our own devices, Primrose and I decided that a walk would indeed do us good; and leaving Maurice curled up on my bed but taking the dog with us, we set out to sniff the mountain air and get our bearings.

In fact our bearings were stupendous: jagged vistas of brooding mountains and shadowed valleys, expansive skies and trailing clouds, sudden meadows, sparkling tarns, sunlit crevices, gnarled tangled thickets, cairns of slatey granite . . . and everywhere, perched perilously and munching imperviously, po-faced mountain goats, their straggling beards moving rhythmically as they stared with blank, indifferent eye. Wild and ruggedly beautiful, it was the kind of mythical landscape that I had read about yet never encountered. I gazed transfixed by the hugeness and romantic grandeur; and for a few precious moments all fears and guilts dissolved – slipped away into some annihilating ether. I closed my eyes . . .

'Well, that's nice, isn't it, Francis?' Primrose's voice rang out. 'Pity I haven't brought my Kodak, it would make a good snap. Shall I let the dog off his lead?'

'Yes,' I replied, 'he could do with a good run.' And dragging my eyes from the surrounding beauty I watched Bouncer lunge at his freedom – dancing and barking, happy as the day he was born. Lucky beggar . . .

For a little while we walked in silence, sniffing the pure air and absorbed in the unaccustomed space and stillness. Bouncer had rushed off on some excursion of his own, reappearing now and again to snuffle at our heels and leer at the goats before darting away for fresh reconnaissance. I took out my cigarettes, and was just about to light one for Primrose when she suddenly exclaimed, 'Oh my goodness, that must be it down there. Look. It has to be the

Fotherington Folly!' And grabbing my arm, she gestured excitedly towards the valley below. At first I saw nothing except trees and remnants of a crumbling stone wall. I strained my eyes, perplexed. 'No, not there,' she urged, 'further on, to the right, past those trees. To the *right*, Francis – you can't miss it.'

And nor I could. Grey, formless, sprawling and turreted, it was a piece of dissipated architecture of a kind that might have been discarded following an abortive attempt at a Disney film. Had it been less monumentally ugly, it might have been risible. As it was, it was simply a large depressing blot on what originally must have been a lovely landscape ... Some folly all right! I thought of Elizabeth and the diary jotting where she had expressed her distaste for the place and her vow never to set foot over its threshold again. Ugly and sinister, she had called it. Well, at least she had been right there; and I experienced a sudden flash of aesthetic kinship. But it was only a flash, for in the next instant the sound of those arch wheedling tones welled up in my mind, and I heard the tinsel laugh, even caught a whiff of the cloying attar of violets wafting around my nostrils. And when Primrose tapped me on the shoulder, I leaped back like a stricken deer.

'Well, don't stand there gawping,' she said. 'What do you think?'

'I think it's awful,' I said bleakly.

'Hmm, pretty grim. Though I suppose having occupying troops in '44 wouldn't have helped much. I wonder who slept in the turrets – Oberstleutnant Schmidt and Hauptmann Braun presumably, or some such. Perhaps we'll meet their ghosts when we're digging up the gold.' She giggled and I gave her a scornful look.

'That treasure business is a load of hooey; and as for selling the place, Nicholas must be mad if he thinks anyone would want it. Total white elephant – which is just as well. The last thing I want is to have my name brought into things, least of all if there's profit to be had.' I stuck my hands in my pockets and scowled down at the monstrous pile.

There was a pause. And then she said, 'Now look here, Francis, you are being a complete wet blanket. Do not, as Pa would say, spoil the party. One hasn't travelled all this way to a most lovely region in France just for you to be gloomy and negative. Besides, we have the right to claim this enormous place for *free*, and even if there's no buyer it could at least be renovated and enjoyed. Also, with a bit of luck – unlikely, admittedly – we might even literally strike gold. Just think of all the hymn books and hassocks you could buy with that . . . even run to a new weathercock for the church spire. Where's your sense of adventure and romance? Take a chance for once!'

I whirled around and confronted her. *'Take a chance for once?* What in heaven's name do you mean! What do you think I took that day in Foxford Wood – a cup of tea?'

She stared back, startled. And then lowering her eyes, murmured quietly, 'No, not tea . . . and not just a chance. You took something else.'

'Pre*cisely*,' I echoed, 'I took something else.' For a few moments we regarded each other in silence, before shifting our gaze to the valley below and my victim's moribund property unlovely in the waning sun. I shivered.

And then Primrose said briskly, 'Yes, Francis, I grant you – some whopping chance . . . Now, let's go back to the inn, find Nicholas and get a bottle of whisky out of the car.' I nodded, whistled Bouncer, and we set off back to the village.

14

The Dog's Diary

Well, I tell you, it's all happening now! Talk about Bouncer the Bold, I'm having no end of adventures! You should have seen the cat's face when we finally met after he had escaped from the car. Looked as if he had been eating lemons smeared in castor oil.

'Bah,' he said, 'trust you to get here, muzzling in on everything! Why aren't you with the Watkins? Borrowed a magic carpet, I suppose.'

I explained that as a matter of fact I had made a small error of judgement which had involved some dog biscuits, and that sometimes mistakes lead to good endings.

'Oh yes,' he said, 'what good endings?'

'Such as seeing you again, Maurice!' And I gave my best friendly bark.

There was a long silence while he flattened his ears and closed his eyes. Then he opened them, and do you know what he said? He said, 'You are most welcome, Bouncer. Things are not good with the vicar and we must guard him closely.' I thought that was pretty good, and I told him he could rely on me all right and would he like to see the way I dealt with rabbits? He said he didn't think that would be necessary but it would be most helpful if I just lay *very* quietly on the back seat and kept an eye on F.O. So that's what I did.

And then of course there was all that business on our first night in that big place with lots of doors and where the vicar was so windy when he took me up to his room. That's where the cat sneaked downstairs to the pantry and overheard those types talking and was chucked off the window sill. He wasn't half in a bait when he came back to the room. Spitting and hissing all over the shop – and you should have heard some of his words! I thought I knew a few like that, but they're not a patch on Maurice's . . . I suppose that's what education does for you. He spent the whole night under the bed planning how to get his own back. But I told him that I thought that was pretty useless because we probably wouldn't see them again and he'd miss the chance. That didn't go down too well and he went into another sulk.

Still, he's all right now because we are at this new place high in the mountains, and there's a table right in the sun where he's allowed to lie, and he's given special pilchards by a chap called George behind the bar who he approves of. They spend a lot of time talking to each other – which is odd for Maurice as he generally ignores most humans. Unless he doesn't like them of course – and then they know it!

But I've found a friend too. He's called Clemso and he's like a brown woolly horse only shorter. Do you know, he's got this collar which plays *music*. How about that! I wouldn't mind having one of those, but I don't suppose I ever will . . . Still, can't have everything. After all, there's always the cat and F.O.

And talking of F.O., he's stewing up again. Got a bee in his bonnet about those two types. Thinks they're out to get him . . . Though come to think of it, he often feels that about people. There's that bishop person, the Mavis woman, the organist, fat Crumplehorn, the Brighton Type, the whole of the Mothers' Union, Violet Pond before Crumple did her in – oh, and lots of others. It must be pretty tiring if you ask me. A bit like always being on the run after you've been caught raiding Miss Dalrymple's dustbin – great hoofs bearing down on you . . .

15

The Vicar's Version

That evening, over a rustic supper of robust ham and vigorous wine, Ingaza gave me my instructions. The following afternoon I was to take his car, drive to the local railway station and meet the fourth member of our party off the train. Henri Martineau, rapscallion curé of Taupinière and long-time accomplice (dupe?) of Ingaza, was evidently an essential part of our enterprise, his principal qualification – other than the linguistic one – being an acute expertise in the art of metal detecting.

'Oh yes,' Nicholas had said, 'set old Henri loose with one of those things and he's like a pig turning up acorns. Makes a small mint out of those Picardy battlefields – though the idiot blows it all on booze and betting. But believe me, if anyone can locate that stuff, he will. Snout and mind like a prime ferret.' I do not often believe Ingaza, but having seen photographs of the cleric during the paintings débâcle and heard a little of his language and manner from newspaper reports at that time, I was prepared to credit every word. The prospect of a rendezvous at the station was not an enticing one, and I asked why Nicholas could not do it himself. He explained that a transaction of some delicacy was being conducted in Brighton and that he needed to keep telephone tabs on Eric to ensure that all went smoothly. 'After which,' he added, 'I intend taking a little nose round the Folie to get the lie of the land – test out the accuracy of the map.'

'You could take Bouncer,' suggested Primrose brightly.

'No,' was the short response. 'Bouncer and I have little in common; and besides, the last thing I need is a dog trailing at my heels when I'm trying to be unobtrusive.'

'Yes,' I agreed, 'discretion is not his finest point, and in any case I doubt whether he would trail at your heels – much more likely to be plunging ahead bellowing his lungs out among the rabbit holes.' I cast a kindly look at the dog who returned it with a grumbling sigh and settled himself deeper into the basket beside the cat. They both began to snore gently.

It had to happen of course . . . Clinker and his entourage. The nightmare I had been dreading, and of which Primrose had been so dismissive, manifested itself the very next morning. (Few concessions from impatient Fate.)

I had risen later than intended and, leaving the others wrangling over the last and rather emaciated croissant, wandered into the village in search of something more substantial at the bakery. However, entry proved difficult, for its doorway was occupied by a woman of enormous bulk, and although she was speaking French to the girl inside, the familiar hectoring tones struck chill to my heart. Voice and girth made her unmistakable: Myrtle, Clinker's sister-in-law and my querulous neighbour at his luncheon table four months previously. I doubted whether she would remember me (not distinguished enough), but where there was Myrtle there was surely Gladys – who most certainly would. I backed away, hunger subsumed by fear; and turning down a small alleyway scuttled into a conveniently placed *pissoir*. Less well camouflaged than a wartime pillbox and affording poorer protection (legs on show), it nevertheless had the properties of both haven and lookout post. Here I skulked, squinting through the narrow slits at the enemy in the square.

Sure enough, as Myrtle lumbered from the shop bearing armfuls of cakes and baguettes, she was greeted by another woman, taller, less huge but beefy: Gladys. The two sisters exchanged a few words and then, as luck would have it, proceeded in my direction. They paused momentarily at the corner of the alley where they seemed to be in dispute over Myrtle's shopping. 'No,' I heard Gladys say firmly, 'there is certainly not room for those things in my bag.' (She was wearing a large canvas rucksack slung over one shoulder.) 'As you well know, it's my best sketching satchel, and I do not propose having my pencils and paints mixed up with all that pastry and flaking crust! If you were going to buy so much I cannot imagine why you didn't bring something with you. Lavinia has endless string bags at the villa – indeed, if you ask me she seems to have an obsession with them. Absurd.' I couldn't catch Myrtle's reply but she looked pretty sour, and in any case by that stage they had drawn level with my sanctuary and I was more concerned with matters of concealment than with bread and bags.

I held my breath and they passed ... but Myrtle had turned round, and in ringing tones announced, 'I think it's disgusting the way their legs are always exposed – so unsettling.'

There was a dry laugh from Gladys, and in an equally scathing tone she replied, 'What else would you expect? Typical Gallic exhibitionism!'

They continued on their forthright way and I slunk from behind my screen, anxiously wondering whether my legs would be for ever recognizable.

The nervous strain of my sojourn in the *pissoir* had produced a ravenous hunger, and the moment the women were out of sight I slipped back to the pâtisserie and bought a pair of almond tarts which I consumed with gluttonous relief. Feeling better fortified but with the prospect of Henri that afternoon, I thought a little peace among the hills would be a good idea. So returning to the inn for stouter shoes, I summoned Bouncer and we set out for a leisurely ramble.

Despite the shadow of the episcopal presence – wherever that was exactly – the first hour of this was delightful. Bouncer was in his element, and we spent a happy time sniffing our way along narrow paths, splashing over rock-strewn brooks and putting up rabbits whenever the chance. The dog's energy was tireless. Not so the owner's: and eventually, despite the interest of the scenery and stimulus of the mountain air, I felt the need for a sit down and a smoke.

I found a comfortable spot with a good view of the surrounding vista and settled my back against a broad tree stump. Above me was a shepherd's hut with a solitary goat tethered beside it, but apart from its occasional bleating and the muted hum of bees, there was nothing to break the enveloping silence. And knowing full well the transience of such peace I leant back, closed my eyes and gave myself up to its ephemeral charm . . .

Ephemeral. Yes, I was permitted about five minutes of it. And then the voice burst down upon me: 'My God, it's not Oughterard, is it? What in heaven's name are *you* doing here!' Clinker's words tumbled indignantly upon my ears.

I opened my eyes: and beheld not a spectacle of the bishop draped with rods and waders as once envisioned in a mild nightmare, but His Lordship in floppy straw hat, open-necked shirt and portly cotton trousers. Slung round his neck was a large wicker pannier filled to the brim with what looked like blackberries. For an absurd moment I wondered if he was rehearsing for some bucolic role in a musical version of the *Eclogues*; but banished it instantly, feeling that at all costs I must keep my grip on grim reality.

'Hello, sir,' I said faintly. 'What a pleasant surprise! Enjoying the mountain air, are you?'

He advanced towards me silently, put down the basket, took a handkerchief from his pocket to mop his brow, and said in measured syllables, 'No, Oughterard, I am not enjoying the mountain air: it is too hot, I am too tired, these damn things weigh a ton and I have just stepped in a mess made by your perishing dog.' He sat down and started to remove one of his shoes and wipe it on the grass. 'Saw the animal a few moments ago ... thought it looked vaguely familiar – hairy hound – but naturally didn't connect it with you. How did you get here? What are you doing? Are you with anybody?'

I cleared my throat. 'Ye-es,' I volunteered, 'if you remember, when we last met in the cathedral, I did mention I was going to France with my sister ... but how amazing our meeting here. Extraordinary coincidence!' Naturally it couldn't be left at that, and he quizzed me for more details; and uneasily I revealed we were staying at the La Truite Bleue in the middle of Berceau-Lamont.

'Oh yes,' he acknowledged vaguely, 'we've passed it a couple of times. Rather a seedy joint, isn't it?' I nodded but said it was all right for a short time.

'Hmm, dare say. Surprising what one can cope with for a short time – sometimes at least. Anyone else staying, or just you and your sister?'

Instinct was to lie of course, but reason prompted otherwise. Just conceivably Ingaza's presence might remain under wraps, but knowing my luck it seemed unlikely; and the embarrassment of such a revelation after the blatant lie would be even worse than the revelation itself. Thus I took a deep breath and said as casually as possible, 'As a matter of fact, Nicholas Ingaza is with us. Hardly ever see him these days – but just now and again we bump into each other ... He, er, rather decently offered the use of his car and a bit of chauffeuring for our French trip, and since he knows the region so much better than we do he seemed a rather useful fellow to bring along ...' My voice trailed off indecisively, waiting for the explosion. Rather surprisingly none came; and at that moment Bouncer appeared from the bushes, evidently tired of his adventures, and trotted over to sit beside me. I was able to pay elaborate attention to brushing the burrs from his coat and adjusting his collar.

Immersed in this I took a covert glance at Clinker. He had gone scarlet in the face and was steadily filling his mouth with the blackberries. I wondered fleetingly whether to mention the imminence of Henri, but felt that this was not the moment.

At last he said, 'Hmm, I seem to remember your mentioning him a couple of years ago –' the memory was mutual: half an hour later the bishop had been nine sheets to the wind on my sitting-room carpet* – 'but I had no idea you were still in touch.' He cleared his throat, adding sternly, 'Not the best of associates, Francis, especially now that you're a canon.' He took another blackberry and stared intently into the far distance. I wondered what he was thinking about – the embarrassing scandal of Nicholas's outrageous behaviour at St Bede's? Or perhaps further back to Oxford before the war and – *pace* Ingaza – their brief dalliance before the melancholy advent of Gladys. Judging from the drumming fingers and the quantities of blackberries being consumed I assumed the latter.

To defuse the awkwardness, I asked him about those blackberries. Did he propose making a fruit sponge perhaps? His features hardened and I fully expected an icy riposte. But instead he gave a sardonic smile, and turning to me exclaimed ruefully, 'Sponge? That would be something. Nothing but fruit, vegetables and sulphurous water since we arrived here – and now I've been sent out to gather these things for a *compôte*, if you please!' The term was rendered as if it were one of Maurice's more distasteful trophies. He must have seen my puzzlement, for after a brief hesitation he lowered his voice and, checking that only the goat was in earshot, launched into a diatribe of protest against his hosts the Birtle-Figgins.

'You see,' he exclaimed earnestly and furiously, 'they are complete nut cutlets. *Complete*. Myrtle's friends or not, if I'd known beforehand I'd have put my foot down and we'd have steered clear. As it is, we are stuck there with a

* See *A Load of Old Bones*

pair of spinach-munching religious cranks who do nothing except rattle on about a cache of desiccated bones. It's too bad!'

I groped for a useful response but could think of none, so said weakly, 'Well, I never.' And since there was no reply added, 'Er, these bones . . . are they very desiccated?'

'Of course they are,' he snapped. 'Nineteenth-century. Been kept in an outhouse for decades. All very hush-hush.' I was none the wiser so tried again; and with a loud sigh Clinker commenced his tale.

Apparently the bones – two tibias, a patella, a single metatarsal, phalanges, a complete set of false teeth and a glass eye – had pertained to the local hermit: one Belvedere Bondolphi, who had lived in the area in the 1830s surviving on roots, berries and impeccable rectitude. Once a novice in a nearby monastery (long since defunct), he had fallen out of favour with the abbot, and indeed the Church itself, by adopting ritualistic practices not normally recognized. So idiosyncratic did these practices become that he was finally dismissed. But undeterred, and convinced he was destined for God's special notice, he had established himself in a hut outside the monastery walls, where he spent the rest of his days singing psalms and banging a tambourine.

'A tambourine?' I exclaimed.

'Apparently. Drove the abbot mad.' Clinker paused in his account and offered the dog some blackberries, while I pondered the idiosyncratic practices. Rather diffidently I enquired what they were.

'What? Oh, I don't know . . . interfering with bees or some such.'

'Interfering with *bees*! What ever do you mean, sir?' I was more than puzzled and a trifle disappointed.

'Yes, seemed he couldn't keep away from the monastery beehives – kept making the creatures swarm when they shouldn't; and then took to wearing one of those beekeeping veils during Vespers and Compline . . . frightened the life out of the younger novices. He had to go.'

87

'Well, I should think so . . . but what has this to do with your hosts and their obsession with the bones?'

Clinker grimaced. 'Boris Birtle-Figgins has got it into his head that the fellow should be canonized. Claims he performed a couple of miracles just before his death. Apparently those plus his lifelong penance of self-denial and silence (apart from the tambourine) make him a prime candidate for sainthood. The Catholic Church won't touch it with a bargepole, but that cuts no ice with Boris. Oh no! He's determined to hijack the chap for the Anglicans and is set on getting him recognized by Canterbury. In fact – and this is the ghastly part – he seems to imagine that I can put in a word with the archbishop.' He closed his eyes and shuddered.

'So where are these bones kept?' I asked curiously. 'Still in an outhouse?'

'No, more's the pity. In a crummy casket on the dining-room sideboard. It's always there leering at one over lunch and dinner. Doesn't exactly help in the digestion of lentils and dandelion leaves, I can tell you.'

'Shouldn't think it would. How awful.'

'The whole thing's awful,' he said tightly. 'And it hasn't helped Gladys's temper either. She can't stand him.' Unsurprising, I thought. There were, after all, few people that the bishop's wife could stand (and Molehill's canon not of the elect).

'But can't you leave? You know – make an excuse and motor on to other parts?'

'Huh!' he snorted bitterly. 'Chance would be a fine thing. Damn car's kaput and the idiot at the garage says it'll take days to fix. We're marooned . . . doomed.' He seemed to enjoy the rhyming assonance and repeated the words sombrely.

A thought occurred. Helpful? Mischievous? I don't know – but I heard myself saying, 'Well, sir, of course Ingaza is pretty good with engines, always has been. Amazing the number of old jalopies he was able to resuscitate at St Bede's. Don't you remember when the Bishop of Pontefract's Rover gave up the ghost in the quadrangle, and Nick fixed it in a couple of seconds despite all the false starts from the AA?'

This was greeted by a massive clearing of throat that rumbled on for some time. 'Well,' he said at length, 'one will have to see about that. Might be useful, I suppose . . . I'll, er, let you know perhaps . . .' He had gone pink in the face again and I changed the subject to something less sensitive: Myrtle. I asked how long his sister-in-law had known the Birtle-Figgins and – recalling the armful of bread and cakes – what she thought of their culinary regime.

'Six months and not much,' was the curt answer.

He enlarged on this, explaining that she had first encountered them at some embassy function in Brussels when her husband was still alive. At the time they had seemed normal enough and they had got on moderately well. Later, after her husband's death, they had popped up again and issued a standing invitation to stay at their villa, Le Petit Rêve, should she ever be in the area. 'On the strength of that,' he continued ruefully, 'Myrtle insisted that we change our normal holiday plans and the three of us travel down here to stay with "dear" Boris and Lavinia.' He sighed. 'Not a good idea.'

'But aren't there things to do?' I asked. 'The fishing is supposed to be pretty good, isn't it?'

'Oh yes, the fishing's all right, and plenty for Gladys to paint . . . *puys* and such,' he added vaguely. 'But there's too much singing for my liking.'

'Singing?' I asked, startled.

'Yes, mad keen on hymns – always at it.'

I laughed. 'Well, you should be used to that, sir. Plenty of singing in the cathedral.'

'Yes, Oughterard,' he replied testily, 'but not on *holiday*. One's got to draw the line somewhere . . . and besides, I don't recognize them, clearly not out of *Ancient & Modern*. Bizarre.'

'Are there any neighbours? I mean, do people drop in – that sort of thing?'

'Not so far,' he replied gloomily, 'unless you count the campers, of course.'

'Campers? Are there many?'

'No, no. Just a couple. They turned up last night and Lavinia allowed them to pitch their tent in one of the orchards and insisted on supplying jugs of milk. Seems to have taken to them for some reason ... shouldn't have thought they were her cup of tea. Not exactly *comme il faut*, if you get my drift. Still, none of *my* business, of course ... Small world though, I gather they come from Crowthorne and –' He broke off, looked at his watch and scowled. 'Oh Lor', nearly lunchtime. Back to the bones, I suppose.' And shouldering the fruit basket and muttering something about being in touch, he stomped off up the path and disappeared among the beech trees.

16

The Vicar's Version

When I reached the inn I was bursting to unburden my shock on Primrose and Nicholas, but my sister was nowhere to be seen and Nicholas so engrossed in his telephone instructions to Eric that it was obvious I would not get his attention for some time.

I mooched into the bar where Georges, smouldering Gitane stuck to lower lip, was polishing glasses and addressing Maurice in lengthy discourse as if he were some intimate crony. The cat looked surprisingly attentive (more so than he ever does with me), and I hesitated to ask for a drink, not wishing to intrude on their tête-à-tête. However, seeing me, Georges broke off his disquisition and reached for the cognac.

'You look tired. Monsieur should not go on the mountains – too much ees no good. *Il faut rester tranquille ici.* Be like cat and stay 'ere 'appy and *doucement.*' He grinned, pushed the glass in my direction and poured one for himself.

Happy and *doucement* – yes, I could do with a bit of that, I thought grimly. (What the *hell* were they up to, the scheming blighters?) I sipped the brandy, debating whether to order some bread and pâté, but felt too agitated to bother. Instead I asked Georges about Le Petit Rêve. He gave a graphic description – a large eighteenth-century farmhouse recently modernized and refurbished, occupying a broad corniche a mile above the village and replete with meadows and small boating lake. But when I enquired about the owners he was less forthcoming. '*Comme ci comme ça,*' was the indifferent response. 'I do not see zem often, they not come here. She OK – *assez jolie* – but *le monsieur . . .*' He trailed off, giving a mild shrug. I did not pursue the matter.

'Many campers?' I asked casually.

'*Le camping*? Only *les Allemands* – *toujours les Allemands!*' He gave a wry smile.

'No English?' I asked, feigning surprise.

'They have big passion for *les caravanes* – no good for *montagnes.*' He opened his arms wide indicating their size, but then paused and added, 'Ah, I forget . . . yes, some *messieurs* come yesterday with big tent and *très chic moteur.* Vairee fast! They have drink and ask questions about *la grande Folie en bas.* But I am busy and they soon go.' He shrugged again, winked at Maurice and turned to greet a customer.

Big tent and *très chic* motor car? Them all right. Bastards! Bastards! What were they doing? Lying in wait for me? I threw down the dregs of the brandy and wandered morosely into the passage. Nicholas had just replaced the receiver and was jotting something briskly in a notebook. I began to tell him about Climp and Mullion but he waved me aside impatiently. 'Not now, old boy. Got to call my Cranleigh contact. It's his Goodwood day . . . must catch the sod before he goes.' He was about to dial, and then paused. 'Time's getting on, Francis, don't forget old Henri.' I sighed. As if I could.

An hour later I was gingerly steering Ingaza's Citroën round tortuous bends en route for the station. Small and empty, it dozed in the afternoon sun, the single track glinting dully like a basking grass snake. Alone on the silent platform, I wondered if in fact anything would appear at all. But after five minutes or so I detected the faintest sound and in the far distance saw a whiff of smoke. I watched nervously, as rounding the bend the train gradually drew into the station. With clanking wheels and a sigh of exhaustion it came to a juddering halt, steam billowing from the engine. I waited for carriage doors to be flung wide and passengers to alight . . . None did.

The air was still, the train now mute, all exits remaining resolutely closed. Then a whistle blew. And just as it was cranking itself up to depart, a door at the far end finally opened and a small figure clad in black emerged, and in a sort of weaving motion began to amble its way down the long platform. Bearing only a knapsack, the figure nevertheless moved with halting gait and, drawing closer, patently rasping breath.

However, despite being apparently broken in wind and limb, on seeing me it let out a cry of exultation: '*Mon vieux*,' it croaked, '*vous devez être l'idiot prêtre anglais! Bienvenu en la belle France! Je suis enchanté de vous rencontrer.*' And before I had a chance to dodge, I was seized in a vice-like grip and kissed fervently on both cheeks.

Reeling from the bristles and a blast of brandy, I said politely in English (too flustered to try my French), 'Er, good afternoon, Monsieur Martineau, I hope you have had a pleasant journey.'

'*Je ne sais pas*,' was the cheery reply, '*je ne me souviens rien!*' Couldn't remember? No wonder. Obviously tight as a tick the whole damn way.

I eased the tick into the Citroën, and amidst clouds of Gitanes and garlic-laden gabble, none of which I understood, we drove back to the inn where I decanted him into the care of Nicholas. On the way I had puzzled over his lack of impedimenta – Nicholas having assured us that he was coming equipped with metal detector and shovels – and I had begun to harbour hopes that he had left them behind. No such luck. In fractured English (his one attempt) he announced that the luggage was due for collection at the station two days hence. 'You go fetch,' he directed. I do not go fetch, I thought grimly, Ingaza can do his own dirty work.

A couple of hours later, having prised some sleep from my springless mattress, I gathered myself together and went down to the bar. It was empty except for a group at a corner table. There, huddled over a pack of cards and watched intently by Maurice and Bouncer, were Nicholas, Georges, the curé – and, rather to my surprise, Primrose. I could hear low mutterings, and then my sister's ringing voice: 'No, Henri, that is definitely *my* trick. And I'll thank you to remove your sleeve from that ace!' There was an anguished splutter of indeterminate French, an expletive from the barman, and then silence as they bent again to the cards.

I watched for a little longer, and then, fancying the thought of an aperitif, cleared my throat politely and asked Georges if he would mind pouring me a small Dubonnet. He gestured expansively towards the bottle on the counter signalling I should help myself. However, as he did so, Nicholas exclaimed, 'Good idea, Francis, I'm tired of this – and old Henri is such a bloody cheat, it's like having to play two games at once, the one on the table and the one in his thieving head.'

'*Moi*, sheet?' the latter expostulated. '*Jamais ma foi!* Henri Martineau ees virtue eemself. He *nevaire* sheet!'

'All the frigging time,' replied Nicholas cheerfully.

With grumbles and mumbles, the curé got up from the table, blew a mouth raspberry and shook his fist at Maurice. The cat stared back bleakly and then closed his eyes – though whether through drowsiness or disdain it was hard to tell.

Over supper we discussed logistics – or rather Ingaza instructed us in how we should proceed once Henri's 'contraption' had arrived. An unsubtle plan: under cover of darkness the three of us (Primrose having obdurately opted out) would proceed to the Folly, and equipped with the priest's shovels and metal detector embark on an intensive search of the areas marked on the plan.

'I know exactly where they are,' said Nicholas. 'My reconnaissance yesterday was most fruitful: it's a surprisingly clear map and seems to tally precisely with the estate's terrain and features. One of the places is under a ring of oak trees close to the perimeter wall, and the other is inside what looks like an old dairy – a ruined shed next to the house. The spot under the trees should be easy enough, but the shed will be tricky. I took a squint inside and it's full of rubble and shattered tiles . . . Good for those etiolated muscles, Francis!' He turned to me and grinned. I did not.

Instead I said, 'And suppose there's nothing there?'

'In that case, dear boy, you will go straight to the notary, stake your claim and say you want to sell the whole kaboosh.' Given the two prospects – the physical cost of delving for gold or parleying with a French *notaire* – the former seemed the preferable. But both were daunting and I was less than eager.

'Oh, but I thought we might keep it for ourselves,' exclaimed Primrose. 'You know, do it up and then use it as a holiday home. It would be lovely!'

'With all due respect,' Nicholas murmured, 'such an undertaking would be prohibitive. And charming though they are, I very much doubt whether your sheep paintings, even with the Canadian market, would run to the renovations that your exquisite taste would require.' He beamed and she nodded reluctantly. 'So,' he concluded firmly, 'it's gold or sale.'

'Neek is right: gold or sale, sale or gold,' Henri chanted. 'Le Curé de Taupinière – 'ee say, strike while 'ot bird ees in zee 'and!' We regarded him in cold silence.

'Good, that's settled,' announced Nicholas briskly. 'We'll have a cognac on it.' And he waved to Georges.

'Wait a minute,' I broke in, 'what about Climp and Mullion? I've told you, they are camped somewhere on the

Birtle-Figgins' land, and it can't possibly be a coincidence again. They're watching us, waiting – I know it.'

'Yes,' agreed Nicholas coolly, 'you are very probably right. But there's two of them and three of us – four if you count Henri. We must just keep alert and see that we're ahead of the game. Shouldn't be too difficult.'

'It's all right for you,' I protested, 'but it's me they're interested in. I'm the one that is going to suffer.'

'Nonsense,' declared Primrose, 'there isn't going to be any suffering. Don't be so melodramatic, Francis. It's disgraceful them harassing innocent travellers, and if they try any monkey business I shall have no hesitation in going straight to the police.'

'Er, actually, Primrose, I would rather you didn't,' I said hastily.

'What? . . . Oh, I see. Well, I shall certainly do something.' She took out her lipstick and applied it with grim force.

We were just thinking it was time to call it a day and retire to bed, when the telephone in the lobby rang, and a few moments later Georges appeared to announce that a gentleman was seeking Monsieur Francis. I froze. Oh my God, I thought, it's them. They're at me already!

In fact it was Clinker. He had muttered something that morning about getting in touch, but I hadn't taken it too seriously and was surprised at his speed.

'Is that you, Oughterard?' the bishop enquired warily. I assured him that it was. 'Ah good . . . I thought I might stroll down to the village tomorrow morning – stretch my legs a bit and, er, perhaps call in for a coffee at your inn. Are you likely to be about? You might like to join me – you and your sister of course.' He paused, and then added casually, 'And er, bring uhm . . .'

'Ingaza?' I said helpfully.

'Yes,' he replied shortly.

I asked what time would suit him and we agreed on eleven o'clock.

'Good, good,' he said briskly. 'All news then.'

News? What news? I had not realized we were on such matey terms, but before I had a chance to enquire further he had rung off.

I returned to the dining room where fortunately only Primrose and Nicholas remained. This was just as well as somehow I did not think that Clinker's invitation for coffee stretched as far as Taupinière's illustrious incumbent.

'It's Clinker,' I said. 'Wants to have coffee with us tomorrow. I think the combination of Myrtle and his hosts is getting him down, he needs a break.'

'Don't suppose Gladys helps either,' added Nicholas waspishly.

'Probably not. Anyway he seems very keen to see you after all this time,' I replied in mild exaggeration.

He grunted. 'Aren't I the lucky one.'

17

The Vicar's Version

I was tempted to lie abed the following morning. But mindful of Clinker's visit, plus the fact that Bouncer was desperate to be loosed into the yard to romp with Clemenceau, I resisted the urge and presented myself at the breakfast table geared for the demands of the day. I was slightly worried that Henri might be around when the bishop arrived. It was difficult to imagine them having much in common. Keeping Clinker in temper was an exacting task at the best of times and unlikely to be helped by the priest's anarchic presence.

Thus I was about to ask how the land lay, when I was pre-empted by Nicholas saying, 'Old Henri has taken himself off to Vichy for the day. According to him there's a church there with some incredible stained glass that he's been wanting to see for years.' He must have seen my look of surprise, for he went on, 'Yes, I know, artistic discernment is not something to be associated with Henri, and I suspect that the real reason is that he's arranged to meet a pal who is due to stand him a gargantuan meal. Can't think why – something to do with a lost bet, I gather.'

'How did he get to the station?' I asked. 'Did you run him there?'

'At that hour in the morning? Like heck. No, he hitched a lift with some nun driving a Studebaker. Told her he had to get to confession tooty sweety.'

'Huh,' I remarked, 'not before time, I shouldn't wonder.'

Nicholas gave me what used to be known as an old-fashioned look and said mildly, 'Yes, the Roman Catholics do have the convenience of that particular outlet – *unlike* those of the Anglican persuasion ...' Thus rebuked I buried my blushes in the newspaper and my coffee cup.

Eleven o'clock arrived – as did Clinker, on the dot. This time, unencumbered by heat and blackberries, he looked less weary; but there was a tension in his face, which relaxed somewhat when he saw me. Indeed, a tolerable smile spread across his features. Goodness, I thought, things must be bad.

The weather being still mild, I took him out on to what passed for the veranda, a cramped area with rickety chairs and tables, desultory stone pots and a rather moth-eaten sunshade. However, the views were good, the coffee strong, and Georges had thrown in some madeleines in honour of *'milord l'évêque anglais'*. For my sweet tooth these dry Proustian specialities have little appeal, but Clinker set upon them with gusto and I was reminded of his earlier reference to his hosts' diet of spinach and lentils ... Suffering from daytime starvation, presumably.

It was not, I learnt, the only thing he was suffering from: the Belvedere bones were proving tiresome. 'The fellow's obsessed with them,' he grumbled, 'and seems to think that he and Lavinia have some special responsibility for their care. I mean, it's bad enough having to sit with the things in the dining room, but he now tells me he has recently built a special shrine to the chap somewhere in the grounds, and along with other crackpots intends parading the bones in front of it as some form of con-secration ceremony. Seems to imagine I would be inter-ested – even participate. Really, Oughterard, what one has to put up with!'

I was about to commiserate and enquire who the other crackpots were, when Maurice emerged, picking his way along the balustrade; seeing me, and with an uncharacteristic mew of welcome, he launched himself upon my lap. This rocked the table and upset my cup (empty fortunately). Clinker grimaced. 'Wretched cats, you never know what they are going to do next. Myrtle has one, a most contrary creature ...' He broke off and stared hard. 'I think I've seen that one before. It can't be yours, surely, not *here!*'

I confessed that it was, and began a stammered explanation as to why the cat was with me in addition to the dog. He cut me short. 'Extraordinary that you seem incapable of travelling except in the company of a menagerie of animals. However, I suppose ...'

I did not learn of his supposition, for just then Primrose and Nicholas appeared, and all conversation stopped as Clinker confronted the erstwhile bane of St Bede's and his pre-war amatory adventure.

I was amused to see that the object of his gaze had clearly made careful sartorial preparation. Despite the thin frame, gaunt cheeks and grey-streaked temples, in a louche sort of way Nicholas Ingaza still cut quite a decent figure – at least to my unpractised eye. Doubtless the slightly crumpled linen suit was more in keeping with the Riviera (or Singapore), and the glistening brilliantine and carefully arranged neckerchief too ostentatious for the purest of tastes, but one had to concede that the overall effect lent a certain raffish distinction to the scruffy veranda – and mercifully diverted the bishop's attention away from me and my 'menagerie'.

I was glad of my sister's presence for it made the handling of the preliminaries less awkward, and in answer to Clinker's polite enquiries about her painting career Primrose spoke with wit and animation.

Initially quiet, Nicholas gradually insinuated himself into the conversation, biding the cues, murmuring appreciatively in the pauses, contributing a nod, a decorous chuckle, even a mild joke. Thus little by little, rather like calming a nervous horse, he made the bishop at ease with his presence. It was a deft little manoeuvre of tact and nice judgement, and not for the first time I had a glimpse of those qualities which made him such a consummate rogue . . . and which presumably had disarmed Clinker all those years ago at Oxford.

We ordered more coffee and Clinker told us a little more about the people he was staying with and their ascetic habits. 'It's not that they aren't hospitable,' he said, 'but frankly, it's all a bit *intense*, and with those bone relics staring at me across the breakfast table sometimes it's downright uncomfortable.' He paused, and then said hesitantly, 'As a matter of fact I have a confession to make. Mrs Birtle-Figgins – Lavinia – is inviting one or two people to lunch tomorrow: her cousin Rupert Turnbull who owns a local language school, and a couple of neighbours. Gladys seemed to think it would be nice if you and your sister could be included too, and Lavinia says she will be delighted.' He coughed apologetically. 'I think my wife thought it might help things along – er, make it all a bit jollier . . .'

I was astonished that Gladys Clinker should regard me as being remotely jolly. She had certainly never given any indication of that view before, and was obviously out of sorts. However, if in a moment of abstraction I was seen as some sort of court jester, then I supposed I had better oblige.

Primrose laughed and said we would be only too happy to help out. Then saying she had some letters to write made her excuses and slipped away.

Left alone, we started to reminisce about Oxford before the war; although by tacit accord the post-war events at St Bede's theological college were tactfully skated over. Relaxed though he was, I doubted whether the bishop would take kindly to that particular turn in memory lane. As it was there was a sticky moment anyway, for at one point in the conversation Nicholas sailed rather too close to the wind (deliberately, I think) and it looked as if our guest might stalk off in dudgeon.

I cannot recall exactly what was said but it elicited an irascible response: 'You were always difficult!' the bishop had snapped.

'Ah,' replied Ingaza slyly, 'but you were such a tease.'

There was silence, and for one moment I thought Clinker was about to explode. He seemed to go puce around the edges and I noticed the vein in his temple working fit to burst. But when something finally issued from his twitching mouth it was a sound not of wrath but of mirth, and in a tone of mingled fury and fond nostalgia he cried, 'My God, you little bugger, you haven't changed a jot!'

Nicholas gave a self-deprecating shrug, sleeked his hair and offered Clinker a cigarette. The latter muttered something about never touching the things these days and took it swiftly. The three of us leant against the balustrade smoking in silence and regarding the distant dome of Le Puy. It was a moment of rare peace broken only by the bleating of a goat and the distant strains of the French national anthem.

18

The Vicar's Version

My anxieties about the lurking presence of Climp and Mullion had left me feeling jaded; and thus after supper that night I decided a little walk might help settle my mind and refresh the spirit. It was a pleasant stroll down to the village, the evening's quiet broken only by the occasional cluck of duck and a distant braying of donkey. The fireflies were out, puncturing the dusk with eerie darting gleams, and now and again I caught the whiff of wood smoke and the insidious sweetness of late lilies.

At the pond's edge I stood gazing at the reflection of the rising moon, savouring the silence, feeling a wave of rare tranquillity and wishing it could be ever thus. A firefly winked, a frog plopped and I could just catch the faint chirruping of an early nightjar.

'Not a bad sort of place, is it, Canon? Leastways, not if you want to get away from things it isn't.' The voice came suddenly from the gloaming behind me and, startled though I was, I did not need to look round to know it was Mullion's.

'Not bad at all,' I agreed easily, 'very attractive in fact.'

He came and stood beside me and lobbed a pebble into the middle of the pond where it made an explosive splash and set up a protest from one of the ducks. He studied the widening ripples and remarked casually, 'Water, it's like life really, one disturbance leads to another ... messes everything else up. But then I expect you'd know about that, wouldn't you? I mean, I expect it's the sort of thing you tell your congregation during your Sunday sermons.' I made no answer. 'Isn't it?' he persisted.

'Not specially,' I replied evenly, 'there are quite a lot of topics which –'

'I bet there are,' he said quickly. 'All that good and evil stuff you vicars have to preach about. Must get a bit boring sometimes – or *worrying*, more like.' He laughed loudly and added, 'You know, when I was a nipper I always thought it was the parson's job to prick consciences – other people's, I mean. Never occurred to me to think that even a vicar might be tarred with guilt. Funny really.' And he laughed again. (Oh yes, side-splitting, I thought . . . and thought too of Bouncer, Nicholas, Primrose, even Clinker, and wished to God they were with me.) 'You know what?' he continued, and paused.

The question was clearly not rhetorical, and reluctantly I asked, 'What?'

'Our Mr Crumpelmeyer – now he's a one that's interested in good and evil too; and with him spending his days inside it has – how shall I put it? – sort of unleashed his imagination. Keeps making up odd stories, very odd. Want to hear one?'

'Haven't got time,' I mumbled, 'must get back to the inn.'

'Oh, but you'll like this one, it's worth waiting for. Right up your street, I should say. All about a vicar and the murder of an old lady – in a wood.' He gripped my elbow; and turning my head I saw the smile . . . and the menace.

'Look,' I said stiffly, trying to ease my arm, 'I've no idea what you are talking about, and as I said, I am in rather a hurry.'

'Really? But you've only just got here. Been watching you, Mr Oughterard, been watching for some time . . . and thinking.' The grip tightened, the smile vanished and was replaced by a sneer of hostility.

'What is it you want?' I asked as coldly as I could.

104

He relaxed his hold. 'That's better. Like I always say to old Victor when he gets on his high horse, things go much easier when you co-operate. Much easier.'

My heart was starting to race, and absurdly the only thing I could think of saying was to query his use of the adjective. But I doubted if the observation would be well received and so kept silent.

'You see,' he went on softly, 'Ken and I, we know what you're doing here. Same as us: you've come to sniff out that Nazi bullion. I was in these parts during the war and heard a lot of the local talk. Didn't think much of it at the time, but I have since; and when old Victor comes along ranting and raving about you and his ma-in-law and the lost deeds and all, I put two and two together. Ay, ay, I thought, he's on the make, on the bloody make! There was something else I thought too – but we won't bother to go into that now, will we? Not *just* now . . .'

Apart from the surge of indignation at the injustice of his words 'on the make', my immediate reaction was one of craven despair . . . At last, after all this time of cringing fear, all the evasions and subterfuge, I was being directly confronted about Elizabeth's death. Sparring with the police had been tense enough; but whatever their suspicions, no one had actually *voiced* them so explicitly as this man now, standing close and confident in the gathering gloom. The flat sardonic words, 'all about a vicar and the murder of an old lady', hammered in my head and struck ice in my gut. He might not have the proof but he had the conviction, and wouldn't hesitate to use it.

Thoughts reeled helplessly. What to do? What to say? Think, Francis, think! The self-assured voice of my father echoed in my mind: 'When in doubt, my boy, stay still. Wait for the other bugger to show his hand . . .' All very well, but suppose the other bugger had already shown his hand and you hadn't a clue how to act? What then, for God's sake? I heard another voice – Ingaza's – nasal, bantering: 'Never admit a thing, old chap, not a thing. Laugh it off – gives you time and they get confused.'

But I was too flustered to cope with that, and instead said feebly, 'A bit beyond me, I'm afraid, you're not making a lot of sense. I really must be –'

'Then I'll spell it out for you, Dumbo,' he suddenly snarled. 'That stuff is there all right and we want it. I've been waiting for a break like this all my life and I'm not having some grasping parson foul things up!'

'I am not grasping,' I began angrily, 'I –'

'Shut up and listen. We know you've got the plan with the places marked and we're pretty sure it's reliable. You can do one of two things – either hand it over to us now or deliver the stuff when you find it. It's a gamble but I'm not passing up a chance like this, and if there is anything going, *I'm* getting it.'

'And Climp,' I murmured.

'Yeah, there's always Climp,' he replied indifferently.

'But even if what you are saying is true – about us seeking the treasure – suppose we don't choose to comply with your request?' I waited, knowing and dreading the answer. It came.

'Well, we'll have to think about that, Mr Oughterard, won't we? Have to think about that very carefully. I mean, things could turn nasty, *really* nasty. And we're not just talking about a broken nose, are we?'

I took his point ... No, not a nose – a broken neck on the scaffold. And again I heard Ingaza's advice: *Laugh it off* ...

'Good Lord, Mullion,' I chuckled, 'you're like something out of Laurel and Hardy!' And I launched into a peal of carefully calculated laughter. The only problem was that the mirth did not remain calculated. It grew in power and intensity until, with tears coursing down my cheeks, I became doubled up in helpless paroxysms, lurching and hooting uncontrollably at the water's edge. Nervous tension, I suppose.

'Streuth!' I heard Mullion mutter. And in his surprise he must have stepped back and lost his footing, for the

next thing I heard was a curse and a colossal splash . . .
And there he was: floundering and snorting like some
befuddled hippo. Clearly it was time to beat a tactical
retreat.

Thus moderately sobered, and to the cries of indignant
geese rushing to appraise the spectacle, I hurried back to
the safety of the inn – to be greeted by Clemenceau and the
rallying notes of the Marseillaise.

'What ever have you been doing?' exclaimed Primrose as I
entered the bar. 'You look awful!'

''Orrible.' agreed Henri.

They were sitting at the card table, monitored by
Maurice and drinking coffee.

'It's Mullion,' I announced breathlessly. 'He has exposed
himself!'

'Disgusting,' remarked Nicholas. 'Shouldn't be allowed.'

'He's done what?' Primrose yelped.

'No, no,' I said hastily, 'not that.' And I started to explain.

When I reached the part about him falling in the pond,
Nicholas said caustically, 'Well, that's sure to endear him
to you, Francis – you've got a friend for life there. Must say,
I think you could have managed it with a little more
finesse.'

I rounded on him. '*Finesse*? How would you like to be
threatened by that vicious thug? I tell you, they mean
business!'

'Yes, well so do we,' he snapped. 'Blowed if I am going
to be beaten by some toerag of a bent screw. I know that
type, too cocky by half.' He spoke with feeling, and, I suspected, from bitter memory.

'This is too much,' protested Primrose. 'I know you are
not in favour, Nicholas, but I really think we should pull
out before things get dangerous. They are clearly a most
unsavoury pair and I really do not wish to be further
embroiled. We should go *home*.' She spoke with the de-
cisive authority employed for the tiresome and vexatious

107

(and in whose ranks I invariably featured), but I knew it would cut no ice with Ingaza: he had his own agenda. And I guessed that part of that agenda included his resentment of Mullion and determination to beat him at his own game: a rival in the treasure hunt stakes had not featured in the original plan and was fast becoming a personal affront. I recalled our days at St Bede's and how tenacious he had been – not simply in pursuit of his own ends, but in ensuring that those ends should be undiluted by the actions of others. Selfishness played a part, I suppose, but more basic were the goads of challenge and vanity. Thus the greater the opposition, the greater his obstinacy. (There was also, of course, the harridan spectre of Aunt Lil . . . incurring her scorn being, I suspected, the least tolerable of Ingaza's nightmares.)

My supposition was right. There was a pause, and then he said mildly, 'That's not entirely convenient, Primrose. You see, this whole affair has put me to substantial trouble and I do not propose turning tail now.' (Put *him* to trouble? What about me? I was irked by the words but unsurprised.)

She started to argue but was forestalled by an indulgent smile and the offer of a Sobranie. With a resigned sigh and only fractional hesitation, Primrose took the proffered cigarette. There are few people to whom my sister capitulates, and Ingaza is one of them.

'Good,' he said briskly. 'Now we must put our heads together and get down to tactics.'

19

The Vicar's Version

Primrose is more adventurous than me and she was amused at the prospect of 'helping things along' at the Birtle-Figgins' lunch party. 'I say,' she laughed, 'they must be having a tough time if Gladys Clinker wants us there! It could be quite amusing in a masochistic way.'

'Anything must be funnier than rooting around with Henri Martineau and his metal detector,' I replied gloomily. 'I wonder what she'll give us to eat – not much, according to Clinker.'

'No chance of gourmet splendour, that's for sure. But from what your bishop was saying, the house itself is nice and with some lovely gardens. It'll be quite interesting really. Besides, if you are good, Francis, that cranky Boris will show you his bone collection. You'll enjoy the treat.'

We arrived at Le Petit Rêve just before midday and were met in the gravel drive by a tall man who introduced himself as Rupert Turnbull, a cousin of Lavinia Birtle-Figgins. He at least seemed perfectly normal, and after a brief exchange of pleasantries he took us indoors where we were introduced to our host. Boris was also tall, but thick-set, lumbering and pallid; and to my rather disapproving eye wore his hair far too long for a man of his age – or of any age. It gave him the look of a lugubrious bloodhound.

He did not look like a rabid fanatic, but then you can't always tell with these things . . . However, he gave us a friendly welcome and said warmly, 'Now, you all go in while I mix the drinks.'

My spirits perked up immediately. Perhaps Clinker's tale of the menage being a more than temperate zone had been exaggerated. I mentally prepared my palate for a dry martini or, given the weather, possibly a Pimm's . . . Or what was that nice concoction we had tried on the way down, the cassis and white wine thing? A kir – that's what Ingaza had called it, and very tasty too . . .

My reverie was abruptly curtailed by our hostess thrusting a glass of ochre liquid into my hand saying, 'I think you'll like this – spearmint and Tizer with chopped apple pips, Boris's speciality!' I thanked her and moved dolefully to the window. The view was good at any rate.

Accompanying the liquid libations were miniature rice cakes embellished with what I took to be mounds of wet woven grass. 'Interesting, aren't they?' a voice said challengingly. Myrtle.

'Fascinating,' I agreed.

'I so admire the Birtle-Figgins,' she confided. 'It's not often one meets genuine purists, least of all within the Church, and it is most refreshing to be among true ascetics for once. Why, I was saying to my brother-in-law only this morning what a shame it is that more people don't practise a diet of such cleansing simplicity – the world would be a better place. Don't you agree, Canon?'

I recalled the picture of Myrtle emerging from the pâtisserie, knees bent under the weight of cakes and buns, and avoiding her question asked instead what the bishop had to say on the matter.

'Huh,' she snorted, 'nothing of any coherence – never has.'

I smiled wanly and asked if she was enjoying her stay. 'Yes,' she replied shortly, 'it is always pleasant to *goûter la nouvelle*.'

'I'm sorry?'

She gave a pained sigh. 'To taste the unaccustomed – it is always stimulating. After all –' and she gestured expansively towards the rice cakes and jugs of Tizer and spearmint – 'so different from Brussels and the embassy, don't you think?'

I confessed to not knowing either.

'No,' she murmured sourly, 'no, I don't suppose you would ...' And with a dismissive nod she turned away and lumbered off in the direction of Turnbull.

It had never occurred to me that I should be glad to speak with Gladys, but beside her sister, the bishop's wife seemed almost human – briefly at any rate. She wore the habitual scowl of course, but her opening words were startlingly cordial. 'Nice to see you, Francis,' she began. (How alien the greeting!) 'Horace mentioned he had bumped into you ... Surprising really, I always assumed you took your holidays in Clacton. But I dare say the mountain air may do you some good – although,' and here she lowered her voice, 'you would have done better to stay further *north*.'

'Really?' I said in surprise. 'Why is that?'

'Because then you would have been spared this ludicrous man and his nonsensical notions. All these bones and the mumbo-jumbo are tiresome beyond endurance. Myrtle's fault naturally. She would insist on dragging us down here to stay with these people, and now pretends she's enjoying it when I know very well she can't wait to get back to Brussels. Typical.'

'Oh dear ...' I began.

'Yes, it is oh dear,' she replied in a booming whisper. 'I can assure you, more than vexing!'

'What is Gladys saying?' laughed Lavinia, gliding up and offering to replenish my reluctant glass. 'What is it you find so vexing, my dear?'

'The hill,' replied Gladys gruffly, 'very steep and long in this warm weather.'

'Ah, but you must rest awhile at the allotted stops,'

soothed our hostess. 'Boris had them made specially – Belvedere's Niches for the Afflicted, that's what we call them – holy respites for weary travellers.'

'I am not in need of a niche,' answered Gladys. And excusing herself abruptly, she went off to rattle Clinker.

Left alone with Lavinia I made polite enquiries about the Belvedere relics, saying that I understood her husband was quite an expert on the hermit.

'He most certainly is,' she enthused. 'Devotes so much of his time to the good man. Just as well really, stops him from . . .' She broke off, went slightly pink in the face and cleared her throat, before hurriedly adding, 'But I too help in my small way – organizing the followers and festivities, and telling the village children how lucky they are to have such a pious example in their history. Oh yes, we both hold a torch for dear St Belvedere!'

'But he is not a saint,' I pointed out, 'not even reached first base of a Venerable.' Yes, it was an ungracious remark, but my spirits were flagging, and lack of gin in the Tizer was proving an irritant.

However, she seemed not to notice and prattled on merrily. And then just as my attention was giving up the ghost, she hailed Clinker. 'Oh, Horace, do come and persuade Francis and his sister to join us for the harp and recorder recital this evening, it will be such a joy for them! And then they could stay overnight, and tomorrow Primrose could join us *girls* for the shopping trip to Clermont and Francis could keep you and Boris company while we are gone. Why, you could all go fishing.' She clapped her hands delightedly.

I froze. Harp? *Recorder?* . . . The delights of Duke Ellington swam into my mind, and the brilliance of Bach and the Goldberg Variations, Vivaldi, Brahms, Count Basie, Savage's drumming hero Gene Kruppa. For an instant I even thought of Eddie Calvert (he of the 'golden trumpet') and Gilbert and Sullivan. And what about Alban Berg, Liszt, Dizzie Gillespie and countless other possibilities . . . anyone, any*thing* rather than harp and recorder!

'What a capital idea,' agreed Clinker viciously, and summoned reinforcements from Gladys and Myrtle.

To my surprised chagrin both women seemed in favour
of the suggestion and a distinct expression of relief
appeared on their faces. Myrtle instantly sought out
Primrose to entice her with the delights of Clermont. Just
goes to show, I thought ruefully, when social desperation
drives, even the Oughterards are in demand.

Everything depended on Primrose. If she could stand
firm and think of a cogent reason for our not staying the
night at Le Petit Rêve I should be spared the horror. I tried
to catch her eye as she was being buttonholed by Myrtle.
She must have seen me grimacing but made no sign. And
then to my fury I saw her smiling and nodding in apparent agreement. The treachery of it!

They came over, and Myrtle announced triumphantly,
'Well, that's all wrapped up then. Primrose says she would
love to stay and is *so* fond of the harp.' Liar, I fumed. She
hates it. What on earth was her game?

I glared at her grimly. 'Francis, dear,' she responded, 'we
shall have to excuse ourselves to our friends at the inn, but
I'm sure they won't miss us for just one night. Could you
possibly pop back and fetch my nightdress and vanity case.
It's on the dressing table – and I dare say you'll need something yourself. And perhaps you could bring my spare pair
of shoes from the car.' She smiled sweetly.

The others drifted away and I was able to mutter to her,
'Whatever did you want to do that for? It'll be ghastly.'

'Yes,' she agreed quietly, 'but worth it. I think I've got
that Turnbull man about to place an order for three of my
pictures. Says he's got a mass of wall space at his language
school and it needs filling up. If I turn on the old charm
this evening he might settle for another two.'

I should have known it: Primrose would flog a picture
to St Peter if she ever got that far. 'Huh,' I replied, 'Ingaza
won't like it. Old Henri's paraphernalia is due at the
station this evening and he wanted to get things up and
running tonight before those beggars start snooping.'

She shrugged. 'Well, he'll just have to be patient,' she said, 'or careful.'

After a mournful lunch of limp salad and unadorned blackberries, I hitched a lift from the gardener back to the inn. Here I found Ingaza hunched at the the small writing desk in what Madame fancifully called the residents' salon. He was chewing his pen over a postcard and sighing irritably, and I guessed Aunt Lil was about to receive a rapturous report from *la belle France*. Judging from his mood I rather doubted whether he would take kindly to my news.

'Ah, Nicholas,' I started, 'if you don't mind, Primrose and I have been invited to stay the night at Le Petit Rêve. They've roped us in to listen to some concert by a few of the locals – and I think we're also expected to be around for a while tomorrow. Couldn't get out of it really, they were so insistent, and it was becoming difficult to –'

'Do what you like,' was the careless reply. 'There's a bloody rail strike in Paris and Henri's stuff won't be delivered until tomorrow morning at the earliest – which in Frog lingo means considerably later.' He paused, and adding sourly, 'Give my love to the bishop,' returned to his labours.

I collected Primrose's things and a change of shirt and trousers for myself, and in a frame of mind similar to Ingaza's trudged back to the house. Gladys had been right about the steepness of the hill, and like her I did not fancy stuffing myself into a wayside niche to crouch cheek by jowl with the hermit's effigy.

When I arrived, Primrose was waiting in the hall and took me upstairs to my bedroom. It was splendid: huge, hushed and opulent, with its own bathroom and blissful-looking double bed draped in folds of toile de Jouy. Compared with my rabbit hutch at the inn it was a palace. I began to feel stronger instantly.

'Yes, I thought you'd like that,' laughed Primrose. 'Mine's even better. For a couple so dedicated to a life of lentils and austerity they do pretty well in the sleeping department. Dinner's at seven, so you've got plenty of time for a nice little shut-eye.'

One bonus at any rate. I took off shoes and tie and sank gratefully on to the feathered pillows. My eyes closed and sleep came swiftly.

When I awoke it was nearly seven, and skipping the pleasure of a leisurely shower I changed quickly and hurried downstairs. In the hall there stood a large harp and a number of music stands. My heart sank. Clearly the performers had arrived and preparations were afoot. There would be no escape . . .

With the prospect of the recorders hanging over me, and surrounded by their withered and earnest virtuosi, I found supper an irksome affair – although to some extent leavened by the sight of Primrose trying to seduce Turnbull into purchasing more of her sheep and church pictures. If they learnt nothing else, I reflected, at least his students would graduate with an enriched vocabulary of matters ovine and ecclesiastical. From what I could make out he seemed to be weakening, and I wondered idly whether Primrose would offer much of a discount. Unlikely.

I was also pondering the looming imminence of the metal detecting which, despite the Paris strike, seemed as inescapable as the Birtle-Figgins' recital. And as with the latter, and whatever its outcome, the process was sure to be painful. However, sitting next to my host, and having nothing riveting to say, I asked him casually about the rumoured gold.

'Huh! That old canard!' Boris replied scornfully. 'Thought it had been laid to rest years ago.' He turned to Lavinia. 'My dear, fancy people still pursuing that piece of nonsense. Extraordinary. Still, I suppose it keeps the tabloid press amused. I remember *Picture Post* trying to drum up . . .' He broke off, seeing my look of perplexity, and turning to his wife said, 'You explain, Lavinia. I am

115

sure the canon and his dear sister would far rather hear it in your dulcet tones.'

Underneath her simper I thought I glimpsed a curling lip. However, with a bright laugh Lavinia started to elucidate. 'Oh, Boris is quite right, there is no gold there now, absolutely none at all . . . There was at one point and for a short while – some German commandant had amassed a stack of gold napoleons, and guessing they would be handy after the war had hidden them under the floor of the old dairy. But he wasn't very bright and used to swagger into the local hostelry, overdo the drink, and broadcast their presence to all and sundry. You can imagine! Over the months the coins were simply leached away by the locals, and then at the liberation they strung him up anyway: bully gone and his said bullion spent. So you see, the whole thing is merely a charming little myth!' She gave a silvery giggle, which for one cringing moment reminded me of Elizabeth.

Just as I was deciding whether to be relieved or dismayed by the revelation, and doubting that Ingaza would appreciate the myth's 'charm', her husband broke in: 'But there is of course the diamond-encrusted swastika . . . Now that *is* worth a bob or two – assuming one were ever concerned with such tawdry matters.' And he gave a superior laugh.

'So what's that?' asked Primrose quickly.

'Oh, it's a relic from Hitler's early days,' said Boris carelessly, 'given to a brother of the Folly's original owner in the early thirties. Some English Germanophile – name of Fotherington or something – a reward for sympathies to the Reich. He kept it in a wellington boot in one of the servants' lavatories under the back stairs . . . and do you know, despite the shambles the Jerries made of the place, it remains there to this very day.'

'But why?' gasped Primrose.

'Why what, dear lady?' asked Boris obtusely.

'*Why* is it still in the wellington boot?' interjected Gladys.

'And how do you know, anyway?' She fixed him with a cynical stare.

'I found it,' he replied simply. 'When I was seeking a suitable place to lay the Holy Bones . . . but of course, nothing was really appropriate which is why we had to prepare a special –'

'Yes, yes, we know that, but why leave the swastika in the *boot*?' boomed Gladys impatiently. 'If it's so valuable why did you not remove it to a place of safe-keeping?'

'Far better,' Clinker agreed. 'By Jove, Boris, it could be treasure trove – you know, finders keepers. Play your cards right and they'll probably give you permission to claim the thing. I'd get it out of the gumboot if I were you!'

Boris looked pained. 'I have more pressing matters to give thought to than the vulgar swag of Mammon,' he declared sententiously.

'Such as?' demanded Gladys.

'The revered Belvedere, of course,' he exclaimed in surprise, 'and my mission to restore his memory to its proper place: to ensure he receives the recognition, nay, the canonization he so richly deserves.' He turned to Clinker, adding, 'And with the help of the good bishop here I am sure that can be achieved. After all,' and he dropped his voice in earnest confidence, 'the paltry treasures of man are nothing to the treasures of the spirit. Wouldn't you say so, Bishop?'

Clinker coughed. 'Absolutely,' he replied.

20

The Vicar's Version

It is enough to say that like all things, good and bad, the recital passed. And punch drunk on tinkling harp and mewling recorders, I was left thankful and longing for bed.

Flushed with success and unadulterated Tizer, the performers tottered into the night twittering about Belvedere and his custodian's proposals for the shrine's inaugural ceremony. Much was being made of the harpist (alas, no Harpo Marx), who, after Boris and the hermit, was billed to be the star turn of the great occasion. Thus laying plans to absent myself from the area for the entire day, I retired stealthily to bed.

As arranged, the next morning the women were whisked off by Lavinia on their shopping spree, leaving Boris, Clinker and myself to our own devices. Lavinia's suggestion of a few hours' fishing was not pursued, Boris being far too heavily engrossed in polishing the bones' casket in readiness for its public display. Clinker too was otherwise occupied, muttering something about going down to the village to supervise the progress on his motor. Although there was no reason why he should, he did not invite me to accompany him, and set off from the house at a brisk, even eager, pace. His manner had struck me as slightly furtive, and I surmised that, like Myrtle earlier, he was intent on raiding the pâtisserie and stocking up on carbohydrates.

I wandered into the garden, found a deck chair, and lighting a cigarette gave myself up to peaceful contemplation of the still colourful flower beds and sweeps of well-tended sward leading down to the meadow and its improvised swimming pool. I grinned, thinking of Bouncer and his mania for water. Just as well the little beggar wasn't with me: he would have been down there quick as a flash, plunging in to do his frenzied dog-paddle convinced he was a battleship or Moby Dick.

However, as I visualized the dog besporting himself in the water, another image superimposed itself: that of Mullion in similar circumstances, not sporting but snorting furiously. My smile vanished and I flinched in recollection of that flat menacing voice.

Well, I brooded, there was one thing to be thankful for. According to Lavinia's tale they were on a fool's errand as far as the gold was concerned . . . As, of course, were we. I thought uneasily of Ingaza and his likely anger at being baulked of the 'treasure', not to mention his wasted arrangements with Henri for its detection and excavation. Indeed, Henri himself would be less than pleased, and already I could see the saturnine scowl on the curé's face and hear the enraged imprecations as he fulminated against all things connected with perfidious Albion – in particular its clergy and Oughterard of Molehill. One way or other there was bound to be a shindig, and the fallout could be interminable . . . Clearly there was nothing for it but to tell them of the existence of the booted swastika: with luck it would be a mollifying substitute, and presumably more accessible. Also with luck, any efforts to 'liberate' the thing would be less likely to attract the attention of our competitors.

Competitors? A feeble term. Avenging Furies more like, out to get me whatever the means! Or were Climp and Mullion simply the vanguard of heaven's infantry, dispatched to harry and discomfit the guilty before the final submission? But, I wondered, would celestial emissaries be quite so louche and prosaically thuggish? It seemed unlikely – but one could never be sure. Doubtless a case could be made . . .

Unwrapping a peppermint preparatory to reflecting further, I became aware of something glinting. I looked up. There was nothing obvious, and I scanned the windows of the house thinking one of the panes might be catching the sun's rays. Nothing there either, and I was about to settle to the newspaper when there was another sudden flicker. I scrutinized the field below and the trees beyond. And that was where I saw it – the darting flash of a lens. Yes, somebody was surely there with a pair of binoculars, trained, it would seem, on Le Petit Rêve . . . or perhaps more specifically, on me.

I recalled uneasily that to the right of the trees was the apple orchard, the area where, according to Clinker, Mullion and Climp had been permitted to pitch their rotten tent. I groaned. Whether Furies, thugs or heavenly infantry, they had me in their sights and I was clearly a marked man. I got up hastily and hurried back into the house imagining my sister's dismissive voice telling me not to be so melodramatic. Maybe she was right and I was overreacting – although judging from the duck-pond encounter, it seemed doubtful. Despite the morning's warmth, I shivered, and thought enviously of my locum back in Molehill with nothing more to harass him than Tapsell's tantrums and the pallid inanities of Mavis Briggs.

In the salon I picked up a book from the coffee table on local lore and legend by one Herbert Castris, described as 'a notable authority', and trying to banish all thoughts of the 'Watchers in the Orchard' settled down to read. A large part of the legend seemed to be devoted to Belvedere Bondolfi and the author's tireless search for the hermit's lost tambourine. It was quite entertaining; but I was soon startled out of my absorption by the sound of the front door being banged and heavy footsteps: Clinker, returned

120

from the garage and fortified by the pâtisserie. I braced myself for the interruption.

'Ah, Francis,' he began (first name always a good sign), 'surprised to find you here. Thought you might have been persuaded by our host to help him walk the bones, he's holding a dummy run.'

'Walk the bones?' I echoed. 'I don't quite follow –'

'No, neither does anyone in their right mind,' he replied drily. 'It's some ritual he has devised as part of the ceremony, a sort of prelude to the installing of the casket in the shrine. Apparently the idea is that Boris, plus casket and assorted fellow zealots, will perambulate about the area pausing at those spots where the hermit is said to have prayed or uttered sage words. The lid of the casket will be opened, the bones exposed and the faithful fans invited to sing a *Te Deum* – or rather, a paean penned especially for the occasion by Lavinia. So he wants to get the route sorted out first.'

'Good Lord,' I murmured.

'My sentiments exactly,' said Clinker. He dropped his voice. 'Actually, he seemed to think that I should be eager to accompany him on the dress rehearsal, said something about a bishop being able to give him tips on the processing protocol. More than I can face, I'm afraid, and I've told him my gout is playing up.'

'Oh dear,' I replied innocently, 'didn't realize you suffered from gout. Is it very –'

'Well, I might do,' he said truculently. There was a pause while he cleared his throat. 'Anyway, Oughterard, the man is clearly deranged, though harmless enough I suppose. A bit of a prig, if you ask me, which wouldn't be so bad if he weren't such an awful bore ... no conversation at all except about this Belvedere chappie. It's getting on my wick, and I have no intention of traipsing around this afternoon playing gooseberry to him and his ossified companion.' I smiled sympathetically. 'Mind you,' he continued, 'Gladys can't abide Boris – says I don't know the half of it, and if he were her husband she would put

121

bromide in his fruit juice . . . or arsenic.' He gave a modest guffaw and stomped out into the garden, while I was left pondering why on earth Boris should be in need of bromide.

A little later the man himself appeared, clearly pleased with the results of his polishing and eager for me to inspect both container and contents. The former was dazzling, the latter grey and grisly. However, I showed suitable appreciation and asked how long it would take him to 'pace the course'.

'About an hour or so,' he replied, 'but I might have to attend to one or two matters in the village first, before – ah – before Lavinia returns. Might be some time . . .' He trailed off vaguely, and clutching the precious casket and telling me we should help ourselves to the fruit bowl and dandelion soup for lunch, he left the room. I stared after him, feeling the pangs of hunger already jostling, and wondering if the housekeeper could be prevailed upon to produce some sausage and mash . . . Fortunately she was more than co-operative, for taking pity on the two starved guests she presented us with an enormous baguette and some splendid rabbit pâté, the shared product of her own oven and her husband's gun. Coffee too was brought, accompanied by a surreptitious bottle of cognac (an act of charity which even now features in the bishop's nostalgic memory).

After lunch, sated with cognac and pâté, Clinker took himself off for a nap, while I reapplied myself to Castris's book. I had been tempted to take a stroll around the gardens but was becoming paranoid about our companions in the orchard – assuming of course that they were still there, and not prowling fruitlessly within the grounds of the Folly. Either way, it seemed best to remain indoors.

An hour later, and just as I had started to wrestle with the previous week's crossword, Clinker appeared from his slumbers wearing a towelling dressing gown and carrying a rubber bathing cap. After giving abortive advice regarding some of the clues, he announced he was off to take his daily plunge in the pool before 'the dear ladies' returned. Again the picture of Bouncer swam into my mind, and I wondered if the bishop favoured the same manic stroke as the dog . . . Quite possibly.

Alone once more, I had discarded the crossword and returned to the book; and was just at the part describing the hermit's fondness for his tambourine, when with an almighty crash the door was flung open, and an extraordinary spectacle met my startled gaze. Clad only in vest and dripping bathing shorts, Clinker stood there wild-eyed and mouthing.

'Boris has been bludgeoned!' he cried. '*Murdered!*'

I gaped at him and then said the first thing that came into my head. 'Who by . . . Gladys?'

He also gaped. 'Gladys? What in God's name are you talking about, Oughterard! By persons unknown, of course. Who else? Give me some brandy and don't be absurd . . . This has spoilt everything!' He held out a quivering hand.

Yes, it had been a thoughtless response and I tried to retrieve the gaffe by pouring him nearly half the bottle.

'But how? Where?' I exclaimed. 'Have you told the police?'

'Police? No, of course not . . . I've only just found him – down at the pool where I was floating, behind the bushes . . . And – and what's more – he is surrounded by bones.'

'*Bones!*' I cried in disbelief. 'What bones?' He was clearly hallucinating, and I felt convinced he must be deluded about the body as well.

'The Belvedere bones, of course! Tipped all over him. The casket's there, empty! It's appalling – I'll never hear the end of it, never.' He thrust the brandy to one side and covered his face with his hands, rocking backwards and forwards on his chair while the sodden bathing shorts dripped a small pool at his feet.

I stared at the accumulating wet, thinking that Lavinia would be none too pleased when she returned from the shopping trip. It also occurred to me that Clinker was mad . . . or failing that, that he was somehow responsible. But I banished the latter notion, thinking it too much of a coincidence for us both to be assassins. No, obviously the man was unwell, the rigours of the holiday had unhinged him. I should have to be very gentle . . .

'Horace,' I ventured, thinking that use of his first name might be a soothing antidote to his obvious strain, 'perhaps before anything else you should get out of those wet clothes, and then when you are nice and dry we'll go down together and take a look.' I patted his shoulder reassuringly, picturing my old nanny dealing with similar traumas from my boyhood. Yes, I recalled fondly, she had been good at that . . . calming the enraged and afflicted.

'I don't want another look,' he moaned, 'it's ghastly. Head staved in. Gladys will never forgive me.'

'But it's nothing to do with you, is it?' I said firmly. 'And once you are ready we'll go and investigate and see what's what.' I nodded confidently.

Somehow these words seemed to steady him, for in the next breath and with biting emphasis he said, 'I know exactly what is what, Oughterard. Boris is dead on the bank and I shall be blamed. Now go and get me some dry clothes and be quick about it. We haven't got all day!' He fixed me with a withering glare and took a swig of brandy.

My head in a whirl, I raced upstairs, found the right bedroom and a change of clothes, and returned to the salon. From thence we made our way down to the stream and the bathing area. I was curious rather than nervous, feeling sure that whatever was there (if anything) it would not be a dead body, least of all Boris's.

But he was there all right, all six foot of him, inert and solid. And just as Clinker had described – with his head staved in.

124

'You see,' the bishop said accusingly, 'I told you so, and there are the bones as well.' He jabbed his finger at the spectacle on the ground.

I closed my eyes but could not erase the reality: our host lay spreadeagled on the paving stones, his skull a sickening mess. And strewn randomly across and about his torso were the sacred bones of St Belvedere . . . plus the teeth, top and bottom.

I stared mesmerized by the sight – bones, casket, cadaver – and experienced that same feeling of dream-like absurdity which on an earlier occasion had assailed me in Foxford Wood. But at least this time I was merely the spectator . . .

Soberly it occurred to me that Lavinia would have more to disturb her than the patch of wet on her drawing-room carpet, and I made such observation to Clinker, saying that at least she could count on the sympathy of Gladys and Myrtle in her hour of need.

'Hmm,' he muttered, 'I doubt it. The last time I saw the three of them they were in a huddle working out how she could divorce him. She seemed to have it all in hand.'

'Divorce him?' I exclaimed. 'Goodness, I had no idea . . . whatever for?'

'Oh, I don't know,' he replied impatiently, 'you know how women are, they get these ideas . . . although,' he added (I thought a trifle wistfully), 'it never seems to have occurred to Gladys . . .' He paused, scowling at the corpse. 'Well, it's too late now, and in any case she'll probably find that being a widow is socially easier than being a divorcée – it certainly is in the Mothers' Union.'

'But she may not belong to the Mothers' Union,' I objected, 'especially here in France. I'm not sure if they have –'

'It really doesn't matter in any event,' he snapped. 'The point is, Oughterard, the whole thing will be laid at my door, i.e. refusing to go on that stupid walk with Boris and choosing a nap instead. They'll say that if I had been with him none of this would have happened.'

I brooded for a moment on the logic of 'none of this', but in the circumstances felt it best not to question the bishop's turn of phrase. There were, after all, more pressing matters to attend to.

We retreated to the house and broke the news to the housekeeper, who after a brief bout of hysterics telephoned the police. These arrived just as the shopping party's car was drawing up at the front door, and the resultant furore was exactly as one would have expected. The turbulence lasted for a considerable time, during which the victim was examined, statements taken, the pool area cordoned off, a search (fruitless) made for the weapon, and – as predicted – Clinker blamed by all three women (Primrose for once keeping resolutely out of it). Lavinia, I noted, seemed not so much heartbroken as peeved, and I wondered vaguely if she was feeling cheated of the retributive pleasure of the divorce court . . . until Primrose, taking me aside, asserted in a loud stage whisper that doubtless the wife must have done it.

'Nonsense,' I whispered back, 'she was with all of you in Clermont.'

'But she could have *arranged* it,' replied Primrose darkly.

My sister has always had a vigorous imagination. Nevertheless, I found myself contemplating our hostess with new eyes. Had she really been responsible for having her husband bludgeoned to death? Surely not, the idea was absurd! Besides, she was far too other-worldly to harbour such desires let alone instigate an actual attack – or, as I believe the modern phrase is, to have 'taken out a contract'. No, I mused, Primrose might have an artistic way of looking at things but she clearly had little grasp of human nature.

However, even as I formulated this confident judgement, I was shockingly struck by my own outlandish capacity in that sphere. Decorous respectability, it seems, is no bar to homicide . . . And the summer beauty of that awful wood once more darkened my mind.

Fumbling for a cigarette I hastily pulled my thoughts back to the present, and was just about to light up when a quiet voice murmured, '*Permettez-moi, monsieur,*' and a lighter flashed in anticipation of my own. It was the senior police officer, a small dapper man with thinning hair and pale intelligent eyes. He smiled apologetically and enquired my particulars and business in the area. I gave him my credentials and clerical status, and explained hastily that my sister and I were merely passing guests in the house, had only recently met the Birtle-Figgins, and were on holiday staying at the village inn.

He grimaced. 'You have my sympathy, monsieur. La Truite Bleue is not for the faint-hearted. Indifferent wine, questionable food, *le patron* of uncertain temperament, atrocious beds and a crazy dog. For your sake I hope this unfortunate affair can be resolved quickly otherwise I shall have to request you endure your sojourn there rather longer than planned. But in the meantime would you be so good as to account for your movements between the hours of two and five o'clock this afternoon? I gather you had not elected to accompany the ladies on their shopping expedition?'

I agreed that I had not made that election and instead had spent the afternoon reading and keeping the bishop company.

'But he tells me he was asleep and then went for a swim. At what point were you keeping him company, monsieur?'

'At the point between his waking up and going down to the pool. We spent about half an hour doing the *Times* crossword together – three days old admittedly, but a challenge nonetheless.'

He smiled. 'Ah yes, of course, the English and their crossword puzzles; a national obsession, so they tell me . . . And was there anyone else in the house when you and the bishop were playing your word games?'

I thought I detected the merest hint of a sardonic stress on the word 'games', and felt a flash of irritation. Anyone would think I had confessed to playing Clinker's beloved tiddlywinks! However, I told him firmly that the housekeeper had been in the house the whole time and had even brought us tea at some point. He seemed happy enough at that, and after murmuring that he hoped the clues to the present sad puzzle would prove less intractable than those of *The Times*, he moved off to interview Myrtle. She was clearly bursting to speak and I wished him well of it.

After the questioning and a caution not to leave the area without official sanction, Primrose and I at last managed to slip away back to the inn. In the circumstances it had seemed best not to trouble our hostess with our farewells ... although I doubt if we would have had the chance in any case: for far from lying down sedated, Lavinia Birtle-Figgins seemed permanently draped around the telephone busily broadcasting her husband's demise hither and yon. It struck me that it was less the desecration of Boris that troubled her than that of the scattered bones. 'You see,' she kept wailing, 'he was their chosen custodian!'

We reached the inn to find Maurice asleep on top of the bar counter, and the dining area deserted except for Henri and Nicholas. They had obviously finished their supper and were busily attending to one of the latter's whisky bottles from the boot of the Citroën. Both looked tired and the curé's eyes were distinctly bloodshot.

'About time you turned up,' said Nicholas rattily. 'We've had a hell of a problem with that sodding metal detector. It made a fearful racket screeching and whining, and did nothing but turn up bottle tops and Boche tunic buttons. It weighs a ton and now it's seized up – battery's dead or something. Bloody useless!'

'I thought they made them so light and reliable these days – at least that's what the advertisements claim,' I ventured.

'Nothing connected with Henri is reliable,' he retorted scathingly, 'and as to being light, I can tell you it's blooming industrial-size and I've nearly broken my wrist.' He glared at Henri who smiled sweetly and said something very, very rude.

'Anyway,' he continued, 'it's jolly well your turn tomorrow, Francis. Don't think you can get out of it by swanning off again to those bloody Fig people and sleeping on feather beds while the rest of us are toiling down here – rather defeats the object of our visit, old boy.' He looked sullen and took another slurp of whisky.

Primrose walked briskly to the bar and returned with two glasses. 'It would be very nice, Nicholas,' she said, drawing up a chair, 'if you were to offer us a little of what you are drinking – I think we have need.'

'Can't think why,' was the answer.

'I will tell you why,' she said, taking out her compact and powdering her nose. 'You see, while you two were grubbing about in the earth with that absurd contraption, Boris Birtle-Figgins was being battered to death. Now would you please pour me a drink.'

There was a silence. And then as an automaton Nicholas picked up the bottle and did as he was bid. Both men stared in disbelief, and then Henri laughed and spluttered, *'Menteuse!'*

Primrose took a sip of her whisky and fixed him with a glacial eye. 'I do not know what tales your Norman parishioners may spin you in those murky confessional boxes, but I can assure you that Primrose Oughterard is not given to lying.' She spoke in the imperious tones which I knew from old and which had so often squashed my grosser larks as a schoolboy. Henri slumped back in his chair suitably chastened, while I mentally explored the fine distinction between downright lying and supplying gullible Canadians with fake canvases . . .

'She's right, 'I chimed in, 'it really happened. There's been an awful shindig and we've even been fingerprinted. Swarms of gendarmes and so on. I think perhaps we ought to abandon the digging business, far too much palaver going on. Best to keep our heads down and then scarper as soon as we're permitted.' I spoke with some feeling.

'I see,' said Nicholas, 'you mean scuttle back to England empty-handed? No fear, Francis, I haven't gone to all this trouble for nothing – and besides, Aunt Lil will play merry hell. She's already accused me of losing my touch, and I'm not going through all that again. No, we will proceed as planned . . . just have to be a little more careful, that's all. As a matter of fact it might be to our advantage. With all that fuss going on at the house we can probably work undisturbed down at the Folly.'

'No point. It's a fool's errand,' said Primrose casually.

'What's that supposed to mean?' asked Nicholas.

'What it says. There *is* no gold – pillaged years ago by the local peasantry. The Birtle-Figgins told us. They were most emphatic and seemed to know all about it.' She continued with the details that Lavinia had supplied, her listener maintaining a stony silence, face impassive except for the twitching of a nerve in his cheekbone.

'*Mon Dieu!*' expostulated Henri. '*Pas de trésor? C'est toute la faute de François!*' (Just as I had expected.)

'Shut up,' snapped Nicholas. There followed a lowering pause broken only by rhythmic snoring from the cat.

I took a deep breath and said brightly, 'But there is of course the bejewelled swastika in the gumboot – that could come in handy.' To my relief Nicholas showed more than a flicker of interest and I hastily proceeded with the tale.

When I had finished he emitted a low whistle of disbelief. 'Are you trying to tell me that that chap Figgins actually left the thing in the wellington all this time without doing anything about it? Why on earth didn't he fish it out? Must be mad!'

'Dead actually,' I reminded him, adding pointedly, 'Besides, unlike some people he didn't seem all that interested in matters of crude commerce: a type whose mind moved on higher planes. But you might not grasp that.'

'You bet I wouldn't,' he replied, grinning.

'*Alors,*' burst out Henri, '*qu'est-ce qu'on fait?*'

Ingaza turned to him, and enunciating with studied precision said, 'What one does, old cock, is to get the blithering swastika out of the effing boot.'

130

The curé digested this in silence, a small gleam of excitement in his eye. And then I ventured, 'Yes, but how? Presumably we'll have to break in somehow.'

'Don't need to,' murmured Primrose. 'After all, I've got the key to the Folly.'

'What do you mean? You couldn't possibly,' I exclaimed.

'Perfectly possible,' she replied coolly. 'You see, when we got back from Clermont and there was all the furore with the police and everything, and that nice little inspector was being so busy and charming, I slipped into Myrtle's room, rummaged about a bit, and took the key from the back of the wardrobe door. Myrtle was so busy telling the inspector what he should do and how to do it that she didn't notice a thing.' Primrose spread her fingers and inspected her nails as we stared at her in amazement.

'*Menteuse* –' began Henri.

'*Don't* start that again!' she retorted, fixing him with a withering glare. He subsided, muttering.

'But Primrose,' I said in bewilderment, 'what gave you the idea? How on earth did you know that a key was there?'

'Lavinia told me when we were in Clermont. Apparently years ago some sort of fête had been held in the grounds and the Birtle-Figgins had been asked by the municipal authorities to act as unofficial overseers of the place. Nothing onerous, they just had to ensure that everything was conducted in an orderly fashion – you know the sort of thing, seeing the doors and windows were kept locked and no damage to any of the furniture or fittings. Once it was all over nobody asked for the key back, so they put it in one of their spare bedrooms for safe-keeping and it's remained there ever since.'

Nicholas fixed her with a thoughtful look. 'And this key is now in your possession?'

'Yes, I told you.'

'Oh well,' he said briskly, 'that's it then. We'll raid the place tomorrow.'

21

The Cat's Memoir

'*I have done it again!*' the dog thundered, pawing the ground like some frantic water buffalo. 'I've found another one, just like before! What do you think of that, *Maurice!*'

I closed my eyes, composed my ears and nerves, and enquired gently as to what he might be talking about.

'There's a stiff,' he bellowed, 'laid out by some water – blood and stuff all over the shop, and . . . and *bones!*' He danced around in an ecstasy of triumph and excitement, flailing his tale and trampling wildly over my neatly arranged pilchards.

That did it. 'Enough, Bouncer!' I cried. 'I do not care how many stiffs there are, I will not have my fish interfered with. Now, sit down and be silent, and when you are col-lected I may listen to your news.' Surprisingly my words had the desired effect, and for a few merciful seconds he was quiet.

During the pause I did what I could to rearrange the mangled pilchards, and once they were in some semblance of order indicated he could continue his tale.

'You see, Maurice,' he burbled, 'you know when F.O. and the Primrose went up to the big house and stayed there all night – well, I got a bit bored with them being away like that and I thought it would be quite interesting to go and see what they were up to – sort of have a sniff around. So that's what I did, this afternoon. There were masses of jumbo bunnies everywhere looking all pop-eyed and –'

'And in the course of your sniffing you encountered the stiff,' I interrupted quickly.

He frowned. 'Who's telling this story, you or me?'

'Well, you of course, but I hardly think we need to hear about the rabbits, jumbo or otherwise.'

'Can't think why not,' he growled. 'You should have seen me – put the fear of bears in them, I did.'

'Oh yes,' I said wearily, 'with your usual war cry, I suppose?'

'You bet. "Bugger off, Bunnies! Here comes Bouncer the Brave!" And do you know, they went like –'

'Yes, yes, splendid. Now what about the corpse?'

'Well, *he* wasn't going anywhere – what you might call a bit late.'

'Ah, so it was a him this time?' He nodded. 'But where exactly? You mentioned water.'

'Yes,' he explained eagerly, 'just below the house. There's a big field with a stream, and they've damned some of that up to make a sort of pool – the kind humans use for splashing around in. In fact I was just thinking I wouldn't mind having a bit of a splash myself – when I suddenly saw it, all spread out on the stones just by the water's edge behind a couple of bushes. I thought he was sunbathing at first – they seem to like doing that – but then I thought it was pretty odd lying in the sun with all those bones around you. I mean, if it was me I'd have shoved 'em into the ground first. Can't be too careful, there are some very dodgy customers about ... Anyway, when I got a closer look I realized why he hadn't buried 'em. Not in a position to.' The dog gave a throaty laugh.

'This is not funny ha ha,' I reproved, 'but distinctly funny peculiar. What sort of mood was F.O. in when you last saw him? Perhaps he's been at it again. It's all this travelling, probably taken its toll. Besides, there is that pernicious pair who were so rude about *me* ... they're skulking around here somewhere. Enough to turn anyone to homicide, I should think!'

'Hmm, hadn't thought of that,' said the dog, looking anxious. 'Just our luck for him to do it here in a foreign country where we don't know anyone . . . and what about my grub?'

'Kindly raise your mind to higher things, should that be possible,' I admonished. 'This is a situation, Bouncer, that requires careful handling . . . Now, did you touch any of the bones?' He looked shifty. 'Did you?'

'Not so as you'd notice,' he murmured.

'What does that mean?'

He explained.

'I see,' I said, and smiled.

22

The Dog's Diary

Well, of course he had to see for himself. Couldn't be satisfied with me just telling him. Oh no! Wanted piric evidence or some such, and wanted it there and then. Typical. Didn't care that I had nearly busted a gut racing all the way back in that heat and needed a kip and some water. Couldn't have cared less! 'Show me immediately,' the cat ordered, all prick-eared and bossy, 'we haven't time to waste while you loll around here slurping and snoring.' I told him he wouldn't like it – all those bones and patches of wet (he can't stand either), but he just flattened his ears and said there were certain things in life above which one was required to rise ... yes, that's just how he said it. Couldn't make out what he was on about at first, but I think it means something like grinning and bearing. Anyway, I asked him if we could take Clemso, but he said it would be bad enough having to cope with the wet and the bones without music as well.

So we set off on our own, and because by then I'd got the smell of things it didn't take too long. But cor, was I hot! So hot, in fact, that after I had had a good sniff at the biggest bone and cocked my leg against the box thing, I jumped in the pool and did some very nifty paddling from one bank to the other. When I was a puppy my first master, Bowler the bank manager, used to say 'Little bugger's like a blooming beaver!' and people would nod and say they were sure there was water spaniel in me ... Well, that's as may be, but all I know is that I like ponds and splashing about and such; so while Maurice was being important and checking the corpse and pussy-footing over the puddles, I was having a high old time in the water.

Didn't last of course. I'd only been in a couple of minutes when there was a great shindig from the trees on the edge of the field, and who do you think hurtled out? F.O. and that Clinker person, rushing and crashing in our direction as if wolves were after them. 'Dive, dive!' the cat screeched and took off like a mog on a broomstick. Dive? What did he think I was, some sort of submarine?

No, what I *did* do was to scramble up on the bank, and then just like those Welsh collies herding sheep, I dropped my flanks and haunches and inched along on my belly in the long grass ... got through the hedge and scarpered like hell. Those Taffies, they think they're the only ones who can do that – but Bouncer knows a trick or two as well. Champion swimmer, champion crawler, that's me!

When I got back the cat was in a bad mood, i.e. *nearly* having one of his sulks but not quite. Kept muttering that he was fed up with F.O. going around murdering people and that it was putting him to a great deal of inconvenience. Well, I'm not too hot on counting so I had to think about that for some time; but when I had finished thinking I said it seemed to me that our master had only bumped off one person so far – which wasn't to say he wouldn't have another go in the future. Maurice looked huffy and said that one or many, past or future, it was all the same as it messed up his routine and got on his nerves. What's new? Things are always getting on the cat's nerves.

Still, I felt a bit sorry for him as he had missed his evening milk and didn't seem his usual cattish self – all this foreign stuff, I expect, getting him down. So I decided to tell him where I had hidden the thing that I had nicked from under the stiff's ear ... And that did it! Perked him up no end and he whizzed off like a kitten on skates. Just goes to show, play your biscuits right and things can change in a trice!

136

23

The Vicar's Version

With the swastika project hanging over me, I had slept badly and was in no mood to appreciate Ingaza's badinage at the breakfast table. The prospect of imminent gain and being one ahead of Climp and Mullion had put him in high spirits, and over the coffee and brioches he indulged in a waggish humour not entirely to my taste. It was too early, and the circumstances too disturbing. True, one had been spared the tedium of the excavations, and in comparison retrieving the swastika should not have been too difficult. But I was shocked by what had happened to Boris, and rattled at being the likely target of the previous day's surveillance. Were the two incidents connected? Was it possible that my pursuers were also Boris's killers? I brooded into my coffee seeing no obvious link, but fearful nevertheless . . .

'Right,' said Nicholas briskly, 'are we all set?' We were gathered outside the inn, a quartet of innocent ramblers about to savour the delights of the Auvergne and meander its winding paths. Admittedly the air of innocence was rather spoilt by Henri, who, clad in black from head to toe (though minus his priestly collar), somehow managed to look like a diminutive Al Capone. However, the rest of us appeared respectable enough; and so chatting casually we

moved off down the hill in the direction of the Fotherington Folly.

Halfway along the narrow road, Nicholas said that he
knew of a short-cut discovered on his earlier reconnaissance. It lopped off a good quarter of a mile and was worth
the hazards of the long grass and muddy cart tracks. Thus,
watched by a bevy of mercifully mild-eyed heifers, we
clambered over the stile and made our way down the steep
path. It had rained the previous night and the ground was
damp underfoot, and at that hour of the morning – much
to Primrose's horror – one's shoe would be met with the
occasional lolling slug. However, as assured by our guide
and amidst gasps of disgust from Primrose, we quickly
reached the château's perimeter wall.

Close up the place looked even more hideous than when
first seen, and I surveyed it with fading spirit – the same
response presumably as Elizabeth's on her visit there just
after the war. I shared that distaste . . . as I had shared her
final moments in Foxford Wood. Yes, we were inseparable,
she and I. And however hard I tried to arrange it otherwise, nothing could alter that fact. I put my hand on the
crumbling wall, feeling its wet roughness and dank cling-
ing ivy, and not for the first time wondered what on earth
I was doing – or had done.

'Chop, chop, old man!' urged Ingaza, digging me in the
ribs. 'I don't care what the poet said, we haven't got all day
to stand and stare. Work to do.' He led us towards a cor-
roded iron gate which creaked in protest as we levered our
way though. 'Better skirt round the edge,' he instructed.
'Can't be too careful – eyes in every bush and gully, I
shouldn't wonder.' He chuckled softly.

'Don't be so absurd, Nicholas,' whispered Primrose,
'there's not a soul anywhere. Another crack like that and
you'll give Henri the vapours!'

Personally I did not think he was being in the least
absurd. Images of Boris's fate and my fears of being spied
on at Le Petit Rêve had made me more than jittery; and I

suspect that, far from looking the part of a casual rambler, I projected an air of furtive terror.

Keeping in the lee of the wall and picking our way carefully, we eventually broke cover and wandered as nonchalantly as possible towards the front entrance, a large imposing portico of raddled and poorly reproduced Doric pillars. With what he clearly thought was a deft sleight of hand, Ingaza whipped the key from his pocket and inserted it in the lock. Nothing happened. He tried again with the same result. The thing was immovable; and despite twisting and pushing it remained so.

'It not work,' pronounced Henri.

'Sharp of you,' snapped Ingaza. We stared at key and door nonplussed.

'But it's obviously the right one,' said Primrose. 'Look, it's got a label with "Folie" written on it.'

'Oh, for God's sake,' muttered Ingaza, 'this is absurd.' He shoved the key in once more and rattled it angrily. Useless.

I cleared my throat. 'I say, do you think that it's simply the wrong door? Surely there must be another entrance, at the back or somewhere.'

Circumventing nettles and bits of broken drainpipe, we scouted along the building's flank, past boarded windows and flaking sills. Still no sign of a door, and despite my reluctance about the whole venture I felt an illogical pang of disappointment. But at that moment, there was a shout from Henri who had nipped ahead around the corner: '*Venez, venez!*' he commanded. '*J'ai la porte!*' We hurried after him. And sure enough, there it was: small, weathered and peeling – but displaying a gleaming, and presumably newly fitted, lock.

Before Nicholas had a chance to try the key the curé had seized it from him, and with a couple of twists, and for good measure a hefty kick, flung the door wide, and in beaming triumph exclaimed, '*Sapristi! Victoire!*' A trifle theatrical, I thought, but at least a variation on the usual maledictions.

We jostled our way into what seemed to be a narrow passage, freezing cold and almost pitch dark.

'There must be a light,' hissed Primrose. 'Do find it, Nicholas, I've just stubbed my toe.' We edged along, feeling the walls for a switch; but nothing presented itself and I rather suspected that in all probability any electricals would have long since fused or been dismantled. But as we shuffled through the gloom, darkness gradually gave way to a pallid murk as the passage opened up into a large vestibule feebly lit by a grimy skylight. There seemed to be little there: a flagstoned space with a few ramshackle wooden chairs, a decaying sofa and a couple of trestle tables. On one of these, rather incongruously, stood a large hot-water urn and some randomly stacked plates.

'Goodness,' Primrose giggled, 'do you imagine the Jerries held a farewell tea-party before they left?'

'No, not them,' I said, 'the Birtle-Figgins. They must have used this area when they were catering for that village fête Lavinia was telling us about. Do you remember? She said they had been allowed access to the kitchen quarters as a special concession.'

'Yes,' Primrose replied excitedly, 'and somewhere in those quarters is the back staircase and the lavatory with the wellington boot! We must be pretty close.' She started to prowl around. 'I wonder where –'

'Over here,' said Nicholas's voice. 'Look, these are the stairs.'

We peered into a further recess where he was standing, and I could make out the curve of a banister and the outline of newel posts. A door was there as well.

He grasped its handle and gave a tug. The effort was unnecessary: it opened easily, and from the light of a small unboarded window we had no difficulty in seeing a tiled floor, basin and lavatory bowl, and all the usual accoutrements of an ancient cloakroom. Dusty and musty, it presented a view of cobwebbed gardening tools, a collection of mouldering wicker baskets, two mackintoshes hanging like stiffened corpses on a gibbet, a single gym shoe, and a surprisingly large assortment of galoshes. Of the gumboot there seemed no sign.

'It must be here somewhere,' protested Primrose, 'unless of course Boris was having us on, or hallucinating. The latter probably – he seemed to be living on another planet.'

'Not any more he isn't,' said Nicholas drily, 'unless he's plucking a harp in some celestial sphere.'

'Or banging a tambourine like Belvedere,' tittered Primrose.

In desultory fashion we began to rummage among the bits and pieces, dislodging layers of debris and scuttling spiders. The search yielded nothing, and I was just about to suggest that possibly Boris had meant a different cloak-room, when I became aware that the place had become lighter. I glanced up at the window and saw a small patch of blue, a reminder that beyond these oppressive walls the world had grown bright and warm ... But I also saw something else: on a shelf just below the window stood a pair of elderly rubber boots.

For some impractical reason the shelf was fixed too high for normal reach, and Henri was dispatched to fetch one of the chairs from the hall. Balanced precariously on its wob-bling legs, I reached out, clasped the boots and clambered down. One of them felt distinctly heavier than the other, and with a sudden image of bran tubs and lucky dips, I plunged my fingers into its depths. There was something bulky wedged between heel and toe. Watched in silence by the others I gradually eased the thing out. It lay in my hand: the proverbial brown paper parcel tied up with string. However, it was not long in my grasp, for with a grunt of satisfaction Ingaza had whipped it from me, and with a pocket penknife was eagerly slicing at the bind-ing ... I hoped for all our sakes that the 'dip' would prove lucky.

It did. From the wrappings Nicholas extracted just what Boris had described: a dark metal Nazi swastika, about six inches in diameter and studded with pearls and what appeared to be rubies.

There was a gasp from Primrose. 'Well, I must say, that's a nice little trinket!'

'It's no trinket,' said Nicholas slowly, 'I think the stones are genuine.'

We continued to gaze at it. And then Henri, who had been uncharacteristically quiet, spat out a single word: *'Salauds!'* It was the first truly relevant oath I had ever heard him utter. His eyes held a look of pain and fury; and like him, one was reminded of that awful time and those terrible events. The invaders may have been driven from French soil, but they could never be entirely expunged from the mind of Henri or thousands like him . . .

'Let's get going,' I said. 'We've got what we came for, no need to hang about.' I had a sudden need to get out into the sunshine, into the fresh air and away from dust and fetid memory.

24

The Cat's Memoir

Exquisite! Smooth, spherical and brilliantly shiny, it was a toy of infinite, gleaming charm. I teased it with my paw, flicked at it with my tail, nudged it delicately with my nose, dribbled it across the floorboards where it skidded and spun in the most tantalizing way. It would tap, patter and rattle, gyrating in such a manner as to make me almost dizzy. And then when it was stilled and silent I would creep up from behind, and with the merest touch of my claw set it going again, rolling, spinning, shimmering. Sometimes I would pounce as if it were a mouse and toss it in the air, and then when it had landed give merciless chase among the chair legs . . .

Such were my activities when the dog's voice interrupted as he wandered in from the veranda. 'Ah, you found it then,' said Bouncer. 'Thought you might like it.'

I felt a flash of irritation to be so distracted but, being a cat of breeding and impeccable manners, I paused in my entertainment and thanked him profusely for producing such a rarity.

'Yes,' he said, 'you don't find many eyes like that, do you? A good bit of glass, I should say. Don't know what it was doing under the stiff's ear but it seemed a pity to leave it there, thought it might come in useful.'

I congratulated him on his prescience, said that it was indeed an excellent piece of glass and probably less to do with the corpse than with the upturned box which had contained the frightful bones. 'That's where it came from,' I said, 'along with those teeth.'

He nodded, and then emitted an explosive laugh. 'You're not good on bones, are you, Maurice?'

I agreed that I was not good on them.

'Yes,' he said, still chortling, 'I remember when you discovered my special collection in the vicarage, it didn't half give you a fright. I thought you were going to peg out!' The memory clearly afforded him great satisfaction and normally he would have risked a claw to the snout, but my gaiety with the glass eye had made me benevolent and I let it pass.

Then as I was about to return to my plaything, the air was rent with a sudden blast of music from the hallway, and before I had time to scuttle out of sight, Clemenceau appeared. He stood poised on the threshold, panting and grinning, a fanfare of trombone and trumpet issuing from his collar. I sighed and flicked the eye into a corner. All good things must come to an end . . .

Raising my voice above the din, I addressed him affably in carefully enunciated English (having no intention of pandering to their linguistic peculiarities). 'Good afternoon, Clemenceau,' I said. 'I trust you are spending an enjoyable day.' He seemed not to understand, and with jaw hanging open, continued to grin vaguely while remaining mute. I do not share Bouncer's raucous volume and assumed the dog had not heard me. Fortunately at that moment the noise switched itself off, so I tried again, evincing once more an interest in his day. There was the same response, i.e. nothing.

'It's no good,' said Bouncer, 'he's Frog through and through, you'll have to use the lingo.'

'I most certainly will not!' I exclaimed indignantly.

Bouncer made the equivalent of a human shrug and, going up to Clemenceau, started to grunt and growl in a very peculiar way. At first the dog looked puzzled, but as

144

Bouncer persisted, he slowly began to twitch his ears and then launched into a spate of rapid gobbledygook.

There was silence as Bouncer knit his brows and digested this. Then he trotted over to me and said, 'He's got a different sort of accent from Pierre, but from I could make out he said: "Tell the cat that all my days are enjoyable."'

'Hmm,' I sniffed, 'took rather a long time saying that, didn't he?'

He nodded. 'Yes – what you might call long-winded.' And then pausing, he added quietly, 'Not the only one of course.'

I had no idea what he meant by that – the dog often makes pointless and gnomic remarks. But I have to confess to being impressed by his knowledge of French (my own grasp of the tongue being academic rather than practical). You would think such talent alien to a creature of so little culture; but I recalled that he often spent time with Pierre the Ponce, and presumably some of that garrulous poodle's expressions had rubbed off. There was also his knack of picking up snippets of Latin from his visits to the church crypt, so I concluded he must have a natural aptitude for such things. His ear for music (distasteful to me) could also be a factor ... Well, I mused indulgently, just as well the dog has an aptitude for something! And mindful of his retrieval of the eye, I thought a word of praise might be in order – though naturally nothing excessive.

'That's most helpful, Bouncer,' I mewed approvingly. 'Quite a little skill you have there.' He looked surprised, wagged his tail and said modestly that it was just his sixth sense. As mentioned before, the sixth sense features firmly in the dog's mythology and I did not bother to dispute it. Instead, I told him to convey my compliments to Clemenceau and say that I was delighted to hear that his days were so felicitous.

'What?' he asked, looking baffled.

'Tell the dog I'm glad he's happy!'

'Right-o,' he answered. And clearly proud of his role as interpreter, he bounded over to the other and engaged in more broken mutterings – accompanied by a good deal of mutual sniffing and rear-end reconnaissance.

The hound lifted his head, beamed and uttered something unintelligible.

'What was that?' I asked.

'Didn't you hear? He spoke in English,' said Bouncer.

'Huh! Didn't sound like English to me.'

'Well, it was, sort of. He said: "I like *vairree* much *gingaire* cats."'

'But I am not a ginger cat!' I protested.

'Oh well, not always easy to get your words right first go,' the dog replied philosophically.

An *entente cordiale* is all very well, but the negotiations can be fatiguing and I was becoming a little tired of this trading of pleasantries and eager to return to the glass eye ... Besides, I was fearful that the collar might re-engage itself. Tactfully, therefore, I suggested that as it was a bright day they should continue their parlez-vous-ing on the veranda.

Alone at last I hastily reapplied myself to the eye, suspecting that at any moment my capers would be further thwarted by the entry of F.O. or the Brighton Type.

25

The Vicar's Version

Once in the open we retraced our steps, as before taking the short-cut over the hillside – now fortunately bare of slugs. The climb was tiring, and at the stile into the lane we stopped to draw breath. Henri lit a crumpled cigarette, and Ingaza, clearly itching to take another look at the swastika, unwrapped its covers and began to drool over his find.

'Not bad at all,' he murmured, running his fingers appreciatively over the gems and elaborate metalwork. 'Could be quite valuable. I've got a mate who might –' He broke off, turning it over to inspect the back. 'There's something written here – some sort of inscription.' The lettering was obviously small for he screwed up his eyes and peered intently. There was a long pause. And then he said quietly, 'Good Lord . . . I don't believe it.'

'What?' demanded Primrose. 'What does it say?' He handed it to her silently. After a brief scrutiny she shrugged impatiently. 'It's all Greek to me, it's in German!'

'What would you expect?' I asked.

'Yes, well, we didn't all do Kraut verbs in the fourth form,' she retorted. 'Here, take a look.'

I have to admit that my schoolboy smattering yielded only one or two recognizable words, but in that tiny Gothic script a name leaped to my eyes – 'Rudolph Hess 1940'. I gazed at it incredulously, and then at Nicholas. 'It's to do with Hess!' I exclaimed. '1940 – the year before he flew to Scotland.'

'Observant, dear boy. But it is not "to do" with Hess, it is *from* him. Listen . . .' And he proceeded to translate: 'To my dear friend D.F. in gratitude for our little chats and in fervent hope of amity between our two great nations. You have set my course. Yours, Rudolph Hess 1940.'

'*Mon Dieu!*' rasped Henri.

'Crikey!' exclaimed Primrose.

'How is it your German is so good, Nicholas?' I asked curiously. 'Thought you read classics at Oxford.'

He shrugged indifferently. 'More to the point is what do the initials D.F. stand for? Presumably the father-in-law or his brother of your widowed pal Elizabeth. Quite the eager little collaborator it seems . . . Interesting tale, I should think. You know, this thing could net a fortune in the right hands and with the right contacts.' He smiled musingly, in that silky, heavy-lidded way that with Ingaza invariably precedes images of lucrative gain.

I was piqued by the phrase 'your pal Elizabeth', but before I could respond I saw his smile vanish as he looked up towards the figure coming down the hill. 'Wouldn't you know,' he muttered. 'Here comes our revered prelate. Quick, give me the bloody thing!' He snatched the swastika and stuffed it in his pocket.

'Ah,' Clinker hailed us, 'enjoying the last of the sunshine, I see. Been for a stroll, have you? Amazing how hot it still is.' He was about to mop his brow, but seeing Henri, paused quizzically. The latter was not at his best. Unshaved, uncollared, black garments besmirched from his recent exertions and nether lip adorned by the inevitable Gauloise, he looked less like Al Capone than an inmate of Alcatraz.

'This is the Reverend Martineau, curé of Taupinière – a village just north of Le Touquet,' I explained. 'He is having a little break down here.' Henri removed his cigarette and gave a friendly leer.

'Breakdown?' asked Clinker warily. 'Yes . . . well, I hope he gets over it soon. These rural parishes, they can take their toll . . .' And with a cursory nod in the curé's direction, he turned hastily to Primrose.

'I must say, this Birtle-Figgins business is all rather dreadful – I mean, not the sort of thing one expects to happen to one's host, especially when one doesn't know him very well.'

'Ah, you mean it would be easier if he had been a close friend of yours?' said Primrose.

'Er . . . well, no, er, of course not,' he replied uncomfortably. 'I mean, it's just that one doesn't know quite how to play it. Ideally we would tootle off pretty quickly – a sort of tactful retreat, if you get my meaning. But the wretched motor is still in dock. And in any case, there's that police inspector who seems to think we should stick around while he pursues his enquiries. Myrtle is furious, says she's never been suspected of anything questionable in her whole life.' (No need for suspicion, I thought, the evidence was only too patent.)

'Mind you,' he said in a muttered aside to me, 'one good thing has come out of it – at least now I shan't be continually pestered to suck up to Canterbury about that canonization idea. It's an ill wind . . .'

'How is Lavinia coping?' enquired Primrose politely.

'A bit dazed, of course, but on the face of it quite well – spends a lot of her time in the kitchen trying out recipes.'

'Recipes?'

'Yes. I've noticed the food seems to have taken on a new lease of life. We actually had steak the other day.' He lowered his voice. 'Although it wasn't terribly good; and to tell you the truth, it rather played havoc with my digestion. Been so used to nothing but carrot gruel and lettuce stalks, the old tum must have taken fright!' He laughed heartily.

'Hmm,' Primrose said, 'A sort of therapy, I suppose – cooking can be very soothing.'

'Don't know about that,' he replied, 'she gets enough soothing from that Turnbull fellow. He's done nothing but dance attendance ever since Boris's death.'

'Good to have friends,' remarked Primrose vaguely.

'What about the campers?' I interjected nervously. 'Seen much of them?'

'Odd you should ask that,' he answered. 'As a matter of fact I saw them only this morning – or rather that plush car of theirs. Whizzing down the road hell for leather towards that Folly place. Bit of an eyesore if you ask me – but perhaps it's part of the tourist itinerary. No accounting for tastes . . .'

I froze. 'You – you saw them this morning?'

'Yes, I've just said so – going towards the Folly. Lavinia told me she had been jawing to one of them last night about a Nazi dagger or some such hidden in the château. I wasn't listening really – far too occupied trying to stop my stomach playing up. Gladys has found some excellent pills, they –'

'Christ!' I gasped.

He looked at me, startled. 'Really, Oughterard, that hardly seems the appropriate –'

The rebuke was never completed, for at that moment another voice intervened, one gratingly familiar. 'Well, well, well! Good afternoon, gentlemen – and *lady*, of course.' We spun round. And there, emerging through the trees from the path to our left, came Climp and Mullion, the one smirking, the latter with a set expression that belied the genial tone.

'So we meet again,' continued Mullion sardonically. 'What a coincidence! But then, as we've all been seeking the same thing, perhaps not. Well, not that we were actually *seeking* – just waiting and watching. Oh yes, we saw you go in and waited for you to come out – easy really. Let others do the dirty work, I always say . . . you wouldn't believe how often chance favours those who bide their time.'

'Well, you can go and bide your time somewhere else,' snapped Nicholas. 'Buzz off!'

Climp sniggered. 'That's the jammy one. A right hoity-toity bugger he is.'

'Got the right word there, Ken,' laughed Mullion mirthlessly. '*Just* the right word, I shouldn't wonder.'

Nicholas flushed. Not, I think, from discomfort but from mounting anger. Before he had a chance to retaliate, Clinker thrust himself forward. 'Now look here,' he said severely, 'I have no idea who you are or what you want, but I find your tone most offensive and I should be obliged if you would kindly return to the tent out of which you crawled this morning.' It was a stout effort but horribly counterproductive.

Mullion's eyes hardened, and walking up to the bishop he said quietly and evenly: 'Shut your face, Pop, otherwise you might just find yourself flat on the ground. And you wouldn't like that, would you? Not with my boot in your teeth, you wouldn't.' Clinker gaped at him in stunned silence. Such responses being rare among his clerical brethren, he was unprepared.

As were we all. For in the next instant Climp reached down into the long grass and picked up a short metal rod. Whether it had been lying there by chance or by design I do not know. What I do know is that, gripping it in his hand, he was advancing upon me in a manner far from friendly.

'Look here,' I protested, 'keep that damn thing –'

'Just watch it, *Francis*. Move an inch and you'll get egg on your face – or blood. Hand the swastika over right now . . . NOW!' The word was barked out as if we were on a parade ground, and I think I was more shocked by the sudden bellow than by the weapon. I wondered fleetingly if this was how he handled his wards at the prison.

'Lay off, Ken,' Mullion shouted. 'He won't have it. It'll be the smarmy one – or Pedro here.' He nodded towards Henri who politely raised two fingers . . . a pointless gesture in view of the pistol that Mullion suddenly produced.

151

'My God,' cried Primrose, 'you're insane, you can't . . .'

But her words were drowned in a deafening fanfare of trumpets and drum roll, as down the lane hurtled Clemenceau, orchestral collar at full throttle. Seeing us, the truant gave a roar of recognition, swerved, leaped the stile, and to the defiant notes of the Marseillaise rampaged manically in our midst. Mullion jumped back but was too late to avoid the dog's onslaught; losing his balance he fell heavily, dropping the revolver. The combination of canine gaiety and blasts of fervid French patriotism must have struck a chord in Henri, for with a spluttered oath he suddenly biffed Climp on the nose, and in the next instant was scrambling up the bank towards a mass of dense undergrowth. With the aggressors momentarily wrong-footed, we clambered after him and forced our way through the foliage on to a thin track. However, before we could draw breath, Nicholas cried, 'Watch out, he's got the gun again!' And peering down through the brambles we saw the two men charging towards the foot of the bank. A shot rang out, and then another.

Like a ferret out of hell, Henri took off along the narrow track, ducking and weaving among the trees and boulders, his spindly legs moving with the assurance of a mountain goat. Even in my consternation I was struck by the agility of his performance and its contrast with his normally shambling gait. Clearly the survival instinct is an amazing goad. And thus stirred from shock, we followed as best we could: stumbling, panting and cursing over the impossible terrain. Surprisingly Primrose was in the lead (something to do with her hockey days, I suppose) followed by Ingaza, while Clinker and myself brought up a straggling rear.

'I say, Francis,' the bishop gasped, 'this is a bit much, isn't it! Where the hell are we going?'

'No idea, sir,' I responded helpfully, 'but if they go on like this they'll run out of bullets.' Another one whistled close to my ear.

'Assuming they miss,' retorted Clinker, acid even *in extremis*. He was beginning to puff like a grampus and I wondered which would get him first, heart or bullet. I grabbed his arm, physically and mentally propelling him onwards. We pounded along the path, and although the shots had ceased I could sense our pursuers gaining ground. I looked wildly for some gully or recess into which we might fling ourselves but nothing presented itself. In fact, as I glanced to the left hoping for some shelter, I was horrified to realize we were running along the brink of a precipice, its sheer drop only partially veiled by wispy saplings. To our right there loomed a blank escarpment of granite. I peered ahead, trying to catch a glimpse of the others, but saw nothing except the ever narrowing path insidiously mapping the rim of the cliff. The sun was blazing, the air windless; yet I felt like some benighted figure in a bleak allegorical landscape, driven by the elements and the merciless forces of evil: lost, desolate, doomed . . . However, such mental theatricals were cut short by Clinker's voice gasping angrily, 'For God's sake, Oughterard, look where you're going, man, that's my foot!'

We wheezed on, lurching and limping over rut and jagged stone . . . until, rounding a bend, we were brought up sharp by a stark clearing. Trees, scrub, boulders – all had vanished, and were replaced by great sheets of grey unyielding rock. Huddled in the midst of this was a tableau of figures – Henri, Primrose, Nicholas. They were standing irresolute, gazing ahead and downwards into the immeasurably beautiful and horribly vertiginous valley . . . It was a cul-de-sac with no way out except backwards or over the cliff's edge.

We froze, helpless and nonplussed. There was the sound of rushing feet; and turning sharply, we were confronted by the figures of Climp and Mullion sweating and triumphant. Climp was still gripping his iron bar, but Mullion was the one with the pistol. They advanced slowly and confidently – presumably emboldened by years of rounding up recalcitrant Broadmoor residents. And like those residents, we faced them wary and afraid.

'Nicholas,' commanded Clinker in a good imitation of authority, 'give him the wretched swastika and then we can all go home.'

'*Vite, vite*, Neek,' chimed Henri, '*donnez-lui le truc. Je ne veux pas mourir!*'

'Don't care what you want, old fruit,' Ingaza snapped, 'he's not bloody getting it.'

He put a hand in his pocket as if to grip the thing tightly, and Mullion loosed another bullet which, ricocheting off a rock, spun close to his shoulder. Nicholas turned white but stood his ground – though possibly uncertain rather than resolute. We stared paralysed, too shocked to move. Then suddenly I heard my sister's voice.

'Don't be absurd, you stupid little man. You haven't a chance in hell – and in any case, even if we do hand it over, you are far too bonkers to make use of it!' Scathing, excoriating, this was a tone I knew well (having been its recipient often enough), and I felt proud of her nerve – but this time it was sure to cut no ice.

My fears were confirmed, for the next moment and to my horror, Mullion strode towards her, brandishing the gun, his face contorted with fury. 'Stupid, am I, you bitch?' he shouted. 'I'll show you who's stupid – you and your namby-pamby murdering brother and that pink-eyed pansy over there!' (He gestured towards Nicholas.) I felt sick as I saw him lunge at Primrose, give her a hefty back-hander, and then put the gun to her throat and drag her within feet of the cliff's edge. And I just knew that he would shoot – or worse.

'*Please*, Nicholas,' I croaked desperately, 'let him have it!' (An injunction which, even in the midst of such nightmare, brought the wan face of the hapless Bentley to mind . . .) And then, as in some distant slow-motion film, I watched Nicholas Ingaza withdrawing the swastika from his coat pocket, his face taut and furious. Behind him stood Climp, weapon raised ready to strike at the least hesitation.

'Take it, you fucker,' Ingaza murmured, and lobbed it casually at Mullion who, letting go of Primrose, just as casually fielded it in mid-air. He grinned and held it aloft triumphant. For perhaps three seconds he was poised thus, swastika in one hand, gun in the other . . . And then the most extraordinary thing happened.

A small, low dark shadow streaked from behind us and launched itself upon Mullion's boots, tearing obsessively at his laces and turn-ups. Hissing like a demented black hobgoblin, the creature clawed mercilessly at the man's dancing feet. Climp rushed forward, crowbar poised to smash the living daylights, while Mullion, pointing the gun to blast the fiend to blazes, slipped and tripped, pistol arm flailing wildly . . . His companion fell to the ground, the shot wide of its intended mark – but fatal.

We gazed mesmerized at the form sprawled stark on the granite, trickles of blood oozing from ear and temple . . . And then we stared at the spot where only seconds ago Mullion had been so gloatingly poised. Empty.

Primrose was slumped palely on the ground, her nose bleeding from the swipe Mullion had given her. She was dabbing at it with a handkerchief, but with the other hand was clasping a rather scraggy black cat . . . Maurice regarded her impassively, closed his eyes and began to purr.

I ran forward to help her to her feet but was distracted by a movement behind. It was Clinker. He stumbled towards the granite brink and peered down. 'Oh Lor',' he muttered, 'he's gone over.' We gathered round and scanned the depths. There was nothing to see: the precipice was sheer and deep with no apparent outcrops of rock or overhanging trees. From that great height it seemed unlikely that the valley and its distant peat bog could yield up anything living. We stood dazed and irresolute, casting nervous glances at Climp's body and listening to the silence broken only by a distant curlew and the steady purring of the cat.

'Well, that really has torn it,' exclaimed Ingaza, 'he's taken the bleeding swastika with him. Lost for good now,

I shouldn't wonder. I've forfeited thousands.' He turned to me, glaring: 'Another pig's ear, Francis!'

'That's quite enough, Nicholas,' mumbled Primrose nasally, still mopping her nose. 'Francis had nothing to do with this – at least, no more than usual. And kindly don't swear. Remember we are in the presence of the *departed*.' And without looking she gestured towards the presumably stiffening Climp.

'Yes, yes,' bleated Henri. 'Eet is the fault of zee English priest. Ee put great foot in evair-theeng. *Et maintenant qu'est-ce qu'on fait? Jai mon réputation!*'

I looked him up and down with distaste. 'Nonsense, Henri. You don't have one jot of a reputation, except as a card sharper and lush. And you can't even conduct a service properly without cutting whole chunks off the text or slopping the wine down your cassock. Shoddy, that's what!' I glowered at him.

'Peeg,' was the reply.

'Shut up, you two,' snarled Nicholas. 'I'm fed up with all this. We're in one hell of a hole which we've got to get out of, so *think*!' He produced his cigarette case, studiously omitting to offer it around, and started to puff furiously. I thought of my own cigarettes left on the dressing table and regarded his own with envy. I did, however, have a couple of rather hairy peppermints in my pocket which, in the absence of anything else, had to do. I bit upon them grimly.

'Well,' began Primrose tentatively, 'I suppose the decent thing would be to go back and inform the police. I assume that's what –'

'Are you mad!' suddenly spluttered Clinker. He had been silent until now and his outburst was startling. We looked at him curiously. 'We have had quite enough of the police already over this absurd business with the relics – or at least, those of us staying at the Birtle-Figgins' most certainly have – and that includes you, Oughterard. You and your sister were both interviewed, and while none of us may be actual suspects – though heaven knows we might be – we are nevertheless in their sights: we have come to the *notice* of the *authorities* and I for one do not like it. They already associate us with one unfortunate death, and to be shown to be involved with another incident would –'

'Expose us to comment on the platform?' drawled Nicholas.

Clinker glared at him. 'Oh, very funny. Trust you to bring Oscar Wilde into this!'

I could see his point only too well, as I think we all could. Each of us had certain interests and 'reputations' to guard, even the wretched Henri. And although he had not mentioned it, I knew for a fact that Clinker was nursing hopes of a prestigious advancement: episcopal aide to the Archbishop of York no less. Scandal of any kind, even when supremely innocent as Clinker was, could put a swift kybosh on such hopes. It was bad enough his being inter-rogated over the bones affair, but to have this matter added to his curriculum vitae would be the last straw. My own situation of course was perennially perilous, and anything involving the law – home or foreign – put me in a muck sweat. As for Ingaza, he slithered through life on the seat of his pants, dependent on luck and a silver tongue to see him safe: chummy collaboration with the 'authorities' was not part of his policy – 'Never expose yourself, dear boy,' being one of his frequent and ribald precepts.

And so after further uneasy parleying we decided to say and do nothing, reassuring ourselves that if others chose to go around chasing defenceless strangers, stealing their property (admittedly purloined), firing guns, making vio-lent attacks and generally behaving like demented hood-lums, then it was their problem if they made a hash of things and ended up dead. The police could sort it out – if and when they discovered them missing.

There was nevertheless still the problem of Climp's corpse: what to do with it? To leave it where it had dropped seemed untidy and cavalier. To heave it over the edge to join its companion would be gross, while to lug it back to the village was clearly a feat beyond our capacity and in any case dangerous. Thus we decided to move it

157

from the open ground to a more secluded place of rest, make the usual obsequies and leave it to the hands of fate or a passing goatherd. The process was distasteful and brought to mind an earlier event in a far distant wood where I had once been forced to perform a similar manoeuvre.

The task discharged, we returned to the village as fast as possible . . . although actually it wasn't that fast: Primrose's nose was still splashing blood, Clinker had developed a sore heel, Henri, after his earlier burst of agility, had lapsed into his usual wheezing shuffle, and Ingaza, evidently so burdened with his financial loss, appeared to have difficulty in putting one foot in front of the other without pausing to hurl curses at the indifferent rock-side. Only the cat and I were fully fit and unscathed. But it seemed churlish to leap ahead to the haven of eiderdown and aspirin while the others were thus incommoded . . .

26

The Cat's Memoir

'Blimey!' snorted the dog when I mentioned what I had been doing. 'Do you mean you actually shoved the geezer over the side?' He gazed in admiration.

'Well,' I replied modestly, 'not *shoved* exactly, but I was what you might call instrumental in his downfall . . . and pretty far down it was too!' I added with some satisfaction.

'Blimey!' he exclaimed again after I had supplied the details. 'Now I've got a murderer for a master *and* a hit-cat for a mate. Not many dogs can say that!' He regarded me with rare respect. It didn't last of course. Nevertheless, it is always gratifying to be accorded one's proper due, however brief.

Thus I smiled benignly and reminded him I had been plotting retaliation ever since the Coarse One had so rudely slung me off the window sill at the auberge.

He looked puzzled. 'But you didn't know all that chasing stuff was going to happen, did you? I mean, you were kipping most of the morning on the table in the bar.'

'Yes, but at one point the hound Clemenceau came wagging in (fortunately with a flat battery) and started to jabber something abut playing games with F.O. and several other persons on the hillside. Since our master is not given to playing games (not quick enough), it struck me as rather odd – which, as things turned out, it most certainly was. At first I assumed the creature was simply mangling its

159

words or I had misheard – his accent is atrocious – but I was intrigued nevertheless. And so being curious and resourceful, I naturally thought it my business to investigate the matter.'

'Huh,' Bouncer growled, 'just as well you did, otherwise it might have been the vicar who went over the edge – and then where would we have been?'

'Left with the bishop,' I said drily.

A little later, as I was stretched out on F.O.'s bed resting from my cliff-top exertions (and rather savouring the memory), Bouncer pottered in and joined me on the eiderdown. His chops were still sticky from the bone foolishly given him by the bartender. But being in a mellow mood I refrained from comment. Nevertheless, I thought it would do the dog good to hear something instructive. 'You know, Bouncer,' I said, 'since my time here I have reached a certain conclusion.'

'What's that then?'

'The French mouse struts and is sardonic, whereas the British mouse darts erratically and is given to bouts of surly complaint. Both are obnoxious and deserve frequent correction.'

'Cor, you don't say!' was the response. I wasn't entirely sure how to take that, and was just about to ask for clarification when he said slowly, 'What you mean, Maurice, is that you are like me with rabbits – doesn't matter where the bleeders come from, you like duffing them up.'

I winced at the base terminology – while nevertheless recognizing the merest soupçon of truth in what he said. But naturally I received the comment in silence and briskly attended to my tail.

After a while he cleared his throat (a sure prelude to something guttural and garrulous) and announced that he thought himself a lucky dog. I remarked warmly that I was glad he appreciated the merits of feline company.

'What?'

160

'Cats – it's so nice to be with them.'

There was a silence as he snuffled the eiderdown thoughtfully. 'Ah, well that's not *quite* what I was going to say, Maurice. What I was going to say is that I am jolly lucky belonging to F.O. because I get a ringside seat at his circus – and get *fed* into the bargain.' He licked his chops.

This time I felt less disposed to indulgence, and reminded him tartly that there was once a Roman writer who had said something very similar about the tastes of the common herd. As you may expect, the point was entirely lost on him, and after a genial burp he asked if I knew the French for 'marrow bone'. I replied that I most certainly did not and had no wish to find out.

'I'll tell you then. It is *os à moelle*. That's what Clemso says George gave me, an *os à moelle!*' He was clearly pleased with the expression for he muttered it to himself several times. 'You wait till I get home and try it out on Pierre, he'll wonder what's hit him.' For once I felt sorry for Pierre – little did he know what was being stored up for those tiny flapping ears.

Mercifully the dog ceased his burbling and gradually dropped off to sleep, leaving me to wonder uneasily whether we ever *would* get home, and what further acts were jostling for display in our master's manic circus.

27

The Vicar's Version

Eventually, dishevelled and subdued, we reached the inn. Clinker limped up to me, cleared his throat, and asked quietly if he could use my room to wash and brush up before continuing to Le Petit Rêve to 'join the ladies'. He looked strained, and I felt sorry for him. Events had been more than bad enough, but to have to now parry the quizzical attentions of Gladys and Myrtle – not to mention the dazed and crazed Lavinia – would be penance indeed.

I showed him up to my room and indicated the bathroom, but just as he was going to the latter, he turned and said sharply, 'Now look here, Oughterard, we don't want any of this to get out, do we? Quite unnecessary. All very unfortunate of course, but fundamentally nothing to do with us – well, not in principle at any rate. And the principle *is* that those thugs hounded us and took pot shots for no good reason other than for that paltry junk of Ingaza's, and damn near killed your sister! And why that Mullion fellow should call you a murderer I cannot imagine – just goes to show, obviously off his head. Yes,' he added eagerly, 'that's it exactly ... mad as hatters, both of them! So the less said about the whole affair the better. We have quite enough on our plate with this awful Birtle-Figgins business, and to mention anything further would only confuse the police – muddy the waters. Do you understand? *Muddy the waters.*' He glared at me anxiously. I assured him he could rely on my absolute discretion. (My God he could!) I left him to his ablutions, and fetching my cigarettes wandered downstairs to the bar. I felt very tired.

Apart from Bouncer gnawing his present from Georges, and Maurice grooming himself obsessively on the only comfortable chair, the place was empty. The others had obviously sought refuge in their rooms and it was too early for the locals. I sat down wearily on the springless sofa, and tried to rid my mind of the afternoon's events.

Five minutes later there was a clattering on the stairs and Clinker appeared. Still limping, he nevertheless looked mildly improved; and throwing me a curt nod, disappeared through the outer door braced for his return to Le Petit Rêve and its occupants.

I started to brood, trying to work out at what exact point in my life things had gone so disastrously wrong ... Foxford Wood, you might say. Without doubt a spectacular shift. Yet there had been other moments, before and after, which had surely contributed their own lethal input: the Church's decision to transfer me from London to Guildford, the nightmare soirée at Marchbanks House, that chance re-encounter with Ingaza in the bar of the Old Schooner, my overlapping with Ingaza at St Bede's just after the war, the war itself, that dramatic fall from the rocking horse in my nursery which – from what I could recall – had seemed to shatter the grown-ups considerably more than me (certainly enough doctors buzzing around). But the accident had been so long ago, and the finer details blurred in faltering memory ...

However, I thought bitterly, watching the slavering dog and his untroubled companion, the current facts were far from blurred. Only too clear! The whole vivid scenario in all its pungent detail came thrusting before my eyes: Mullion and his menaces, the sniggering bloodthirsty Climp, their gross demise on that sheer and dreadful cliff, dead boring Boris and his stupid bones, the polite probings of the French police, Ingaza's forging my signature on the deeds and his insistence that I should claim possession, sell the property and split the profit both ways – in his favour. Well, at least for one joyous hour the discovery of the swastika had freed me from that particular fear, but its recent fate would surely rekindle Ingaza with thoughts of less princely gain, and once more I could risk danger of public scrutiny:

DEATH STALKS THE VICAR

Canon Francis Oughterard, once substantial heir to murdered widow Elizabeth Fotherington, and knife victim of her deranged son-in-law, yet again finds himself in the midst of violence – this time in connection with the fatal 'Belvedere' incident high in the French Auvergne, and only yards from his benefactor's imposing property which he seems so eager to sell. What quirk of fate, we ask ourselves, plunges the mild-spoken Reverend into matters so deadly?

Yes, the newspapers would enjoy themselves with that . . . and unleash or unearth Lord knew what further lines of enquiry.

I closed my eyes. When I opened them it was to see Nicholas leaning against the bar scowling.

'Feeling better?' I asked brightly.

'Like hell,' he snapped.

He seemed about to speak further, but at that moment Georges ambled in, gestured towards the hallway and announced that Monsieur Ingaza was wanted on the telephone. Nicholas turned grey.

'Oh my God,' he groaned, 'she's found me.'

'Who?' (Not a pursuing girlfriend, that was for sure.)

'Lil. I always give her the wrong number. Must have told her the right one by mistake.' He mooched into the hall. We all have our troubles, I reflected . . .

He was gone a good fifteen minutes, and with little sympathy I assumed the old aunt was giving him an earful. But when he returned, far from being chastened, he wore the smug air of Maurice after a feast of cream and salmon, and held a bottle of whisky in his hand.

At my look of surprise, he gave a broad grin, fetched a couple of glasses from behind the bar and began to fill them lavishly.

'What's this about?' I asked in wonder.

He didn't reply at first, but sat swirling the Scotch and smirking enigmatically. Still reeling from the recent nightmare, I was in no mood to be patient, and asked again what he imagined there was to celebrate.

'Oh, nothing to do with imagination, old fruit, all to do with perception and acumen. You see, that wasn't Lil on the blower, it was Eric – Eric with the goods.' He took a long sip of his drink, grimaced, sighed and added appreciatively, 'Just the job, the very job.'

'I still don't understand, what –'

'He's pulled it off, the little business I was telling you about. Worked like a dream. We're in the money!' And taking a couple more swigs, he launched into the song of that name. It was not a melodious performance, but his glee was infectious and, despite not really knowing what it was all about, rather haltingly I found myself joining in. Release of tension, I suppose.

It was thus that Primrose found us when she entered the bar two minutes later. Both glasses were now empty and we were about to embark on fill-ups.

'What a racket!' she expostulated. 'What *are* you doing, Francis?' Seeing her swollen nose and mottled cheek, I felt shamed, and in sober tone mumbled something about Nicholas having had a little windfall.

'Good,' she said frostily. 'Perhaps now he will kindly pay me the commission he owes for that second consignment to the Canadians.'

'Of course, dear girl. And I'll throw in a bottle of champagne for your birthday, as well,' he rejoined airily.

'Vintage plus lunch?'

He nodded graciously. And leaning forward, explained that while not remotely compensating for the grievous loss of the swastika, the manipulations of Eric and the Cranleigh Contact had generated a 'handy little packet', enough to keep him and cronies in substantial pocket money for some time ... Whether I counted among those cronies I couldn't be sure, and in any case was far from certain I wanted to. But what nudged my hopes was that Ingaza might now be steered away from acquisition of the wretched Folly. After all, as he had frequently observed, cash in hand was so much more comforting than future promise. However, I didn't like to raise the matter just then, sensing it might be wasted in the general merriment. But to my grovelling amazement he later broached the issue himself at supper that night.

Bribed by further whisky from the Citroën's boot, Georges had surprisingly put on a very tolerable spread: bream from the local tarn, mammoth wedges of local sausage, a goat's cheese of ammoniac pungency, chestnut mousse and copious flagons of an obscure but excellent Rhône.

At first things were distinctly subdued, unease about Climp and Mullion weighing heavily upon us – even quelling the garrulous Henri. But as the meal progressed and the alcohol was imbibed, we started to relax, and Nicholas, though guarded about its exact nature, waxed lyrical about his recent coup. We repeated to one another the bishop's view that our attackers had brought the whole thing upon themselves, and that such immoderate behaviour had been bound to backfire. And thus conveniently fortified we focused on the pleasures of the meal and speculations about the murder of Boris. Little headway was made with the latter, and it was at the point when Henri declared that in his opinion it was all the doing of a disaffected papal envoy, that Nicholas made his proposal.

'Frankly,' he yawned, 'I've had enough of this French lark. There's clearly nothing doing at the château, not now we've lost the swastika ... and according to Lavinia the gold was pillaged years ago. In any case, after today's little romp the sooner we put some mileage between ourselves and that plateau, the better. Those two will be found eventually and I don't fancy being hauled in front of Frog magistrates to answer questions about a matter nothing to do with me . . . It was their own damn fault. Besides,' he added musingly, 'it doesn't do to leave Eric too long to his own devices, especially with this latest development and my Cranleigh pal wanting his cut. Uncle Nick needs to be there to supervise matters. Give 'em an inch . . .'

I experienced a pang of relief and triumph; and rather than risk saying anything that might upset the delicate balance of things, nodded sagely indicating my full support.

However, Henri was in less accord, protesting that he hadn't come all the frigging way down from Normandy to foreign parts without getting something out of it, and what compensation was on offer? Nicholas told him he could have a bottle of Scotch and a hundred francs for his collection plate. Such a sop would hardly content this Cerberus, and I could see him opening his mouth to pour scorn and mordant invective. But Ingaza forestalled him by saying nonchalantly, 'You could stay on, and then I'm sure, if you ask nicely, Francis will permit you to grub about on his property with the detector. Anything you happen to turn up – Roman coins, insignia etc. – you could keep all to yourself.' He turned to me. 'You wouldn't object, would you, old boy?'

'Fine, fine,' I replied quickly, still loath to think of the place as being anything to do with me, and yet ready to be more than generous if it meant we could get back to England free of all entanglements. The curé cast me a smile of fawning beatitude and imperiously ordered another ration of the Rhône. Ingaza narrowed his eyes but said nothing.

'Well, I'm glad that's all settled,' broke in Primrose, 'but has it occurred to any of you that we are not free to return, whether we want to or not? You may care to remember we are still under police investigation about the Boris affair and are confined to barracks until they see fit to release us. At least, Francis and I are.'

There was silence as we pondered this; and then Nicholas said to me, 'Why don't you nip over to the gendarmerie tomorrow and find out the lie of the land? Have a word with the investigating officer and see if he still wants you.'

'No fear,' I answered, lowering my voice to avoid Henri's sharp ears. 'The Molehill police are bad enough, I certainly don't want to get mixed up with the ones here more than I have to. What you might call a hostage to fortune!'

'Hmm . . . In that case perhaps you had better go up to Le Petit Rêve in the morning – take Lavinia some flowers or something – and see if she or the Clinkers know more about it.'

I was also reluctant to do that but I could see his point, and prompted by Primrose agreed to pay a visit.

28

The Vicar's Version

'Tell you what,' said Nicholas the next day, 'I'll come with you – give old Horace a thrill.'

'Heart attack more like.'

He grinned, checked the mirror and adjusted his scarf. 'Come on. Let's see what's what. So you got the flowers all right – always a handy gesture. Puts you on top straight away!' I nodded, looking doubtfully at the forlornly ragged dahlias hastily purchased from the village shop.

The weather was bright and the previous night's shower had given a tang to things, so we decided to walk the mile and enjoy the last of the summer air. I had thought of taking Bouncer, but decided against it ... doubtless there would be quite enough to occupy us without the dog's cavortings.

As we climbed the steep hill, a thought occurred – presumably Climp and Mullion's tent and car would still be lodged in the Birtle-Figgins' orchard: a realization that for some reason struck chill, and yet perversely I wanted to take a look – half expecting to see them still there, tending a fire, adjusting guy ropes or whatever it is campers do. I wondered too what Lavinia had thought when, taking them the morning milk, she had found only an empty tent ... *But*, it suddenly dawned, much more to the point was what the police would think – as presumably at some stage the campers too must have been roped in for routine questioning, and like ourselves put under temporary curfew.

'Oh Lord, Nicholas,' I gasped, 'I bet the police have got their eye on them as well, and are bound to come sniffing round asking if we have seen any signs and generally raising a hue and cry. So much for keeping quiet and trying to get out while the going's good. We're bound to be dragged in!'

'Not if you can control your nerve we won't,' he said severely. 'I'm damn sure nobody saw us with them, and if that little Inspector Maigret, or whatever he's called, asks questions, it's just a matter of brazening it out. After all,' he added wryly, 'it's not as if you haven't had enough practice.' I thought the comment unnecessary but said nothing, and instead strode to the other side of the lane and peered down into the orchard below.

There was nothing there. No car, no tent, no clue to suggest that anyone had been present at all. My eyes swept the wide field with its brook, the few apple trees and newly planted saplings. Nothing.

Nicholas joined me and gazed down at the empty space where the campers had been. 'They're alive,' I squeaked. 'Came back, got their stuff and driven off. Oh my God, they'll get me in the end!'

'Shut up,' he said roughly. 'Of course they're bloody dead. You saw for yourself. We all did. My God, Francis, with you in the army, it's amazing we had any chance in the war at all!'

I was stung by that, and retorted quickly, 'Well, at least I was *in* the services – don't know what you were doing during that time.'

'Being considerably more useful than you, I shouldn't wonder,' he muttered, and turned away to light a cigarette.

I went on scanning the orchard, trying to work out what had happened in the hours between our pursuers losing their lives on the high plateau and their things vanishing from the Birtle-Figgins' land.

'There's a simple explanation,' he said, 'which we shall

doubtless discover. Now, stay cool and best foot forward, and let's see what My Lord Bishop has to say.'

We recommenced our climb to Le Petit Rêve – or night-mare, as it was fast becoming.

But as we approached the house I was struck again by how attractive it was. Rustic yet elegant, it wore an air of confident repose, both the building and its surround-ing pastures exuding feelings of safety, civility and rooted ease . . . an ease horribly at odds with the fate of its late owner.

'Hmm,' said Ingaza, gazing around appreciatively, 'this would make a nice little bolt hole from Brighton – a sort of bucolic sanctuary. I can see myself here communing with the blackbirds and a gin and tonic. Just the job!'

'Thought you hankered after a smart town house in Manchester Square,' I replied acidly, the dreadful mission to Claude Blenkinsop's flat still sharp in my mind.*

He grinned. 'That would do too, dear boy – town and country, what could be better?'

I was about to ask how Eric would take to such a 'bucolic sanctuary' and whether he might miss the dartboard at the Crown and Anchor, but I was forestalled by a shout from an upper window: 'If you have come to see the bishop he's in the bath. You'll have to wait!' Gladys.

Nicholas sighed. 'Hell, she doesn't improve, does she?'

'No,' I answered, 'but you want to see the other one, Myrtle.'

'Rather not, old chap.'

At that moment Lavinia emerged, draped in the same trailing garb as she had been wearing on the day of her husband's death, but this time embellished with long strings of green and silver beads. They were rather pretty. I thrust the flowers into her arms, said I trusted she was bearing up, and introduced Nicholas. As always he was lavish in his compliments, and, leaving me to wait for Clinker, she took him off to view the gardens. I wandered

* See *Bone Idle*

into the salon, hoping fervently not to bump into Myrtle, and was about to take a chair when I realized someone was sitting on the window seat: Rupert Turnbull.

He put down the book he was reading and greeted me warmly. 'Good to see you again, Canon, though sorry the circumstances are so tragic. Poor Lavinia, she's being fearfully brave about it all but it's a terrible ordeal, terrible!' He offered me a cigarette and went to ask the housekeeper to bring some coffee.

I glanced down at his book, and was interested to see it was the same one I had been perusing on the fateful day, *Ventures Among the Myths: Haunting Tales from the Auvergne* by Herbert Castris MA.

'Writes quite well, doesn't he?' I remarked when Turnbull returned.

'Too florid for my taste, but he knows his stuff all right – been researching it for years. A prep school master originally – French and History – but he retired early, couldn't stand the little tykes, I suppose, and settled in the valley below to devote his days to cultivation of the Muse and "all things scholarly".' On the last phrase Turnbull assumed a slightly mannered voice and laughed. 'Actually he's not bad, old Castris, but takes himself too seriously. Ought to get out more.' He lowered his voice. 'As a matter of fact, a bit like poor Boris – has a bee in his bonnet about the local hermit. But whereas Boris saw himself as some sort of spiritual advocate proclaiming the man's sanctity and pushing for canonization, Castris is hellbent on scaling the heights of academia with Belvedere as his ladder. Actually, he and Boris were not exactly bosom pals – too many petty rivalries. You know what these zealots are like. Castris has already published one short study of the chap and was hoping to make scholarly capital by uncovering the precious tambourine. Been on its trail for ages – a sort of holy grail, you might say.' He paused, and laughed again. 'But unfortunately just when he thought he had cracked the –'

He was interrupted by Clinker's voice from the doorway: 'Ah, there you are, Francis, Gladys said she had seen you – and with Ingaza.' He coughed, adding, 'At least, that's what I gathered from her description . . .'

Fresh from his ablutions, the bishop looked spruce and almost sprightly, and despite the trials of the mountainside I wondered if Lavinia's sudden culinary interests were taking effect. He certainly appeared more relaxed than when last seen – although in the circumstances, I suppose that would not be difficult. But it also crossed my mind that perhaps the Clinkers had received the order of release from the French police – a possibility that should augur well for ourselves. I was about to make tentative enquiry, when I saw Lavinia and Nicholas approaching the french windows. For one in the midst of dire disaster, our hostess seemed remarkably animated, chatting gaily to her companion and pointing out aspects of the local flora and fauna. Nicholas looked suitably attentive, but I suspected that by this hour his thoughts were largely focused on a Sobranie and snifter. Well, I thought wryly, he might manage the first, but unless he liked Tizer or elderberry, he could forget the drink!

How wrong one can be. As she stepped over the threshold Lavinia gave us a dazzling smile, consulted her wristwatch and exclaimed, 'Oh, a quarter to twelve already! Not too early for a cocktail, I think.' With a gay little laugh she went off to the kitchen, murmuring something about finding some brandy and Cointreau.

Given the dearth of spirituous uplift on previous visits, I was amazed by this turn of events. As clearly was Clinker. 'Good Lord,' he muttered, 'she's going to give us a *Sidecar*.' He emphasized the word with delighted disbelief. And then rather tactlessly added, 'Must be the end of Lent!'

'What are you talking about, Horace?' demanded his sister-in-law as she billowed into the room. 'Lent's been over for months.'

'Speaking metaphorically, Myrtle. Lavinia is mixing *cocktails* for us.'

'Really,' was the acid retort. 'Squash and pineapple?'

'Not at all – a Sidecar.' Clinker beamed.

'Have you been drinking?'

'No, but I shall be shortly.' He gave a gleeful chuckle.

Myrtle evinced surprised interest. 'Does Gladys know about this?' He shook his head. 'Then I suggest you inform her immediately. She could do with a sweetener – been frightful all morning!'

'What a treat,' Ingaza drawled suddenly. 'Yes, do fetch her, Horace, it'll be quite a little party.'

Myrtle regarded him with suspicion. 'Who's this?' she asked. I explained as best I could; but clearly unimpressed with the deftly sleeked hair and raffish tie, she gave a hostile grunt and turned her attention to Turnbull.

Nice though the prospect of cocktails was, it was hardly enough to assuage my fearful perplexity about the disappearance of the campers' tent. But as I was on the point of going into the kitchen to sound out Lavinia, Nicholas sidled up and said, 'I've got the answer to our little puzzle.'

I didn't have a chance to learn more, for at that moment Clinker returned with Gladys, who, having been delivered of the good news, looked mildly pleased. She nodded to me, glared at her sister, and seemed about to say something, when Lavinia arrived with a tray of glasses and a shaker.

'I am so sorry,' she began, 'but the brandy is all gone. Can't think how.' (I felt a pang of guilt, recalling its avid consumption on the day of the murder.)

'Are you sure?' the bishop asked plaintively.

'Oh yes,' she said, 'not a drop – but I've found some gin, so you will have to settle for White Ladies.'

There was an audible sigh of relief from Clinker. 'Better and better,' he enthused. 'I'm rather partial to that particular concoction.' (As I knew only too well!)

'How many?' Nicholas whispered to me out of the side of his mouth.

'Curb your greed,' I muttered.

For my personal taste our hostess had underplayed the

lemon; but they were good all the same, and we sipped appreciatively. Gradually a sort of ease prevailed: the sisters becoming disposed to speak to each other, and Clinker and Nicholas exchanging more (guarded) memories of their Oxford days. I drifted towards Lavinia and Turnbull on the window seat. It seemed the right moment to enquire the state of play re the police investigation. And I was just deciding how I might introduce the subject, when Turnbull pre-empted me. 'You know, Canon, I was just saying to Lavinia how splendid she is being over all of this – attending to her house guests, laying on these delicious cocktails *and* coping with the incessant police presence!'

'Oh well,' she said lightly, 'one can't give in. And as to the police presence, "incessant" is a bit of an exaggeration. That Inspector Dumont has been here only a couple of times and he is always so polite. I am afraid it's just one of those things that have to be gone through.' She looked painfully brave.

'Well, I think you are remarkable.' He looked at me. 'Don't you agree?'

'Rather!' I replied stoutly; and then asked casually how the investigation was progressing.

'Quite swiftly, I gather,' Lavinia replied. 'That's to say, the inspector is expecting to eliminate all those in the immediate vicinity, so he tells me.' She cast a quick look in the direction of Gladys. 'To tell the truth, I suspect the two ladies are getting a trifle tired of their enforced sojourn here. They'll be glad to go home, I shouldn't wonder.'

'Surely not,' I said gallantly.

She laughed. 'I certainly would. After all, it's not quite what you expect on a holiday, is it? Anyway, I think you will all be able to get away soon – Dumont seems to know what he is doing.' There was a pause, and then she said, suddenly pensive, 'Not that that will bring back Boris of course ... Such a shame.' I was struck by that final phrase ... a trifle limp for the loss described?

But I had no time to ponder semantics, for having detached himself from Nicholas (or the other way round),

175

Clinker was moving towards me looking agitated. Excusing himself to Lavinia and Turnbull, he intimated that he had a professional matter to discuss and would I mind taking a stroll with him in the garden. As a matter of fact I did mind. It was well past one o'clock and I was getting hungry and keen to catch the last of lunch at the inn. Besides, having got what I came for, i.e. confirmation that with luck we might soon be off the inspector's hook, there seemed little point in staying. Bouncer too would be bustling for his walk. However, Clinker was evidently determined to get me alone, and reluctantly I followed him out on to the lawn.

'Typical,' he hissed, 'just typical!'

'What is?' I asked, perplexed.

'Ingaza of course. Hasn't changed one iota, just as infuriating!' I had no idea what he was talking about but could certainly identify with the feeling.

'What's the trouble?'

'The trouble *is* that he won't give me a straight answer. When I told him that naturally I had not apprised Gladys and Myrtle of our dreadful experience on the mountain and it was vital that they never hear of it, he had the nerve to say –' and Clinker turned pink with annoyance – '"A bit late now, Hor old chap, the nag's bolted." When I asked him what on earth he meant by that, he kept smiling that maddening smile and said he rather thought that you knew. *Do* you know, Oughterard?'

'No,' I said blankly. 'No, I don't.'

'Are you sure?'

'Of course I am. When would I have had a chance to tell Gladys and Myrtle? And besides,' I added, smiling faintly, 'if I had done so, don't you think you would have heard about it by now?'

He frowned, and then said, 'Yes, you're right ... I would.' He too started to smile, albeit grimly, but then stopped abruptly. 'So what's Ingaza babbling about?'

'Since you ask me, sir, I would say he was pulling your leg.'

'Pulling my . . .? How absurd. Always was puerile! I remember at Oxford when I was dining with him at Merton one night, he . . . Oh well, we won't go into that now,' the bishop said hastily.

I was about to make my excuses and hurry away, when a thought struck me. 'Uhm . . . I don't wish to appear prurient, but what made you say that Lavinia had been on the point of filing for divorce? I thought she and Boris were so compatible.'

'Oh, women and such,' was the reply, 'you know the sort of thing . . .'

The 'sort of thing' was not something I was much acquainted with (unless one counted those instructive afternoons in wartime Brighton with the redoubtable Madge*), but nevertheless I found myself protesting, 'But he was so ugly!'

Clinker gave me a withering look. 'If you knew anything about the fair sex, Oughterard, you would know that that doesn't stop 'em.' He coughed delicately and added, 'Well, some at any rate . . . not all of course.'

Of the latter I assumed he was thinking of Gladys and Myrtle whom, I imagine, most things in that department would have stopped – but thought it unwise to enquire. We got on to firmer ground: the Belvedere bones.

'In my opinion,' pronounced Clinker, 'he was asking for it.'

I was startled. 'You mean he invited the attack?'

'No, no, not *invited*, but behaved in such a way as to lay himself open to alien forces.' He obviously saw my look of puzzlement, for lowering his voice said, 'I never really cared for Birtle-Figgins – a rum sort in more ways than one. But then of course, being an acquaintance of Myrtle's, what else could you expect?'

This may have been the bishop's opinion of his host, but as a means of shedding light on either Boris or those 'alien

*As recalled by Francis in *A Load of Old Bones*

forces' it had little value. I tried again. 'I am sorry to sound dense, sir, but what exactly do you mean by alien forces?'

'Oh, all those fakes and fantasists he cultivated, crackpots of one sort or another: spiritualists, communists, Rosicrucians, druids, vegans, the Jung squad – all the usual woolgatherers. You saw some of them the other evening . . . I must say, Francis, I wouldn't like to meet that harpist on a dark night!' He gave a snort of mirth. 'Yes, Boris certainly had a mania for the esoteric all right – hence his obsession with that absurd little hermit. And besides,' he continued, 'as Lavinia let drop, the man was a *libertine* – out and out, if you get my meaning.' The term was articulated with conviction and relish.

I pondered the information. 'Ah, so some of those alien forces might also have been the cuckolded husbands?'

He raised his eyebrows. 'If you don't mind my saying so, Oughterard, you have been watching too many French films . . . No, I do not mean the husbands – though I dare say a few may well have borne grudges. As a matter of fact, it is far more likely to have been one of his fellow enthusiasts, some rival crank piqued at having his chances scuppered as Master of the Bones.'

'That's a bit extreme, isn't it – to kill him simply for loss of professional kudos?'

'Not at all. You would be surprised at the flimsy motives people have for such activity. I haven't been a bishop for all these years without learning a little about the vagaries of human nature. Of course, as a lesser canon, your own insights are necessarily limited.' He gave a genial and superior laugh.

Disregarding the inevitable put-down, I reflected sombrely that Clinker was right. My own 'activity' in that area had been an unpremeditated act of desperation triggered by a longing for quiet which had come to dominate my whole being . . . The sudden dispatch of Mrs Fotherington had taken me by surprise, and I wondered whether Boris's assailant had been similarly wrong-footed. Was he too now paralysed by incredulity – stunned at his own capacity and flinching at every footfall and gendarme's shadow? Or perhaps he was at this very moment calmly taking stock of his action and meticulously planning the next move. The second response I had read about, the first I knew only too well . . .

As I ruminated I realized that the bishop was similarly engaged. He wore a look of frowning concentration as if tussling with some recalcitrant puzzle.

The silence was eventually broken. 'Yes, that must be it,' he intoned triumphantly. '*Cherchez la femme!*'

'What?'

'It's the woman, Clothilde de Vere,' he explained. 'Turnbull has told me all about it: apparently a local widow of impeccable respectability and stupendous poitrine. For some reason her uncle owned the hermit's tambourine – a sort of heirloom, I gather – and gave it to her as a fiftieth birthday present. And Castris – that historian fellow writing the life of Belvedere – dazzled by her physical endowment but even more by the said instrument and eager for both, had been paying court for several months. Apparently the campaign met with great success, and at the very point when both desires were about to be satisfied, Birtle-Figgins stepped in and snaffled the lot.'

I cleared my throat. 'Er – you mean spectacular poitrine *and* musical instrument?'

'Precisely,' replied Clinker. 'Sex and laurels – all vanished in a puff of smoke. Yes, the good widow transferred both her endowment and the tambourine to Boris . . . Triumph for one, ignominy for the other. Just goes to show, Oughterard,' he observed sententiously, 'nothing is certain. One would do well to remember that.'

Thanks for the tip, I thought sourly, and asked how Castris had taken it.

'Badly,' was the reply. 'Wrote a vitriolic letter to the *Church Times* castigating religious charlatans, and has cut Boris dead ever since.' There was a pause, and then lowering his voice, he confided, 'In fact, Oughterard, it is my belief that there was a cut too far – i.e. it is highly likely that Herbert Castris is the *slayer*!' He flourished the last word as a conjuror might pull a rabbit from a hat.

'Good Lord!' I exclaimed. 'Do you really think so? When did you get that idea?'

He hesitated, and then said with a tinge of regret, 'Well, it wasn't me really . . . Gladys's view actually, she's good like that – all those trashy novels. I didn't take much notice at first, seemed pretty far-fetched. But the more I look at it and remember what Turnbull was saying, the more I think there may be something in it. *She's* certainly convinced all right.'

She would be, I thought. Once Gladys gets an idea in her head wild horses wouldn't dislodge it. A mule by any other name . . . But still, recalling the homicidal jealousy of Victor Crumpelmeyer when also baulked of what he felt to be his, I reflected that in this instance she could just be right.

'Have you said anything to the police of your suspicions?'

'Certainly not!' the bishop snapped. 'I told you the other day, the less we have to do with any of this business the better. There is much at stake, Francis. You may not be fully aware, but my chance of selection as the archbishop's adjutant is no small matter.' I nodded respectfully. 'Besides,' he added, 'given your unfortunate involvement with that Crumpel fellow and all the unsavoury press attention, I'd have thought you would recognize the need for reticence. After all, there is the reputation of the Church to consider!'

Ah yes, I mused, the reputation of the Church . . . safe in the capable hands of H. Clinker and F. Oughterard.

29

The Vicar's Version

I walked back to the village on my own, for by the time I left the house Nicholas had already taken off, presumably sated with small talk and the pronouncements of Myrtle and Gladys.

Back at the inn I attended to Bouncer, ate what little was left on the lunch menu and then went in search of the others. But to my surprise Georges reported that Primrose and Henri had borrowed bicycles and gone for *'un petit spin'* to the neighbouring village. I had not expected such freewheeling fraternity and wondered what on earth they would have to talk about. I was also a little fearful for any pedestrians they might encounter. 'And Monsieur Ingaza?' I asked. 'Has he been back for his lunch?' Georges shook his head and said not as far as he was aware. I was slightly put out by this, being anxious to hear what he had discovered re the vacated orchard. What was he doing – buying more postcards to send to the insatiable Lil? Stepping over Maurice lolling on the threshold, I settled on the ramshackle veranda and lit a cigarette; but then sleepy from the White Ladies and the walk back from Le Petit Rêve, stubbed it out and shut my eyes.

I was awoken by a soft voice saying, 'My apologies for intruding, monsieur, but Georges said I might find you here, and I would be grateful for your time.' I looked up to see the smiling face of Inspector Dumont.

Over recent years I have developed a nervousness of the police, a Pavlovian response engendered by earlier events and my dealings with DS Sidney Samson. But this was no quivering whippet ready to sniff and pounce at my least hesitation, but a mild-eyed spaniel, polite and almost companionable. Thus I said he was more than welcome and invited him to sit down on one of the rickety chairs.

He began by confirming Lavinia's assumption that our group was on his *liste d'élimination* and would soon be free to collect the passports. 'However, these things always take more time than one hopes, and as you are perhaps aware, we French have a system of bureaucracy which is *très pénible* – or what I think in English would be termed red tape most bloody. But I am sure it will not be long before you can continue with your well-earned *vacances*. In the meantime I would appreciate if you could give me your thoughts – quite informally – on one or two small matters.' I gave a co-operative smile.

'You see, I am trying to establish a picture of Monsieur Birtle-Figgins, the unfortunate victim of this frenzied attack. Without an image of the victim it is impossible to deduce the murderer.' I nodded agreement, wondering vaguely if March and Samson had been so intent on establishing an 'image' of Elizabeth. 'In the case of Monsieur Birtle-Figgins,' he continued, 'it is rather perplexing – there seem to be a number of incongruities . . .' He paused, looking at me quizzically. 'And I wonder if you as a "man of the cloth", to use your Anglican phrase, could shed some light. I have of course spoken to the good *l'évêque* Clinker, but the two ladies, they make rather a noise and it is not easy . . .' He trailed off and I smiled sympathetically. 'For instance, perhaps you can explain his rabid passion for those hermit's bones. I always assumed such interests alien to the Protestant mentality.'

'Oh, they are,' I said firmly. 'Absolutely!' (I have never been drawn to bones myself, and ever since the Crumpelmeyers had threatened to have Elizabeth disinterred my wariness of them has increased.)

'Yes, that is what I thought. So I am inclined to suspect that Monsieur's concern for those relics was less the product of religious conviction than of an uncertain *psychologie*. During your sojourn at the house had you noticed any signs of this?'

'He didn't eat much,' I said.

He looked surprised. 'No – well, I wasn't really thinking of his appetite ... although,' and here he leant forward, dropping his voice, 'in some ways I suppose I am.'

I looked at him blankly. 'You see, *entre nous* I think the bones were a form of sublimation, a surrogate for *autres choses.*'

'What other things?' I asked, not quite clear what he was getting at.

'For *la sexualité* of course.' Of course. What else? Trust the French to put that construction on things!

'Well, possibly,' I replied, 'but maybe he was just a bit eccentric, what we call a harmless crank. Quite a number of people are – they just get bees in their bonnets about things.'

'Yes,' he said doubtfully, 'it is true there are a lot of English people like that. We have a number living in this area. That writer Castris for example, he too has a fixation but in his case it is for a tambourine. Yes, the English are very inventive and rarely logical ... But as for our victim at Le Petit Rêve, I think you will find there is some truth in what I say. It is my belief that he had not been getting – forgive me if I use a crude expression, I encountered it when studying at Cambridge – he had not been getting his fill of oats. And bereft of oats he turned to bones.'

'Really?' I gasped. 'Is that so?'

'Undoubtedly,' he replied gravely.

There was silence while I tried to formulate a suitable response, but I was forestalled by a voice behind us saying, 'Who's not getting his oats?' Ingaza stood there grinning.

'Boris,' I explained. 'The inspector feels that his concern for the Belvedere relics was a sort of substitute for, er – sexual relations.'

'Oh well,' Nicholas said blithely, 'any port in a storm, I suppose. Though I must say, that's not exactly what I have heard. I have heard various –'

'Ah,' said Dumont, 'that has been a more recent development. I think the bones were only a partial diversion – or they were beginning to provide diminishing returns. For all his earnestness – dullness, one might say – he appeared to be cultivating a taste for the local ladies. In fact we are beginning to work on the possibility of a *crime passionnel*. But naturally I have to keep an open mind. You see, there was also the question of status and power: the relics may certainly have been a form of sublimation, but it was quite obvious that the man was greatly enjoying his role as Guardian of the Bones and leader of the *culte de Belvedere*. Thus he could have provoked enemies of a political nature. Or conversely, it may simply have been a question of personality: it is amazing how mere dislike can grow into loathing. I remember being on a case once in Aurillac where the wife poisoned her husband for no other reason than she found his presence distasteful and the prospect of divorce tiresome . . .'

As Dumont continued to speculate about the ramifications of Boris's psyche, my own thoughts were increasingly occupied with Climp and Mullion. I was longing to have it confirmed by Nicholas that there was a perfectly simple explanation for the disappearance of their things in the field, and that Mullion, at least, had not somehow survived and was still at large and poised to resume his harassment. I recalled only too well his less than veiled threats by the duck pond, and felt again the cold clawing of fear . . . Besides, I argued to myself, even assuming that all was well, there was still the problem of a search being made if the men were needed for further questioning or if it was thought they had left without sanction. Presumably, like us, they would have been required to surrender their passports, and thus their failure to collect these would surely be a matter of immediate concern. It would be just our luck for someone to have seen us with them, talking perhaps on the hillside before the dreadful chase, or me with Mullion by the pond . . . Supposing there had been a witness to his fall from the bank – it might be assumed we had been fighting and I had knocked him in! Any such sightings would inevitably unleash a whole mass of officious probing; the bodies would be ferreted out and our chances of an unobtrusive exit – of just driving off from the area and 'throwing away the key' – completely wrecked.

With hindsight and now at a safe distance in my study at Molehill, such anxieties seem a trifle excessive. But I have discovered that murder sharpens the sensibilities and makes one uncomfortably alert to whatever attracts attention or leads to curiosity from officialdom, however irrelevant. Thus I wondered if the pair were also on Dumont's elimination list, or whether he was intending to question them further.

'Very complex,' I said, 'but at least you have been able to narrow down the search a bit. Some of us can very nearly rest easy!' And I laughed genially, adding, 'I suppose any strangers in the area are bound to widen the range of suspects and increase the work. Must be difficult.'

Dumont laughed. 'As a matter of fact I was rather pinning my hopes on those campers in the Birtle-Figgins' orchard. It would have been most expedient: their tent was close to the bathing area and they could easily have got through the hedge and given him *un bon coup* – or as you English would say, a right bashing. But there was no obvious motive . . . and besides, unfortunately they had what I think your police call a watertight alibi. On that afternoon they were drinking in a bar in Aurillac – and causing a bit of trouble too: singing questionable songs and disturbing the card players. Nor did it go down too well with the locals when one of them continually bragged of having liberated the town at the end of the war. *Le patron* was most indignant and said that it was de Gaulle himself who had done them that honour.' He sighed ruefully. 'No, we had to eliminate them almost immediately, and I fear must look closer to home for our assassin than among passing strangers. *Quelle dommage* – or to quote Monsieur Gilbert, a policeman's lot is not a happy one!'

He stood up, shook our hands vigorously, and giving Maurice several fond strokes, took his leave. The cat exhibited glazed shock, while Nicholas laughed and exclaimed, '*What* a nice man – just your type, Francis.'

'He is at the moment,' I said in some relief. 'Now, what about their things? Why on earth aren't they still there?'

'Because, dear boy, being freed from police surveillance, they packed up the car, said bye-bye to Lavinia and buggered off ... She mentioned it when we were together in the garden and said they meant to do some local exploring before heading on down south. What they didn't tell her, of course, was that they would stop at the Folly gates and hang about in the hope of spotting us – as of course they did.' He gave a sardonic laugh. 'Presumably they thought they could relieve us of the swastika – which in the course of her milk round your talkative hostess had so thoughtfully told them about – nip down to Cannes and make hay on the proceeds. And if for some reason that didn't work they were obviously planning to make trouble for you anyway. They were chancers whose chances backfired. Lucky escape for you, old fellow, if you ask me.'

'Yes,' I said faintly, 'it was.' However, just as I was beginning to feel the stirrings of safety a thought struck me: 'But I say, what about the Austin-Healey, it must still be at the Folly gates or somewhere around there. It's bound to be noticed, especially if it's got all their gear inside. Oh my Lord!'

'Don't panic, old cock, all in hand. I've been rather busy.'

'What do you mean?'

'Uncle Nick has deposited it in a place of safe-keeping – temporarily safe, at any rate.'

'What do you mean? Where?'

'When you were gassing with Clinker in the garden at Le Petit Rêve I nipped down the road to the Folly entrance (plodded, actually, it took a hell of a time), located the car parked behind some trees and drove it back to that makeshift barn in the corner of the orchard. Given the current preoccupations, it is highly unlikely that Lavinia or anyone else will bother to go near the place for quite a while, weeks probably, by which time we shall be well away knowing nowt about owt.' He looked pleased with himself.

'But the car – was it open? How did you get in or start it?'

'It is amazing,' said Nicholas reflectively, 'how living with Eric can be such an education. Best lock-picker and car mechanic on the whole of the south coast ...' He winked slyly.

30

The Vicar's Version

There were still a couple of hours before supper, and I thought it would do both myself and Bouncer good to take a brisk walk. Ingaza was occupied on the telephone, presumably keeping tabs on Eric and the Cranleigh Contact, and it was unlikely that he would choose to accompany us in any case – having suffered quite enough exercise on the mountainside only recently. Bouncer of course was as always raring to go. So, careful to choose the opposite direction from the plateau, we set off at speed and in strong voice.

I was still nervous about the discovery of Climp's corpse and knew it could only be a matter of time. However, at least we were off Dumont's suspect list, and if luck held could soon be away before questions were asked. But a very real delaying factor was Boris's funeral. Forensics had done their job and the body had been released to the family, i.e. Lavinia. The interment was scheduled for a few days hence, Clinker having been invited to conduct the service himself; and shortly after Dumont's visit he had telephoned to ask if I would also lend support. In the circumstances, and given the Birtle-Figgins' hospitality, it was hardly something I, or any of us, could refuse.

I strolled along a well-trodden goat track, watching the dog throwing himself among brambles and bushes, putting up rabbits and worrying fallen branches. He was a companionable creature and I envied him his energy and freedom. I just hoped he could be smuggled back to England without trouble. Maurice would be less of a problem; but when it came to repatriating Bouncer things could be a mite tricky. I wondered about a strong sedative. Perhaps Georges could recommend a vet . . .

I also started to think about Boris. Shocking though his end had been, our escapade with Climp and Mullion had rather pushed his particular event to the back of my mind. But now, safe from their threats, I once more started to ponder his fate and reflect upon the killer. Had our host really been the roué that Dumont and Clinker suggested? To my untutored eye it seemed improbable, although maybe the odd fling with a desperate female was not beyond the bounds of likelihood. Still, would that have been sufficient to goad an enraged husband to bump him off? A biff on the nose should have done the trick. Who on earth could have wanted to risk their neck to dispatch that pompous and more than ridiculous bone-keeper! . . . But then, I thought soberly, who on earth would have wanted to dispatch Mrs Elizabeth Fotherington?

Yes, I mused, perhaps the ones who escape detection longest are those with the least or flimsiest of motive – flimsy at any rate to the uninitiated outsider. Naturally, gain of one sort or other was at the root of all such activity. But (as in my own case) it was perhaps gain of the negative kind which made the motive most difficult to grasp and gave it an elusiveness protective to the perpetrator. What I had needed was privacy and freedom from noise and interference, and I suspect few would see that as a likely reason for murder; yet at the time it was so desperate a need that, willy-nilly, I did what I did.

Was Boris's assassin cast in the same mould – prompted by some seemingly minor cause that went out of control? I remembered what Dumont had been saying about personal distaste sometimes turning to hate, and I thought of his example of the woman in Aurillac who had poisoned her husband because she was tired of his presence and found divorce an inconvenience. Well, presumably quite a

189

few people may have become tired of Boris's presence – a feeling one had little difficulty in sharing.

I stopped and gazed at the distant *puy*. If the lady in Aurillac could do that, how about the lady in Berceau-Lamont? I reflected upon Lavinia: she was not dislikeable. Despite the air of abstracted other-worldliness, the woman was perfectly affable and, while sharing his earnestness and under-developed humour, certainly did not project the unctuous piety of her erstwhile spouse. Had the sudden serving of a cocktail and conspicuous display of glittering beads been a private celebration of his death? Death maybe . . . but murder? Anyone's guess.

And what about Herbert Castris? A disaffected would-be scholar with a thwarted fancy for a hermit's tambourine and a spectacular cleavage (I made a mental note to keep my eyes scanned for Madame de Vere), was he really the *slayer* as Clinker – or rather Gladys – had asserted? True, he had held a grudge all right: after all, you would need to be fairly exercised to find time and a writing pad to pen a letter to the *Church Times*. But whether that was enough to prompt such an extreme reaction as murder was surely questionable . . . A question which made me reflect once more upon my own experience.

Such cogitations were interrupted by Bouncer who had bounded from the bushes, jaws firmly clamped on the centre of a fallen branch. Several times his own length, it clearly put him in mind of an unduly protracted rat, and I emitted the required gasps of amazement as he proudly deposited the trophy at my feet. Such heroics had obviously induced hunger, for instead of bounding further into untapped territory, he turned briskly, and with firm foot set off for home. Shelving thoughts of Boris and his attackers, and sharing the dog's desire for food and drink, I followed his example.

When I reached the inn, I met Primrose at the foot of the stairs. She had obviously survived the bike ride with Henri and was making a beeline for the bar.

190

'Did you have a good time?' I asked doubtfully.

'Oh yes,' she said, 'and you will never guess who we met and had tea with.'

'Who?'

'Go and get changed first – there are burrs all over your trousers. I'll tell you when you come down.'

When I rejoined her in the bar Nicholas was also there – though no sign of the curé. Perhaps the conjunction of pedals and Primrose had proved too much and he was recovering quietly in his room. I asked who it was they had met in Villiers.

'Well, Turnbull at first and then later Herbert Castris. He lives there and we went to his house and had tea – jolly nice it was too: real Earl Grey and proper bread and butter. Even Marmite. Not at all French!'

'So how did that come about?'

'Villiers is quite a large village and they've actually got a second-hand bookshop. I wanted to buy some nail polish at the hairdresser next door but Henri insisted on dragging me in to look at some ancient horse-racing books. And that's where we met Rupert Turnbull, browsing among the dictionaries – wants some cheaply for his language school, I suppose. He was very chummy and said our arrival was well timed as he was just on his way to take tea with his friend Castris, and would we like to come too. I was slightly hesitant as it seemed unfair on the man having a couple of strangers suddenly thrust on him like that. But of course, never one to pass up a free meal Henri agreed like a shot. So we joined forces with Turnbull and it all proved very pleasant.'

'So what's he like, Castris?' I asked, picturing him belabouring Boris at the poolside, *Church Times* in one hand, cricket bat or Belvedere's tibia in the other.

'Small and grey with a distinctly acid tongue. Quite amusing really, in a rather cynical way. But he was most hospitable, and really very interesting about his researches on local customs and folklore.

'Did he mention the tambourine?'

Primrose laughed. 'Well, yes, in a roundabout way. Naturally one of the topics of conversation was Boris and his grisly end, and although Castris was fairly civil about his rival (perhaps because Henri and I were there) you could see he was hardly grief-shattered. However, he made a point of saying how sorry he felt for Lavinia, and that despite their former differences, did Turnbull think it would be in order if he went over to Le Petit Rêve to pay his respects. Turnbull said he was sure that Lavinia would be very touched. At which point Castris immediately asked about the tambourine: was it being kept in a safe place and did Lavinia have any particular use for it . . .' Primrose grinned. 'I must say, he couldn't have been more transparent if he had tried!'

'So what did Turnbull have to say about that?'

'Oh, he was suitably diplomatic – said he wasn't really sure on either count, and there was so much going on with the funeral arrangements that the question of personal effects hadn't really arisen.'

'And is Castris going over there?'

'Oh yes,' laughed Primrose, 'pretty pronto I should think – and trying his luck with Clothilde de Vere on the way back, no doubt!'

At that point Henri appeared, evidently rested from his exertions and moderately shaved. He went over to the bar, ordered a cognac and then hailed Primrose fulsomely.

'Bonsoir, ma vieille. Ça va?'

'Ça va bien, merci, mon vieux,' answered Primrose gaily.

'Goodness,' I exclaimed, 'you have been getting on well!'

'Henri is all right,' she replied, 'provided he is kept in his place. With that achieved he can be quite entertaining.'

'Really?' I said drily. 'You mean like a marmoset in a cage.'

'Quite an intelligent one actually.'

Over supper that night Primrose told me that Turnbull had offered to show us round his language establishment in the nearby town. 'I've twisted his arm into buying some more of my pictures and he seems eager to show me where they will be displayed.'

Nicholas grinned. 'Play your cards right and you could supply all of his schools. I gather he has plans afoot to set up some more, one in England I believe. I shall have to watch out – you'll be so busy selling stuff to him that the Canadian market will run dry.'

'At least it won't be fakes this time,' I remarked.

'*Francis*,' Primrose cried. 'How many times do I have to tell you that the term fake is a total misnomer! What I send to the Canadians are highly artistic and sensitive reconstructions of the eighteenth-century mode. If the discerning connoisseurs over there choose to see them as originals that is their lookout. *Caveat emptor*, I always say. Now kindly pour me some more wine.'

'You must indulge your brother,' observed Nicholas, 'his mind is not of the most subtle in matters aesthetic; and besides, he has had a hard day.'

'*Moi aussi*,' declared Henri, getting up from the table. 'I go to bed now.' He shambled towards the door, where he turned, and addressing himself to Primrose, said: 'Kindly remove your unsavoury feet from that seat or I shall be forced to summon the guard.' With that he left the room.

There was a stunned silence. And then Nicholas gasped, 'What the hell was that about?'

'Don't know,' I replied. 'Finally flipped, I suppose.'

'I think he was practising,' said Primrose. 'You see, when we were cycling to Villiers this afternoon, we passed the time by teaching each other useful sentences in our respective tongues. I think he quite liked that one. He's certainly remembered it very well.'

I stared at her. 'What other sentences did you teach him?'

'Well, uhm . . . let me see now, there was: "Have you *any* idea the trouble this has caused me?" and: " No, I am not prepared to give you a five per cent discount on my paintings." As a matter of fact, he had difficulty with that one. Can't think why, it seems perfectly easy to me.'

'Ah,' said Nicholas, 'and I suppose he taught you how to say, "How much longer are you going to keep me hanging about in this confessional box!" and "What are the runners for the two thirty?"'

'Yes, something like that,' said Primrose.

31

The Vicar's Version

Our visit to Turnbull's language school was fixed for the following morning. The town was only three kilometres distant, but Primrose was not keen on the walk and had organized a lift from Madame Vernier who was taking Clemenceau to have his teeth scrubbed by the vet. 'He is always *very* good,' she explained with pride, 'and afterwards Maman gives him a special treat ... Don't I, *mon petit*,' she cooed, planting a smacking kiss on the animal's bear-like head.

'What sort of treat?' I asked, envisaging a romp in the park with the other dogs.

'He has *une grosse pâtisserie* from Le Café Vert in Le Grand Place – it is the best in town,' she confided.

I asked if the dog had any particular preference in the cake line.

She reflected, and then replied, 'He likes very much *les choux à la crème* and *les bombes meringués*, but his most special favourite is *un éclair au chocolat avec des fruits glacés – ça il adore!*' (Clearly a dog with a discerning sweet tooth, I thought. The vet must be laughing all the way to the bank.)

Thus we drove into town with Clemenceau sitting eagerly alert on the back seat. I noticed he was wearing a different collar. Was this a muted one for social visits? I hoped so. She drew up outside a large building surrounded by a beech hedge, black railings and elaborate wrought-iron gates, one of which displayed a shiny brass plate. *'Voila!'* she announced. *'L'Institut de la Langue et Culture Anglaise. Il a une bonne réputation, ici en Fleurville.'* We thanked her for her help and, wishing the dog well with his dental ablutions and ensuing treat, made our way through the gates and towards the front porch.

Turnbull's establishment was impressive – bright, airy and spacious, with wide corridors, polished floors and comfortable classrooms. At every turn there seemed to be bevies of projectors or glass-fronted booths full of tape recorders and earphones. The place had an aura of gleaming efficiency, and I imagined that it appealed to local businessmen as much as to younger students. It all seemed a far cry from my own memories of language tuition at the hands of an ancient French schoolmaster with a rickety blackboard and wind-up gramophone.

Primrose spent a happy forty minutes with Turnbull, scanning walls and classrooms to select those spaces which would display her rural landscapes to maximum effect. The idea, our guide explained, was to convey to students the essential placidness of the English character as depicted in the rustic charm of the artist's nestling churches, languid water meadows and gently grazing sheep ... Clearly Turnbull's use of entrepreneurial rhetoric was on a par with my sister's.

The tour over, we were taken back to his office where a cafetière of good coffee was ready but accompanied by a plate of rather desiccated biscuits. I wondered how Clemenceau was enjoying his pâtisserie at Le Café Vert and if he had managed to grab the éclair.

After we had chatted and sipped our coffee, Primrose and Turnbull got in a huddle over purchasing details and freight arrangements, while I browsed the bookshelves. It was an eclectic assortment, but I was surprised to note that, for one whose business premises were so orderly, Turnbull's reading material – like my own – was conspicuously ill sorted. Reference books, gardening books, volumes of poetry, biographies, detective novels, histories and two well-thumbed French cookery manuals by an Englishwoman called Elizabeth David – all jostled haphazardly cheek by jowl: a collection puzzling to negotiate, but at least having the element of surprise.

Like Primrose, I was not particularly looking forward to the trek back to Berceau, and was relieved when Turnbull said he was lunching at Le Petit Rêve and would drop us off at the inn. As we drew up I was startled to see Inspector Dumont's car parked in the yard, and a moment later Henri darted out exclaiming, '*Venez vite, l'inspecteur*, he ees *ici. C'est très urgent*! He want to speak with Primrose – and Monsieur *aussi*.' He beckoned to Turnbull who hastily got out of the driving seat.

I groaned to myself. 'Oh my God, they've found Climp – now it begins!' And with weary foot I followed the others inside.

Henri led us to the residents' salon, a dispiriting place well suited to bad news. Dumont was there plus a gendarme with a notebook, and unexpectedly Clinker also. His presence confirmed my fears about the discovery of Climp: we were all to be interrogated about our involvement with the missing campers – and we hadn't even worked out a story!

Dumont looked grave. 'I am sorry to be the bearer of sad news. But a man has been found dead, one of your fellow countrymen. We found him at six o'clock this morning.'

We? ... What on earth were the police doing on the mountain at that hour? Dishing out speeding tickets? The inspector continued. 'You will probably be acquainted with the gentleman. His name was Herbert Castris. He has been found hanging from a lintel above one of the doors in his house.'

There was a heavy silence while we assimilated his words. And then Primrose burst out, 'But he couldn't have! Are you sure? I mean, we were with him yesterday. He was giving us tea!'

'Yes, madame, I am quite sure,' replied Dumont, tactfully refraining from saying that he knew a dead body when he saw one.

'But why in heaven's name should he have done that?' exclaimed Turnbull. He sat down abruptly on a nearby chair, clearly upset. I gathered they had known each other for some years, and could see it must have been a dreadful blow. 'I mean, I assume it was suicide?'

The inspector nodded. 'Very probably. That is what we are trying to ascertain, and why I need to ask Madame Oughterard, yourself and Monsieur le Curé a few questions about his demeanour when you were taking tea with him yesterday. The housekeeper said you arrived at about three thirty and stayed for an hour or so. During that time did he show any signs of agitation?'

The gendarme signalled that Clinker and I were not required, and we went out leaving the other three to give their version of the previous day's visit.

'Ghastly, ghastly,' exclaimed the bishop as we stood irresolutely in the foyer. 'It's really too much, all this mortality. Gladys will be most put out – not to mention Lavinia. She was expecting him for supper, you know. The man rang up last night and asked if he could come and give his condolences. Considering he and Boris had been at daggers drawn over that de Vere woman, it seemed a little excessive. Still, a decent gesture all the same ... Of course, the women won't have heard yet – I just happened to be in the village when that Dumont fellow drove past and gave me the news ... No, Gladys won't like it at all. As a matter of fact I was buying her some aspirin at the village shop. Gets through 'em at a rate of knots. Can't think why – strong as a horse. Says she likes to take them on principle ... Suppose I'd better go back for another packet after this business, one won't be enough.' He glanced around scowling. 'Where's Ingaza? I could do with a Scotch.'

'Here,' said Nicholas coming in from the front entrance. I was surprised to see he was accompanied by Bouncer on a lead. 'Just been taking your hound for a little spin in the car. He seemed at a bit of a loose end after you and Primrose had gone, and his mate has disappeared as well.'

'Yes, having his fangs scrubbed prior to being stuffed with cream buns,' I explained. I asked him how Bouncer had behaved.

'Little tyke was as good as gold. Sat up on the front seat like the Queen of Sheba. The only thing is that sometimes when we went past another dog in the road he set up a most peculiar falsetto keening. It was rather disconcerting really.'

' Yes, that's his special front seat noise. It happens whenever –'

'Look,' broke in Clinker testily, 'when you two have finished jawing about these wretched animals, I should appreciate a small reviver. It is all extremely unsettling, and there's the painful task of breaking the news to the ladies.'

Ingaza regarded him wide-eyed. 'I say, Hor, you don't look too good. What news? May one ask what is perturbing His Lordship?'

'The *suicide*, of course! And kindly refrain from calling me Hor. It may have been all right at Oxford but it certainly isn't now. Most indecorous.'

Ingaza's smile faded as he looked at me for explanation. Clinker and I accompanied him out to the car to fetch the requested Scotch, and standing around the Citroën's boot told him what had happened.

'Poor old bugger,' he observed. 'Just goes to show the power of a tasselled tambourine.'

'Do you really think it was to do with their feud and all that?' I asked. 'It seems a bit extreme.'

'All depends on your point of view,' he replied soberly. 'Loneliness plus dashed hopes can be a killer. One's seen it often enough.'

'Yes, but his rival was dead. Who knows, given time he may have been able to reclaim both widow and instrument.

And according to Primrose, he seemed chirpy enough yesterday.'

'Ah,' interjected Clinker, 'what you are overlooking, Oughterard, is that for some people the existence of an irritant is precisely what keeps them going: fury is a good galvanizer. I've often seen it with Myrtle. Remove the cause of annoyance and she becomes prostrate with boredom.'

It was, I thought, one of the bishop's better observations, and I was just about to pursue it, when Nicholas tittered and said: 'Better watch it, Francis, if anything happens to me or Mavis Briggs, you'll be as dead as a doornail!'

At that moment Turnbull, Dumont and the gendarme emerged from the inn, and with a nod in our direction the two latter got into their car and drove off. If anything Turnbull looked shakier than before, but offered the bishop a lift back to Le Petit Rêve. 'Poor Lavinia,' he said, 'another blow for her. This is all very disturbing, but good of you to conduct the funeral service – one less thing for her to worry about at any rate.'

'Not at all,' said Clinker, 'glad to be of help. I'll prepare a few words for an address this afternoon. Of course, I didn't know the poor fellow really, so you may be able to give me a few pointers . . .'

Nicholas and I returned indoors where we were met by Primrose and Henri. 'How did it go?' I asked. 'Were you able to help the inspector?'

'Well,' she replied slowly, 'I think we probably just confirmed what he suspected already – that Castris had committed suicide. His questions to us were just a formality.'

'But does he know why he should have done it?'

She hesitated, and then said, 'As a matter of fact I think he does. You see, he is pretty convinced that it was Herbert Castris who murdered Boris and that in a fit of remorse he took his own life.'

'Goodness!' I gasped.

'That's a pretty swift assumption, isn't it?' said Nicholas.

'It's one thing to recognize that the chap committed suicide, but quite another to link him with the murder.'

'Rupert has been filling him in about his relations with Boris and their rivalries, but that was only after he had shown us the note.'

'What note?'

'The suicide note. It was found on the dining-room table. What it said was . . .' Primrose frowned, trying to recall the words. 'Uhm . . . yes, that's it: "That nincompoop B.F. has blighted all my hopes and I have done for him now. He deserved his end as I do mine. H.C." I remember clearly because it had a rather old-fashioned ring to it.' My sister has an almost photographic memory which stood her in good stead in her Courtauld days, and indeed for her sheep paintings, and I guessed her version of the note was accurate.

'*Mon Dieu,*' suddenly chimed Henri, 'I, le curé de Taupinière, was drinking tea next to a maleficent English murderer. *Quelle horreur!*' Despite the last words, I detected little sign of horror in Henri. Glee, perhaps. I wondered what terms he would have used had he known of other such proximities.

Ingaza must have had the same thought, for he gave a brief smile, and then said briskly, 'Well, at least this should finally let us off Dumont's hook. Once the funeral is over we can scarper off home pronto. As said, there's a nice little packet waiting for me there, and Eric says he has already netted a likely purchaser for a rare miniature I just happen to have access to.'

Later that afternoon, accompanied by Maurice and Bouncer I had a quiet shut-eye on my bed which, with the pressure off and the prospect of imminent departure, now suddenly felt almost comfortable.

When I woke I started to peruse again Castris's book, which I had borrowed from Le Petit Rêve. Despite the slightly mannered style, it was really a very interesting exploration and I suspected that once the author's role in the murder became generally known its intrinsic value would more than double. I took it downstairs with me to show to Primrose before supper.

There was a strong whiff of Gitanes in the foyer and I guessed that Henri had already preceded me to the bar. I entered to find him in animated conversation with Georges, obviously giving a graphic and doubtlessly embroidered account of his questioning by the police and tea with Castris. On seeing me Georges said it was time he went off to supervise the preparation of the rabbit. 'It is Monsieur's favourite, I believe.'

'Oh yes,' I enthused, 'with plenty of garlic!' On the whole the inspector had been right about the quality of the cuisine at La Truite Bleue. It was not the most remarkable, but the rabbit stew was one of its better offerings. Leaving me to administer the drinks, Georges wandered off towards the kitchen.

Primrose and Ingaza came in from the veranda and I busied myself with the bottles.

'What book you read?' demanded Henri.

I explained, and he took it from me with interest. As he did so a slip of folded paper fell out from where it had been clipped to the inner flap. I had seen but overlooked it earlier, assuming it to be some sort of improvised book mark. Henri picked it up and smoothed it out. He frowned, trying to decipher the words, gave up and handed it to Ingaza. '*Qu'est-ce que c'est que ça?*'

Ingaza glanced at it indifferently, and then suddenly began to peer more closely. 'Streuth,' he breathed, 'extraordinary.'

'What is it?' I asked. He passed me the paper. It was in pencil and looked like a roughly scribbled draft for a letter.

My dear Rupert, I have it from a reliable source (which I choose not to name) that you have been exerting financial pressure upon some of your students, who, I gather, do not have the requisite papers for residence in this country. Penalties for such an offence can be serious and would most likely involve the transgressor being permanently debarred from domicile in this country. Personally I have little time for the pedantry of French officialdom and cannot say that I am unduly bothered when it is flouted.

However, what I do find objectionable is that these vulnerable and earnest young people should be made to dance to your sordid tune. Unless you desist in your blackmailing activities I shall be forced to mention your nefarious practice to the Board of Education, who would take a dim view of a college principal who cynically exploits the peccadilloes and meagre pockets of his pupils. I am sure you are aware that there is such a thing as 'withdrawal of licence'.

In passing, I must also make it plain that I did not appreciate the tasteless joke you made the other day regarding my relationship with the splendid Madame de Vere – or indeed with the other ladies who have been so kind as to accommodate my urgent needs. The terms 'moral humbuggery' and 'randy old goat' do not fall happily upon my ears and it ill behoves you to employ such terms. Further references of that kind will only ruffle Lavinia whose sensibilities in that sphere are of the most delicate, and who has little understanding of my passionate nature. However, the consequences to me of your aspersions are nothing as compared to the effects upon your own career should I be disposed to publicly question your professional fitness.

Yours in sorrow and sincerity,

Boris Birtle-Figgins

PS As you know, the Belvedere Bondolphi Canonization Project is always in need of funds. Were you to make a substantial donation to this worthy cause I might be prepared to overlook the above matters.

'What ees meaning of all thees blah?' asked Henri.

'Well, old fruit, this blah is what you could call dynamite,' replied Ingaza thoughtfully. 'It tells us, for example, that Boris was a sanctimonious, lecherous mountebank, and that Turnbull is a shit and quite possibly his murderer.'

There was a silence, and then a gasp from Primrose. 'But he can't be the murderer! It's obvious that it was Castris, it all fits in. That is certainly what little Inspector Dumont thinks. I mean to say, there was all the ridiculous sexual rivalry and the quarrelling over that piddling tambourine; and when Boris made it on both counts Herbert Castris was beside himself with rage. Not surprising really – who on earth would like to be ousted by that bore! And surely the final proof was that suicide note. It was a dead giveaway – what could be more self-explanatory?'

'Hmm ... He didn't wrap it up, did he?' Nicholas conceded.

'No, he didn't. Castris was a man broken by disappointment and humiliation. Mad for revenge. And so – perhaps still hoping to win back the widow and get his hands on the tambourine – he waited for the hated rival and did him in. Afterwards, racked by guilt and unable to live with himself, he wrote the note and took his life. Obvious.'

'So what about this letter? Are you saying Boris never sent it?'

'I don't know whether he sent it or not, but it merely confirms that Birtle-Figgins was a narcissistic hypocrite and that Turnbull is a nasty piece of work. But it doesn't mean he would go so far as murder.'

'It might if he was about to lose a nice little earner from milking those students *and*, courtesy of Boris, saw his whole professional career hanging by a thread. We know from what he said recently that he has grandiose plans to develop the language school and open branches in Paris, Holland and England. It's a big project, and if successful likely to net him a lot of dosh. Boris only had to say the word and the whole thing would be up the spout and his future reputation in shreds. Quite a lot at stake, I should have thought.' Nicholas paused, studying the letter again.

'Added to which, judging from the way those bones and gnashers were strewn over the body, it looked as if the assailant had been in a bit of a paddy – the result perhaps of this charming *postscriptum*. Enough to get anyone steamed up. It's a wonder he didn't cut off his head as well and ram it in the casket!'

'That's all pretty speculative,' said Primrose doubtfully, 'and there's no proof; whereas Dumont has got something tangible on Castris.' She looked at me. 'What do you think, Francis?'

I said nothing for a few moments, being too preoccupied trying to clarify a blurred memory nagging away at the back of my mind. For some obscure reason it had to do with the word 'nincompoop', one of the words Castris had used in his rather stylized note. I had seen the term some-where else only recently.

Primrose sighed impatiently. 'In one of your trances as usual – what Pa always used to call your "blooming brown study".'

'No,' I replied slowly. 'No, I am not in a trance, I have just thought of something ... and you know, Nicholas could be spot on – except I don't quite understand about the suicide ...'

'Yes, well, don't keep us in suspense, there's a good chap,' said Ingaza cheerfully.

'You remember when Primrose and I visited his school? Well, while we were in the office and he and Primrose were discussing her paintings and making arrangements for their shipment, I was looking at his books and some unusual figurines on the desk. He needed to jot down an address or something, because he turned and asked if I could find a pen which should be in one of the drawers. I couldn't see anything there so started to move some of the papers on the desk top, and found one lying under a writing pad. At the time I barely registered the fact, but there were some words scribbled on the page. Naturally I didn't give them a thought – except that *now* I suddenly remember what they were.'

'And . . .?'

'"That nincompoop has blighted all my hopes".'

There was a silence. And then Nicholas observed, 'My, my, you're a right little Autolycus, aren't you? Talk about being a "snapper up of unconsidered trifles" – Oughterard the bloodhound!'

'Didn't Castris say something like that in his note?' exclaimed Primrose.

'Exactly – and old Hawk-Eye here has made the vital connection. What do you know!' He flashed me a mocking grin.

'It all sounds a peculiar coincidence to me. I mean, what on earth –' Primrose began.

'Hardly a coincidence,' I said. 'I think it can mean only one thing: Castris was Turnbull's scapegoat. He killed him to make it look like suicide – throttled him first, I suppose – and planted the note which he had already been rehearsing on that pad. Probably wanted to make sure he had the form right: it's a bit precise and literary, typical of Castris's written style.'

Ingaza nodded. 'It adds up all right. Boris was putting the frighteners on Turnbull, who promptly silenced him and then went on to kill Castris as cover. This draft letter of his together with Turnbull's jottings would seem to be pretty good proof . . . Besides,' he added slyly and to my discomfort, 'you're the expert, old chap. Doubtless we can rely on your judgement in such matters.'

'That is most uncalled for, Nicholas!' Primrose protested.

'Why ees François expert?' asked Henri.

'He writes detective novels in his spare time,' she snapped.

32

The Vicar's Version

We sat on the veranda after supper smoking feverishly. 'So what on earth are we going to do?' exclaimed Primrose. 'Show Dumont the letter and tell him our suspicions?'

'No fear,' replied Nicholas. 'There's been enough trouble as it is. Let Dumont know and we shall be stuck here till hell freezes over. There'll be no end to the questions and entanglements. We'll have to write affidavits or even appear in court – and the longer we remain the greater the chance of our being around when they find Climp and Mullion, and then we shall have that to cope with on top of everything else ... And another thing,' he added fiercely, 'for God's sake don't tell Hor. It'll give him a stroke and we'll be left with those two frightful harridans!'

It was one of the rare occasions when I agreed wholeheartedly with Ingaza. All I wanted now was to slip back to Molehill unknown, unseen and untroubled. I thought of the vicarage and its stolid ordinariness, a place of refuge and embalming peace. I longed to get at my piano and immerse heart and fingers in the notes of Bach and Duke Ellington; saw myself slumped with the *Times* crossword in the shabby confines of my study; could hear the sound of St Botolph's bells floating across the graveyard, and smelt the polish on the vestry floor after it had suffered the frenzied attentions of Edith Hopgarden and her cohorts. Even the penning of an improving sermon seemed a welcome task after the recent rigours . . . Yes, I wanted to get back rather badly. I looked at Bouncer and wondered what he was thinking. He returned my gaze blankly, but through the gathering dusk I could just discern the slow wagging of his tail.

'You are so right,' I replied. 'As Clinker said earlier, don't let's muddy the waters.'

Apart from Henri muttering something about Turnbull being yet another example of English perfidy, the consensus was absolute, and we turned our minds to the forthcoming funeral and the difficulties of not letting our guard slip re the Castris/Turnbull business. To my relief, Henri said that since he had never met the deceased nor his wife, he had no reason to attend the burial and would thus spend his time more profitably with his metal detector at the Fotherington Folly.

'You do that,' said Nicholas 'and if you turn up some coins with that useless contraption you can buy us drinks when we get back.'

'*Tu crois!*' replied the curé indignantly.

'Actually,' said Primrose, 'I quite like Rupert Turnbull, he's always very affable and has an extremely discerning taste in pictures. But it's going to feel pretty peculiar making small talk with him when one knows the truth.'

'You talk to Francis, don't you?' said Nicholas.

'Oh yes, but that's different. He's family.'

I was grateful for that, but could see her point. It would be awkward all right! And of course we would also have to play along with the grieving widow and try to make out that Boris was no end of a fine chap . . . Although on reflection I suspected that that was not necessarily her own view. I wondered if Clothilde de Vere would attend, and whether the coffin would be crowned with the troublesome tambourine. It could make quite a decorative feature laced with ribbons, lilies and autumn-flowering pansies. Perhaps too there would be a tasteful display of the reassembled bones bedecked with –

My reverie was interrupted by Primrose saying, 'Oh Lor', I've still got the key to the Folly. What shall I do with it – chuck it away?'

'Don't suppose it matters really,' said Nicholas. 'I mean, when Lavinia eventually discovers that it's missing we shall be back in England. And I don't imagine she would be much bothered anyway. She seems pretty vague about most things.'

'Wait a minute,' I broke in anxiously, 'we can't be too careful. Both she and Boris told us all about the swastika that evening at dinner. And who knows, perhaps now that he's dead she might get a sudden urge to fish it out from the boot. Death focuses the mind in the oddest ways. If she can't find the key and discovers the thing gone, when she finally gets access she might put two and two together and assume it was us. I really think you ought to put it back, Primrose.'

My sister sighed impatiently. 'You are such a fusspot, Francis. Besides, Lavinia also told Climp and Mullion about the swastika. She will probably think it was they who whipped it. After all, they would have been *far* more likely to than us – just the types.' She gave a superior smile.

'But they didn't,' I pointed out, 'we did – or you, rather. And although Lavinia let them know the thing was hidden in the Folly, it is highly unlikely that she mentioned the key was hanging on a hook in the wardrobe of Myrtle's bedroom! That particular detail she helpfully revealed to you in Clermont. And vague though she is, she may just recall it.'

'Oh really . . .' Primrose grumbled.

'Nothing like belt and braces,' said Nicholas briskly. 'There's a good girl, Primrose, put the key back – it will be good practice.'

'Practice for what?'

'Who can tell?' he replied enigmatically. 'These little sleights of hand are always useful. One never knows what difficulties they may resolve.' He gave a heavy wink.

'Oh, all right,' she conceded, 'just as long as I don't encounter Myrtle climbing out of her stays ...'

The weather broke on the morning of the funeral. Up until then we had enjoyed a mild Indian summer, but now the mists came down and there was a dankness in the air redolent of autumn. The distant *puys* were blotted out and the valley below looked grey and uninviting. A classic interment day, I thought gloomily. However, I brightened at the prospect of our impending departure. Dumont had rung to say our passports would be returned by a passing gendarme, and already Ingaza was checking the Citroën and clearing the boot of the now denuded whisky crates. There was of course still the problem of Bouncer and his concealment, but as I had hoped, Georges had kindly offered to seek counsel from a veterinary friend, and it seemed likely that the poor little blighter could be sent off to the land of nod with no ill effects. Whether Primrose would be prepared to shove Maurice into her classy travelling case was another matter, but if I made the right pecuniary gestures perhaps she would ...

I was impressed by the funeral service, which, given its subject, was surprisingly conventional, with the usual Anglican prayers, hymns and ritual. Knowing Boris, I had expected something fey and cock-eyed but this seemed the model of decorum and normality, and I wondered if its swift and businesslike procedure was due to the organizational powers of Turnbull rather than the hand of Lavinia. Clinker delivered a deft, even generous address, and Boris's coffin (unadorned by either tambourine or bones) was lowered into the earth with due precision and solemnity. I am rather particular about the matter of obsequies, and in that respect the handling of Boris Birtle-Figgins' final passage struck me as exemplary.

Solemnity over, we returned to the house for the usual bun fight. To my surprise Lavinia had laid on some caterers from Fleurville, and while there was no repeat of the earlier cocktails, there was a lavish supply of tasty French canapés and delicate *bonnes bouchées*. Gladys and Myrtle were being moderately useful in dispensing these, and it crossed my mind that while the latter was thus occupied it might be a good moment for Primrose to slip into her bedroom and return the key to its rightful place. I looked around for her to suggest this, but was caught by Clinker intent yet again on impressing upon me the need for silence regarding the Climp/Mullion affair. I assured him that he should have no qualms on that score and enquired when he expected to leave.

'As soon as possible,' was the answer. 'Gladys is fractious and Myrtle talks of nothing except getting back to Brussels.'

'But I thought she had been so keen to come here – to the Auvergne.'

'Not any more, she isn't,' he replied darkly. 'Says she wasn't brought up to be associated with suicides and murderers or their victims, and that staying here any longer will bring social death. No, she's champing at the bit to return to her embassy cronies. I don't think Lavinia will encounter her again. Some people have all the luck.' He melted away to consume some sausages on sticks.

There was a light tap on my shoulder. 'It is very good of you to come, Canon,' breathed Lavinia. 'Boris would have so appreciated it.' I mumbled some appropriate response and took stock of my hostess. It may have been a trick of the light, but she struck me as being fuller in the face, more physically animated than when I had last seen her. Although draped in black, she still wore the glittering beads that she had sported on our last visit, and her hair was swept up in a rather becoming chignon. I noticed too that her nails were painted a discreet silky pink. The result was not unattractive.

'So what are you going to do now?' I asked. 'Carry on here, or do you have other plans?'

'Oh, other plans,' she replied emphatically, 'but first I am going to have a little holiday. These things put one at such

211

a low ebb. I think I need a tonic – you know, some sort of break from the norm to get my bearings as it were.' I did know, having needed just such a respite after the Spendler débâcle* – but alas, thanks to DS Sidney Samson and Nicholas Ingaza, never achieved that luxury.

'Very sensible,' I said, in my best soothing voice.

'Oh, but I don't want to be sensible, that's just it. I feel it is time I was rather *un*sensible!' She gave a soft giggle. I was slightly taken aback by this, not used to recent widows responding with quite such liveliness. She clearly saw my surprise, for she then said, 'But haven't you ever wanted to behave outrageously? You know, break out from your chains – drive fast cars, go to Monte Carlo, tango till six in the morning – live *dangerously!*'

'No,' I said firmly. 'All I have ever wanted is peace, quiet, seclusion and safety. And so far none of those has come my way.'

'Oh dear,' she said, 'how sad.' And giving me a puzzled look she drifted over to join Turnbull.

Behave outrageously? Live dangerously? Huh! She didn't know the half of it . . . In some irritation, I followed Clinker's example and moved in the direction of the sausages. Thwarted again – the bishop had scoffed the lot.

I was on the point of choosing a canapé instead, when I saw the harpist from the musical evening making a beeline towards me. Admittedly it wasn't a dark night, merely a gloomy afternoon, but I thought it prudent to take evasive action all the same, and looked about for an outlet. Unfortunately the nearest one was Gladys. But working on the principle of better the devil you know, I walked smartly up to her and embarked on some scintillating chit-chat. She looked rather surprised as neither of us is in the habit of seeking the other out – although, at a really loose end, the bishop's wife has been known to hold court even with curates (a practice never embraced by her sister).

* See *Bones in the Belfry*

'Hmm,' she said with her usual forthright charm, 'I don't know what you have to be so bright about. Personally I consider this whole holiday to have been a nightmare – not helped, I may say, by my dear sister. It was her idea in the first place. One would have done far better to stick to the Ardennes. We've been going there for the last thirty years and never a suicide or dead body in sight.'

I nodded sympathetically. 'Yes, it has been rather trying, and most perturbing for the bishop – just when he needed a good rest.'

'Good rest? He does nothing but . . . No, Canon, it is we women who need the rest. But then that's not something you would know about, of course.'

'No,' I agreed humbly, 'perhaps it isn't.'

'A case in point,' she continued, 'being that tiresome Birtle-Figgins girl. What she has had to put up with is nobody's business! Mind you, such a door mat – has only herself to blame, I consider.' She frowned, looking very fierce, and not for the first time I felt mildly sorry for Clinker.

'Er . . . but what did she have to put up with?' I ventured.

'Marital matters,' was the terse reply. 'Again, not something you would understand.'

I cleared my throat and tried to steer us down another route. 'I rather gather she has plans to move elsewhere. Is she intending to leave France?'

'I don't know about that, but what I do know is that she is certainly giving up this awful relics business – ceasing all involvement with the hermit *and* severing her link with that monstrosity down the hill. She and Boris were sort of substitute concierges in the last few years. He thought it gave him additional status in the village. It didn't of course, everyone hates the place.' She stopped, rummaged in her handbag for a handkerchief and blew her nose explosively. I wondered if the hiatus would give me the chance to slip away, but in the next moment she said, 'In fact now I come to think of it, wasn't it built by some

213

relation of that woman who was murdered in your village? I seem to remember her name was Fotherington.'

I looked suitably vague and murmured something to the effect that I hadn't heard of any connection, and that although the name was not particularly common, neither was it rare.

'Hmm, perhaps not. But in any case they are going to pull it down soon – well, half of it apparently. A good thing too.'

'*Really?*' I was startled.

'Yes. The locals can't stand it – think it's haunted. You know how superstitious these people are. Apparently the authorities have been trying to trace the owner for some time – or at least, so they say. Technically of course they need his or her permission, but with typical French pragmatism they've decided to demolish it first and deal with complaints later. All very high-handed no doubt ... but that's the way with the Frogs. I remember during the war when ...' She prosed on, while I felt a rush of grovelling warmth towards the French and their high-handedness.

'So what's going to happen to it?'

'Assuming no claimant materializes from the wood-work, I believe they have plans to turn it into a holiday home for deprived children from the slums of Nice and Toulon. A worthy cause, naturally – though I must say if I were a local I'd be a trifle nervous. After all, you never know these days, do you? But quite a constructive idea, I suppose. Anyway, I hear the bulldozers are all ready.'

Making a mental note to remain well within the wood-work, I said I thought it an excellent scheme, and then asked her what Lavinia was going to do with Bondolphi's bones. 'She's going to donate them to the children's home. The plan is to display them in a large showcase in the central hall. Grotesque! Frankly, if I were one of those young inmates I would heave a brick through the glass.' And so saying she stomped off to argue with her sister.

Looking around, I noticed a number of people were beginning to leave and saw Lavinia by the door shaking hands and nodding graciously. Turnbull was still there, in animated conversation with Primrose. (Were *more* paintings being negotiated? Surely not, not now!) He looked confident and relaxed. And I felt a pang of guilty envy of one who could remain so poised having just committed (presumably) so dastardly a crime. Nevertheless, I was glad to have escaped meeting him during the afternoon, for I suspect I might have made a hash of things – blushed, stuttered, giggled, spilt my tea. It is one thing being a murderer oneself, quite another to be jolly with a fellow practitioner.

I was pondering this and preparing to leave, when there was a disturbance at the far end of the salon, and Myrtle appeared on the threshold breathing fire and apoplexy. 'This is outrageous,' she boomed, 'my room has been ransacked!'

'Oh dear,' said Lavinia vaguely, 'the maid does get carried away sometimes, it's the hoovering, she –'

'It is not the maid,' Myrtle thundered, 'it is someone *else*.'

Fortunately the announcement elicited only mild shock, for half of the residual guests did not understand English (or were inured to the eccentricities of its speakers), while the other half were too familiar with Myrtle's melodrama to take much notice. She hovered by the door, muttering and spluttering and for once largely ignored.

'So you did it, then,' I whispered to Primrose as we moved out into the hallway, 'put the key back.'

'Of course I did.'

'Well, it doesn't sound as if you were very subtle – what was all that about the room being ransacked?'

'Old bat had left an open suitcase on the bed. I was in such a hurry after shutting the wardrobe door that I knocked it over on my way out. The stuff spilled all over the floor – frightful mess!' She chuckled.

33

The Vicar's Version

At last we were free to leave. Dumont had come personally to deliver the passports, and wished us a safe journey
back to *'la belle Angleterre'*. He seemed genuinely sorry that
our stay in Berceau-Lamont had been so alarmingly disturbed, and was at great pains to persuade us that normally that part of the Auvergne was a model of respectable
tranquillity. He was, he said, *désolé* about poor demented
Monsieur Castris and trusted that Madame Birtle-Figgins
would find it in her heart to forgive so wretched a crime.

I had been wondering about Boris's inamorata, Clothilde
de Vere: whatever the dimensions of her *poitrine*, the loss
of two lovers in such violent circumstances must have
been hard for the woman. Thus, affecting a casual tone, I
asked him how she was taking it all. 'With great excitement,' was the dry reply. 'Being on such intimate terms
with both victim and perpetrator, she was one of our key
witnesses and responded to our questions with alarming
enthusiasm.' He paused and coughed discreetly. 'The
account she gave of her relationship with the two gentlemen was most explicit ... rather more than necessary
really – and repetitive. However, monsieur,' he murmured
politely, 'I need not bore you with the details ...'

Lucky escape, I thought. And turning to other matters
said that, with the sad demise of its leader, the cult of
Belvedere would surely lose much of its impetus. He gave

a brief shrug, whispering something that sounded very like *'Zut alors! Tant pis, tant mieux . . .'*

I was beginning to quite warm to the man, and when he mentioned that he was hoping to visit his old Cambridge college the following year, in a rush of thoughtless bonhomie I suggested he visit Molehill as well. But at that moment his attention was distracted by an acerbic comment from Gladys, and I received a sharp kick on the shin from Primrose and her muttered warning, 'Don't push your luck, you fool – he hasn't discovered Climp and Mullion yet!' I coughed loudly, and instead made some polite remark about longing to return to the area in more propitious circumstances.

That afternoon Clinker telephoned announcing they were leaving on the morrow, the two ladies being intent on taking the waters at La Bourboule 'to soothe and pacify the nerves' before embarking on their homeward journey.

'Ah, that'll be nice,' I said encouragingly, 'very refreshing.'

'It won't be nice,' he said testily, 'simply prolong the agony.'

I ignored that and asked brightly if there would be salubrious treatments.

'I do not intend having any treatment,' he replied stiffly. 'But I think the women are proposing some massages or thermal baths . . . With a bit of luck Myrtle may sink.'

There being no answer to that, I wished him a pleasant trip and said I would see him at the annual diocesan conference the following month.

'Unless you forget about it like last time, Oughterard . . . And remember, at all costs be *reticent!*' He rang off.

I started to go upstairs intending to begin some early packing, but was diverted by Georges saying there was still coffee available in the bar and that I was welcome to help myself. I went in, poured a cup and picked up the newspaper. Other than a small article reporting the Birtle-Figgins funeral and brief references to the fate of the 'malefactor' Herbert Castris, there was little of interest. And I was about to put it aside and attend to the packing, when my attention was caught by something small and shiny tucked into a corner under the window seat. Thinking it might be a piece of jewellery dropped by one of the female customers from the night before, I bent down and picked it up. What I held in my hand was no brooch or ring, but a glimmering glass eye with dark pupil and pale blue retina ... I gazed at it with curiosity and a flicker of irrational distaste. However, it looked perfectly clean and 'clinical', and I was suddenly reminded of a similar encounter many years ago at my prep school. That one had belonged to the piano teacher, whose zeal for the keys had invariably necessitated the removal of both dentures and eye before tackling the more rumbustious pieces. But at least in that case one had known to whom the item had belonged. This eye could be anybody's.

Or could it? I remembered Boris enthusing about his casket of bones, detailing the contents which had included Belvedere's false teeth ... and, as he had said, 'that brilliantly azure eye'. As far as I knew, in none of the press reports had there been any mention of an eye, and I certainly could not recall seeing such an object when confronted by the spectacle by the poolside. Nevertheless, might it just possibly be the hermit's – purloined from the casket before or after the murder? Unlikely surely. Obviously it belonged to one of Georges's clientele – slipped from pocket or socket in a moment of bibulous aberration.

As I pondered, there was a heavy padding in the hall. Clemenceau appeared and launched himself upon me with a roar of welcome. The collar was silent but the dog was not, and deafened by the kindly pandemonium I retreated upstairs still holding my find. I put it on the bedside table meaning to take it down later, but in a trice Maurice had seized it, and tossing and dribbling the thing around the room established immediate ownership. Oh well, I thought, if someone is careless enough to leave their eye lying about on the floor that's their problem if the cat gets it ...

34

The Cat's Memoir

'I'll get that bluebottle if it kills me!' the dog exploded.

'Probably will,' I replied indifferently. 'With all those Bonios inside you, you won't have the stamina.' And hoiking my leg behind my ear I resumed my grooming.

'Who says?' Bouncer asked truculently. 'You'll see – I'll settle that bugger's hash, Bonio or no Bonio!' He made a lunge at the fly as it zoomed past, missed, and roared an oath.

'Keep your voice down,' I hissed. 'You'll wake F.O., and then there'll be more hubbub.'

The dog turned his attention to the comatose form on the bed. 'Huh! He's out for the count, won't surface for ages. All that larking about.'

I lowered my leg in mild surprise. 'Larking about? What do you mean?'

'Well, he's done nothing but chase his tail ever since we got here – rushing down to look at that dead geezer by the pool, running away from those nasties, hiking up and down to the big house, arguing with the Frog vicar, swanning off with Clemso in the car and not taking *me*, and then getting all het up about the chap they found swinging in the doorway, and then –'

'Yes, yes, Bouncer, but what's new? He's always in a state and chasing his tail. Tiresome, I grant you, but unremarkable – no different from usual.'

'The difference,' he replied, snapping ineffectually at the air, 'is that over here he hasn't got his *piano*. That's what soothes him in the vicarage and keeps him sort of sane. Bit like a dog basket, you could say. He goes there when things get on top of him and he wants some comfort. When he sits down on that stool he feels at home – like me on my hairy blanket.'

'But in the vicarage he *is* at home.'

'Yes, but *more* at home.'

I regarded him blankly. 'I do not entirely follow your point, Bouncer. And except that both offend my sensibilities I see little resemblance between F.O.'s piano and your basket: the one is noisy, the other smelly. Beyond that the comparison ends. And quite honestly if –' I broke off for the dog had ceased to listen, being far too occupied with making futile attacks on the fly.

It occurred to me that I could do with a little more soothing exercise myself. F.O. had tiresomely confiscated the Special Eye and left it in the ashtray on the bedside table, but with a lithe leap I made a quick retrieval and started to roll and toss it about.

'Look out!' barked Bouncer. 'I nearly got the bugger then, and you've just set it off again!' Naturally I took not a blind bit of notice and continued to hone my dexterity. The dog's antics were far from dextrous and he went on floundering about the room until I was convinced that the vicar would wake up.

'That thing is flying circles round you,' I remarked. 'Why don't you give up and go and find Clemenceau?'

'I think it's my toenails,' he grumbled, 'they've got too long again and they make my paws feel funny. Can't always get a proper grip, so it slows me down. Time we went back to England and I had them cut.'

'But you hate having them cut,' I exclaimed. 'You make such a fuss!'

'Oh no,' he said airily, 'I don't mind the cutting one jot.'

'So why the fuss?'

'Well, of *course* I make a *fuss*! I mean, what are vets *for*

220

except to make fusses at?' He made another aimless snap into the air. 'Blooming toenails,' he muttered.

I refrained from saying that a poor workman blames his tools (or in Bouncer's case, lack of pedicure), and instead, seeing that he was getting fractious, remarked tactfully that it was obvious his true forte was decimating the rabbits and he should conserve his energies for that heroic feat. 'After all,' I added, 'why should a dog of your talent waste his time on piddling bluebottles!' He liked that last phrase, as I knew he would. And muttering 'piddling bluebottles' to himself, he trotted out on to the landing in search of Clemenceau. Peace at last.

I executed a few more twirls with the eye, jumped on to the window sill to survey the wood pigeon, and noting the fly hovering in my direction put up a languid paw and brought it down with one fell smack. Very satisfying.

There was a movement on the bed and I guessed that the vicar would soon be resurrecting himself. I must have been in benign mood for it occurred to me that when he opened his eyes it would be a comforting sight to find the Special Eye resting next to him on the pillow: a little trinket to welcome him back to the land of the living. Thus carefully taking the precious thing in my mouth I jumped up on to the bed – a rather hazardous manoeuvre I must admit, for it very nearly went down my throat. However, all was well and I was able to regurgitate it on to F.O.'s pillow with no ill effects. That done, I tweaked it to a position within inches of his face. Having been in my mouth the eye had taken on an even better shine than usual, all moist and glossy, and I was pleased with my endeavour. Then returning to the window sill, I sat and watched intently, waiting for the first stirrings.

These came swiftly and profanely. 'Bloody hell!' he screeched. 'Jesus, what's that!' And picking up the pillow he hurled it to the floor, adding for good measure, 'Sodding cat!'

Well, *really*! Just how churlish can one be?

35

The Vicar's Version

Henri Martineau's departure for his parish of Taupinière was both complex and voluble. Complex, because although originally accepting Ingaza's suggestion that he should prolong his stay to see what debris he and his contraption could salvage from La Folie, he had now changed his mind and was set on returning to his parish at the speed of light. The reason, I gathered, was something to do with the runners at Longchamp – a kindly (or fearful) parishioner having procured ringside seats and a complimentary ticket 'should the curé be so disposed'.

'You bet the sod is disposed,' sniffed Ingaza. 'Anything for a free handout and a guzzle of top-class fizz. Never misses a trick, our Henri.' Not entirely alone there, I thought . . .

The problem was that the curé's urgency could not be immediately met. His impedimenta of detector, shovels and related items would first have to be dispatched in advance – a chore which fell to me to organize. And since there were only two passenger trains a week to the Pas de Calais, the traveller himself would be required to possess himself in patience for three days. This of course Henri was ill prepared to do, and much noise and energy was expended in trying to persuade us to accommodate him in the Citroën. However, for once we presented a united front and the suggestion was firmly quashed. Undaunted, his response was to seek out the nun in the Studebaker who had helped him earlier. And plying her with flattery and guarantees that his flock would pay for the vehicle's next service, he managed to persuade her to drive him some of the way. It was, I suspected, an act of Christian charity which the nun would take some time to forget.

Our own departure was more straightforward and, apart from some valedictory fanfares from Clemenceau's collar, moderately quiet. We shared with Henri, however, an eagerness to get home as soon as possible, and thus we had decided to attempt the marathon in one day – a proposal which entailed rising at five in the morning. It was a raw experience and all grumbled, humans and animals alike.

For the first hour and a half we drove in smoke and silence, but then spotting a likely-looking workmen's café stopped for a snatch breakfast. Like the other early risers, Nicholas stood at the bar with espresso in one hand and small cognac in the other. Unable to face the grape quite so early in the day, Primrose and I settled for large bowls of café au lait and croissants.

The breakfast interlude did us all good and animation gradually returned. I was surprised how compliant the animals were being. Fed, watered and ablutioned, they settled down placidly, and except for heavy breathing from Bouncer remained uncannily quiet. I just hoped they would be as well behaved when we reached Customs.

A sudden thought struck me. 'I say, did Lavinia or Turnbull make any mention of the Austin-Healey – or any reference to those two?'

'Not to me,' said Nicholas. 'They obviously took care to persuade her they were quitting the area that day and motoring on south. And as for the car, not a yelp. I told you at the time it was unlikely that anyone would bother to look in the shed. There was nothing much there, only some old sacks . . . No, when it's eventually discovered we shall be far away and forgotten, and they'll just have a little mystery on their hands. Lavinia will bleat, but Turnbull won't bother. He'll be far too busy hatching his business plans and covering his tracks re Boris and Castris.' He laughed wryly: 'Mind you, it'll keep little Dumont busy. I don't suppose he sees much action up there, he'll welcome the challenge, especially when the bodies come to light. That Boris business must have been a rare treat for him.'

We were silent for a while. And then Primrose said casually, 'Of course we don't actually *know* that Mullion is dead. Climp yes, but not Mullion.'

'Now, now, Primrose, stop spreading alarm and despondency, you'll give old Francis a heart attack, he's windy enough as it is.'

'Yes,' I said irritably from the back, 'that's an absurd idea. He went straight over. It was a hell of a drop – didn't stand a chance thanks to our friend here.' I glanced confidently at Maurice who immediately closed his eyes.

Primrose shrugged. 'Oh well, I expect you're right –'

'Of course I'm jolly right!' I exclaimed angrily.

'Keep your hair on, old boy, you'll do yourself a mischief. Here, have one of these, it'll calm you down.' With his free arm Nicholas passed a Sobranie over his head and then offered one to Primrose. We smoked in silence and sped on towards the Channel coast.

Eventually signposts started appearing for Paris, and I was just beginning to feel the need to stop for a bite of lunch when I noticed Primrose peering intently into the passenger mirror. 'I say,' she said slowly, 'is that what I think it is?'

'Think what?' asked Nicholas.

'That car behind us . . . it looks like a silver Austin-Healey . . .'

Nicholas glanced in his own mirror. 'Looks like it,' he said easily. 'French number plates, I think, won't be theirs. Stop teasing your brother!'

I craned round, squinting through the rear window. There was indeed a silver sports car – and moving at some lick. I fished out the binoculars from the glove pocket, and after adjusting the focus, trained them unsteadily on the bonnet. Nothing emerged except a large smear on the lens, but after a rub with my handkerchief the image became clear. And what I saw filled me with dread and a numbing sense of déjà vu. 'You're wrong,' I said flatly. 'I think it is theirs.'

'Hardly, old boy,' replied Nicholas.

'What do you mean, Francis? asked Primrose sharply.

'Different number plates, but it has a British right-hand drive – and very few of those are made, most are for the export market. I noticed it in Dieppe, quite a rare feature. And also,' I said, getting more agitated, 'the bonnet badge is missing, just like theirs was, *and* they had shoved on a square wing mirror – the standard one is round. And this one's exactly the same . . .' I moved the binoculars up an inch to scan the hood, and glimpsed what I had feared. 'It's them, I tell you . . . Oh my God, they're after us!' And I shrank down in the seat, fully expecting a bullet in my neck at any moment.

'Well, unless there's a corpse in the passenger seat, it won't be Climp,' muttered Nicholas, pushing the speedometer up to ninety. We hurtled along at the rate of knots, but sneaking a furtive look I saw the Austin gaining rapidly. It must have been doing well over a ton.

Suddenly the sparse traffic thickened and Nicholas was forced to ease the pedal. 'Watch out!' Primrose cried. 'There's a crossroads ahead and it's *priorité à droite*, you'll have to give way.'

'Only a farm cart,' he murmured, 'we can beat that.' With a surge of power he briskly bypassed a dawdling *deux chevaux* and sailed over the intersection. I closed my eyes. What would be worse, the resurrected Mullion or the French police?

We speeded on. 'It's still there,' said Primrose, 'and there's definitely someone in the passenger seat. He must have another accomplice!'

'Bastards,' I muttered, clutching Bouncer nervously. The dog gave me a gormless look.

'Look!' Primrose cried again. 'They're flashing their lights. They must want us to stop – we're going to be hijacked!'

'Like fuck,' muttered Nicholas, slowing slightly as we approached a roundabout. The Austin-Healey sailed up alongside and I recognized the roughly sewn patch on its canvas hood. This is when they do it, I thought, this is when they take us out . . . And then with a blast of its horn, the car veered to the right, screeched into the roundabout and took off in the direction of Paris.

'I am sure that bitch waved,' said Primrose. We were sitting at the roadside, recovering our nerves with the final dregs of Ingaza's whisky. 'What was it she said to you about wanting to live dangerously . . . something about fast cars and Monte Carlo?'

'Yes,' I answered, 'but I guess Paris is as good as Monte Carlo, better probably – especially if one were thinking of opening a language school there.'

Primrose gave a wry laugh. 'You mean business research on the one hand and making whoopee on the other.'

'It has been known.'

'Disgraceful,' Nicholas said. 'So unprofessional!'

I poured him the final drop of whisky. 'If you don't mind my saying – you did rather miscalculate over its hiding place, didn't you? I wonder why they found it so soon.' He shrugged, and looked piqued.

'They must have wanted something from the shed,' Primrose suggested.

'I told you, there was nothing *there*, only some old sacks,' he muttered irritably.

'Containing what?' she pressed.

'How should I know? Fertilizer or some such.'

'Oh well,' replied Primrose, 'that's it then.'

'What is?'

'Lavinia mentioned it at the funeral. She was sick to death of Boris's geraniums. He had insisted on planting them year in year out and always in the same colour. She said that now autumn was here it was just the time to root out the whole lot and establish a shrubbery. The only problem was the soil: it was very poor and would need masses of fertilizer. She said she couldn't wait – was raring to have a go at it.'

'Huh,' I said, 'raring to have a joy ride in that sports car too, I assume, and frighten us all to death.' I paused, thinking about it. 'You know, that Turnbull is a cool customer – bashes Boris's brains out, strangles and hangs Castris, and then, switching number plates, whisks the widow off in someone else's car for a jolly in Paris. Can't think where he gets the nerve – or the energy.'

'Didn't you say something about her wanting to dance the tango until six in the morning? Presumably he's got that in prospect as well. I can't see you doing that, Francis.'

'No,' I mused ruefully, 'a waltz is about my limit.'

There was a discreet cough from Nicholas. 'As it happens, the tango is rather my forte – Snake Hips Ingaza, that's my name in the Brighton Palais. In fact, Primrose, once we get back on terra firma I'll treat you to a night out and a demonstration. Eric won't mind . . . I have cups, you know,' he added modestly.

'How nice,' murmured Primrose.

'So where did you acquire this remarkable talent?' I asked.

'Aunt Lil of course.'

We returned to the car, and at a more seemly pace resumed our journey. I still felt shaken at what had happened, and kept seeing images of the wretched Austin-Healey zipping towards us like some pursuing silver nemesis. Already the memory was assuming a bizarre, surreal quality; but for its short time the experience had been only too palpable.

I ruminated, astonished at how carefree Turnbull and Lavinia had seemed. What on earth had possessed them to zoom up to us so brazenly, with flashing lights and blaring horn? Turnbull had been driving. Had he been experiencing some sort of triumphal rush of adrenalin, a flow of euphoric relief at having successfully discharged his dreadful tasks? . . . I cast my mind back to my own reactions after the Fotherington event, but could recall little except a sense of prolonged numbness and blankness. Somehow everything had seemed very prosaic. Flat really. Although I do remember enjoying a strawberry ice cream on Brighton beach and speaking briefly to a rather inquisitive little Cairn terrier. But I don't think one could have called those actions euphoric exactly . . .

Primrose broke in on my thoughts: 'But you know, what I don't understand is Lavinia. Do you think she was in cahoots with Rupert all along – that it was a joint project and she was as keen as he was to dispose of hubby? Or is she so dense that she hasn't a clue he did it, and is just glad to have found her freedom so she can be whirled off to Paris for weekends?'

'I don't think Lavinia is dense,' I said thoughtfully. 'She may simply be shrewd – i.e. is keeping her head down and deliberately not asking questions or showing suspicions. I think she is exploiting his death while ostensibly, at least, not being complicit.'

'You mean keeping her nose clean and affecting ignorance; acknowledging nothing – either to herself or to anyone else – in the hope it will just fade away? A bit like all of us in fact.'

'Something like that,' I agreed.

'Safest policy, dear boy. Never does to get too involved – can lead to all manner of unsavoury entanglements. I am sure the good bishop would be the first to agree,' said Ingaza. 'By the way, what are the current odds on his promotion?'

'Depends on the height of the parapet,' I said.

'Getting pretty close now,' announced Nicholas. 'Little sod needs his pill.'

I looked at Bouncer, now fully awake and on his haunches, quizzing eagerly the passing cows and poplars. 'It seems a pity,' I murmured.

'It will seem even more of a pity when he is impounded and detained in quarantine for six months,' he rejoined tartly.

'Yes, you are right,' I said. 'But even when he is out for the count, how are we going to hide him? I'm not sure if there's much air in the boot – enough for a cat perhaps, but not for a dog Bouncer's size. Besides, they might open it up.'

'He can be left on the back seat,' said Primrose.

'Oh yes, in full view of every passing passenger and official,' I replied sarcastically.

'Not if we use flowers.'

'Flowers? What *are* you talking about?'

'We can drape him in one of those absurd surplices that Nicholas had the whisky wrapped in, and then smother him in swathes of lilies and late chrysanthemums. It will just be assumed we are en route to a funeral or a wedding. Flowers are like children, always presumed innocent, never linked with the base or subversive. People will take one look and think, Ah, how lovely . . . and pass on by.'

'But suppose he wakes up in this bed of floral pulchritude, and starts sniffing the perfumed air?'

'Well, you will just have to double the dose. Feed him two pills instead of one.'

'Can't we find any other flowers? Those sound a bit death-like to me.'

'Not at this time of year. Besides, that might be to our advantage, especially if we sit there looking solemn.'

There was a snort of mirth from Nicholas. 'Poor old bugger – he's going to be a right little Queen of the May! That'll teach him to hitch lifts to foreign ports. Should have stayed at home with the wolfhound.'

'So where's all this stuff coming from?' I asked sceptically.

'There are a couple of nice-looking florists in Dieppe,'

Primrose explained. 'I noticed them after we docked and when our knowledgeable driver was meandering around losing his way all over the place ...'

'Reconnoitring is the word, my dear,' observed Ingaza mildly.

We reached Dieppe in plenty of time to walk both dog and cat, and for Primrose to buy armfuls of grossly overpriced blooms. And although I had administered the first of Bouncer's knock-out drops, I still wasn't really sure what to do with Maurice. Unlike the dog, he is not amenable to pills of any kind, and though coercion might have worked, I found the prospect both distasteful and fatiguing. Tentative enquiries about Primrose's handbag had been met with obdurate silence.

'Let the cat live dangerously,' said Nicholas. 'He chose to come in the boot and he can take his chance and go back in it. If you remember, there wasn't a peep out of him coming over. None of us had a clue he was there.'

'Perhaps,' I said doubtfully, 'but supposing Customs take a look anyway. I mean, even if he was asleep they would still see him, especially if they were rooting around for smuggled goods.'

Nicholas shrugged. 'Wear your dog collar. Take a gamble. It's what's known as operating on a wing and a prayer – you should know about that, I imagine.'

And so that's what we did: gave Bouncer another pill, spread the white surplice over him and piled on the flowers. He looked like a sort of canine version of St Thérèse of Lisieux. Maurice for once was amazingly co-operative and, with eyes tightly shut and nursing Belvedere's glass eye between his paws, appeared to fall fast asleep curled under Primrose's hat. I closed the lid of the boot gently.

I think it must have been the blend of lilies and dog collar that did it, but whatever the reason, we evidently passed muster ... although I did notice a rather sleeked official with gold-braided cuffs giving Ingaza a beady look, but that may have been merely the glad eye. Ingaza himself registered nothing, for by that time he was already turning an anticipatory green. Once we were parked in the hold, he slid away swiftly to the purser's cabin. Primrose too disappeared, muttering something about ordering her quota of Je Reviens from the tiny Duty Free stall before stocks ran out.

Left alone I strolled up on deck, and in the face of the wind fumbled to light a Craven 'A'. I took a puff and gave a tentative sigh of relief. The quays of Dieppe gradually slipped away, and we chugged out of the harbour into the open Channel bound for Newhaven and the Sussex coast. Last lap, I thought. Hallelujah!

A grateful gin seemed appropriate and I made my way to the saloon, which was more crowded than on the voyage out. But pressing through the throng I managed to place an order the moment the shutters went up. There were few vacant seats at the tables, and in any case at this stage of the journey the idea of fraternizing with fellow passengers was not particularly enticing. I could remember the results from the previous time ...

Leaning on the bar, I was just about to take my first sip, when a familiar voice boomed in my ear: 'That's a bit measly, isn't it, Francis? You can make mine a double, if you please.' I swung round and was confronted by the beaming face of Mrs Tubbly Pole.

Suppressing shock and horror, I said faintly, 'Well, I never!' and mechanically signalled to the barman. Apart from a jaunty French beret and voluminous gabardine now replacing the Bud Flanagan hat and draped fur coat, she looked much as when I had last seen her in the midnight purlieus of Maida Vale, a fugitive from justice after her bulldog's dispatch of a neighbour's Yorkshire terrier.

'So good to see you, Francis!' she chortled. 'How's tricks? Been on some jolly hols, have you?'

There flashed through my mind a picture of Boris bludgeoned at the water's side, Climp's body inert and bleeding on the granite plateau, Mullion being beastly by the duck pond and poor little Castris strung up on his dining-room doorpost. 'Oh yes,' I said, 'very jolly.'

'Good, good! That's what I like to hear,' she exclaimed. 'You parsons, you need to get out and about. Gives you a perspective on things.'

Refraining from saying that I had had enough perspective to last me a lifetime, I asked how her crime novels were doing and whether she had had a successful American tour.

'Excellent on both counts,' she crowed. 'Dear Alfred has read all my books – even my very first one, *Blood Must Flow*, and he's so eager to get going. But of course I said that I would have to ask you first.'

'Ask *me*?' I exclaimed. 'What ever are you talking about . . . and who's Alfred?'

'Alfred Hitchcock, of course. He's going to make a film of my last novel – the one based on my interpretation of the Molehill murder. I told you in my letter. Didn't you get it? . . . Ah, too busy gadding in France no doubt. Anyway, we have both decided that *you* should have a walk-on part – it would give a delightful touch of authenticity if there were a real clergyman in the midst of all the fictional shenanigans, especially one who knew the actual victim so well. You'll love it.'

I closed my eyes; opened them and said woodenly, 'But I thought Hitchcock always did the walk-on.'

'Oh, he will be doing that as usual of course, but the idea is that you should be coming from the *other* direction and you will both meet and cross over in mid-screen. Actually, if I play my cards right I'm sure I can wangle you a small speaking part, you know, just a few words – what do you think of that!'

I began to feel an appalling sense of unreality, and placed a steadying hand on the bar counter not sure whether my whirling head was to do with the motion of the boat or the bombshell of her news. Either way the effect was intense. 'What sort of words?' my voice asked.

'Oh, such as, "If you ask my opinion, the lady was done to death not in the belfry but in the wood."'

I gazed at her in scandalized silence.

'Well, come on, what do you think? Speak!'

I cleared my throat. 'Er ... I say, how's your bulldog these days?'

'Oh, Gunga Din is on topping form, and I can't tell you how *much* the little man is longing to see you.' She clapped her hands excitedly, picked up her glass, and giving it a gay flourish cried, 'Meanwhile, bottoms up, dear Francis, here's to our joint venture on to the silver screen!' She seized my arm. 'Now, there are many things we need to discuss ...'

36

The Dog's Diary

Do you know what? They drugged me up to the eyeballs, up to the eyeballs they did! Yes, just like that time when I was a puppy and my first master, Bowler, took me to the vet's to have a bit of ham bone taken out of my gullet. It was the same thing all over again, except that this time I had cracking dreams. I mean *really* cracking. All about duffing up Maurice and shoving his haddock where you wouldn't normally expect it to go. And then there were some to do with savaging the organist's ankles, and others about chasing a giant bunny who kept yelling, 'Mercy, mercy, Master Bouncer, I'll be your servant for life!' But the best of all was the one when F.O. hung a red ribbon round my neck with a medal that said 'Take note: the best Bouncer in the world.' That was really good. The more I think about it the more I know they were some of the best dreams I have ever had. Wouldn't mind getting my paws on a few more of those pills if that's what they do.

As a matter of fact I think the cat is a bit jealous because when I told him about how nice it all was, he narrowed his eyes and said in that hoity-toity voice of his that it was obvious I was turning into a dope fiend. I said I didn't care what I was turning into as long as it did the trick . . . Mind you, waking up wasn't so good. I thought at first I was in the churchyard along with all those other buggers. I could hardly breathe! There was this mass of flowers on top of me with leaves and twigs and whopping great petals, and a sort of white sheet that my hind legs were all tangled up in. The smell was cat-awful – all sweet and sickly. Thought I might throw up, and the only way I could stop myself was by trying to remember really *good* smells like dustbins, the inside of O'Shaughnessy's kennel, the pig yard at that foreign place we were at, and the gatepost of Pierre the Ponce's house when he has just lifted his leg. As long as I could concentrate on those I was all right – just.

And then there was suddenly the Prim's voice saying, 'Oh look, Francis, he's woken up. I've just seen his eye rolling!' I must have still been pretty dazed because when I heard her say that I began to think about Maurice's new eye, the one he's so pleased with – the one I got for him from under the stiff's head. And that made me think that perhaps one of *my* eyes was made of glass too, and I didn't like that much so started to kick up a fuss. Next thing was I heard the Brighton Type saying, 'Oh, for pity's sake, put a sock in it!' That made me feel better because I knew things must be back to normal and that I was among the humans safe on the back seat of the car – with both my peepers working and F.O.'s fag smoke curling all round my snout. But I still felt a bit uncomfy as there was something stuck in my collar behind my ear. It turned out to be one of those stupid flowers, and for some reason this made them all laugh, especially when the Type said, 'Well, Francis, you've got a right little Carmen Miranda there!' Don't know what he meant by that, but I wasn't having it, I can tell you. So I set up a really good racket, and that brought them to heel all right. Quiet as the grave. That's one of Maurice's tips, you know. 'Bouncer,' he said once, 'when the humans are playing silly beggars and you've had enough, just make it clear who's in charge: be as bloody as possible. They soon get the message.' Of course, the cat's got being bloody down to a fine art – bred deep in the bone, if you ask me. But when he puts his mind to it old Bouncer can show 'em a thing or two as well!

37

The Cat's Memoir

Needless to say the dog was in his element. Sprawled on the back seat, wreathed in flowers and a white shroud, he clearly imagined he was in some sort of celestial basket being borne off to Dog Wonderland. He later described to me the dreams he had been having while in this parlous condition: violent and vulgar, as you might expect. But I tried not to flinch and, apart from one or two mild jibes, assumed a tone of awed interest. This seemed to satisfy him and I overheard him telling O'Shaughnessy what extraordinary adventures he had been having and how much 'the cat' was impressed by his friend's heroic endeavours. Hmm . . .

My own journey back was less histrionic and considerably more decorous. For once F.O. had shown a due regard for my preferences and had been thoughtful enough to ensure that the Special Eye was within my grasp. Indeed, he exhibited unusual sensitivity in placing it right between my paws. This I found extremely soothing and I was disposed to be co-operative for the entire voyage.

When we were eventually returned to terra firma – i.e. the Newhaven docks – there was a great palaver as the humans sorted themselves out, lugging their luggage from one car to the other and generally making much fuss and noise. This seems the usual response when they have little to do. Eventually the Brighton Type took off in a cloud of exhaust and brilliantine, and Bouncer and myself were left with the vicar and his sister. Fortunately they were both tired and so our evening in Lewes was uneventful. However, on our trip back to Molehill the following day I recounted to Bouncer what I had gathered about F.O.'s meeting with the Tubbly person on the boat. The dog was still punch drunk from the drugs they had plied him with and so had some difficulty in recalling who Mrs Tubbly Pole actually was. Patiently I reminded him that she was the person who a little while ago had been so insistent on writing a novel based on the unsolved Molehill murder, and whose beloved companion was the moronic inebriate bulldog, Gunga Din. Reference to this last name perked the dog up considerably and he recovered his limited wits quite quickly. 'Oh,' he growled, 'you mean the loud lady with the bastard idiot!'

'Precisely,' I agreed, 'but from what I overheard of the garbled remarks in the car, when we docked she disappeared immediately up to London. It is unlikely she will inflict further unrest upon our master.'

'Sod our master,' the dog grumbled, 'what about me and you?'

Bouncer's syntax is a constant source of irritation to me, and I was about to make a mild correction, when he suddenly said, 'Hang about a bit, Maurice ... Funny you should mention them because now I think of it, I'm pretty sure she was in one of my dreams ... Yes, that's it, she was! Want to hear about it?'

I told him I had heard quite enough of his dreams for one day and did not think I could cope with any more lurid narratives, and if he would excuse me I had important matters to attend to in the shrubbery.

'Busy cat,' he muttered. And raising his hind leg began to scratch.

Settled once more in our accustomed routine, I took it upon myself to visit Florence the Fermanagh wolfhound. There are few dogs (to say the least) whom I respect but the wolfhound is one of them. She is a creature of great poise and much discernment, and can clearly appreciate a prize cat when she meets one. Thus as soon as I felt in the calling mood I set off to find her.

I didn't have to look far. Much of her time is spent sprawling in the middle of her people's drive, but sufficiently near the gateway to wave a graceful paw at random passers-by. (Not too random, you understand. Like myself, Florence is selective in her companions – although she does exhibit a benignity which sometimes I feel is a trifle misplaced. I wonder whether I should tell her . . .)

Anyway, I gave one of my most beguiling mews, and raising her huge head she beamed and summoned me over. 'Good afternoon, Maurice,' she exclaimed. 'I was just thinking about you and Bouncer and wondering how you were both getting on in France, and suddenly here you are in front of me!'

'But Florence,' I said, 'how on earth did you know that Bouncer was with me? I mean, when he took off in the biscuit van you couldn't have known it was destined for Dieppe.'

She looked vague and said she had heard her mistress saying something about it after being telephoned by the vicar, and that in any case her sixth sense always helped her to keep abreast of things. I have to admit to being taken aback by that and not a little peeved. It was one thing having Bouncer rambling on about his sixth sense but to have the wolfhound at it as well was a bit much. I was surprised that she should harbour such delusions. However, every dog has its flaw(s), even one as distinguished as Florence. Thus hiding my irritation I said we had spent a most enlivening time and would she like to hear a little about it.

She said she most certainly would, but that since I was bound to feature prominently in events it might be best if I related it in instalments so that she could digest things at leisure. That struck me as admirably sensible, so after delivering the bare bones I went away promising to return the very next morning. She seemed to think the evening might be better, and so that is what was arranged. It is rare to find such appreciation from another animal, let alone a dog.

38

The Vicar's Version

Maud Tubbly Pole's plans about my role in the filming of her novel *Murder at the Moleheap* were so excruciating that I wasn't sure whether to give way to wild hysteria or cut my throat. In the end I settled for the middle way – prayer and gin. This combination worked surprisingly well, for it meant that when we disembarked she miraculously vanished up to Maida Vale via taxi and boat train, while I was left in a state of tranced insouciance. So insouciant in fact, that after waving the tail end of the Citroën a thankful farewell, I allowed Primrose to take the wheel of the Singer and drive us back to her house in Lewes. Here we collapsed over Marmite sandwiches and smuggled Beaujolais; and with cat and dog fed and bedded, fell to reviewing the past fortnight.

'If you ask me,' my sister opined, 'it is not a holiday I care to repeat.'

'It was never intended as a holiday,' I grumbled, 'merely an excuse for Ingaza to get his hands on a fat fortune at the expense of the rest of us.' I grimaced in painful memory. 'After this caper I think I shall regard Edith Hopgarden, and even Mavis, as benign saviours of my sanity.'

'Want a bet?'

'Not really.'

For a time we brooded in silence, and then Primrose said thoughtfully, 'I wonder what they are doing now.'

'Squabbling over cups of cocoa, I imagine.'

'No not *them*, silly. Turnbull and Lavinia, of course.'

'Probably preparing for a night on the tiles at some swish Paris hotel with Lavinia practising her tango steps for the Latin Quarter.'

'Very likely. I mean, he obviously thinks he's got away with it, and judging from that merry spate of horn-blowing at the roundabout was clearly feeling pretty confident ... Strange really, us being the only ones who know the dark secret!'

'Suspect, not *know* exactly,' I corrected her mildly.

'Huh! As good as. After you seeing those words on his note pad there's no other conclusion.'

'You're probably right, but it's nothing to do with us now. As agreed, we keep our heads down, stay mum and get on with normal life. We shan't see them again.' I yawned, closed my eyes and contemplated with rare comfort the prospect of compiling the lay-readers' rota. Her next words made me open them in startled horror.

'Oh, but we will. At least I should jolly well hope so! Turnbull has negotiated an order for six of my paintings for his London language school when it opens, and I have no intention of letting him renege on the deal.'

I stared at her incredulously. 'But Primrose,' I gasped, 'the man is a murderer and a blackguard!'

'But so are you,' she replied coolly, 'well, murderer at any rate. Though in your case I am not sure whether "blackguard" is quite the right –'

'But I'm different!' I expostulated. 'I –'

'Very different,' was the dry retort. 'You don't have his money, and even less his business sense. Neither are you fly enough to attempt wriggling out of a contract. He just might, and I am not having it. If I don't hear from him within a fortnight I shall be on his trail.' She spoke with that grim resolution which had so flummoxed Pa in her wilder days at the Courtauld. Like him I tried first dispute and then cajoling, but both were met with calm indifference. Primrose has always been intractable, and it was quite obvious that her instinct for commercial gain had been more than encouraged by her association with Ingaza. It was really too bad. And I retired to bed to dream uneasily of the four of them – Primrose, Nicholas, Lavinia and Turnbull – tangoing with sheep in St Botolph's churchyard while I watched helplessly, pinioned to a tombstone by Mavis Briggs.

As nightmares go I suppose it was relatively mild – but enough nonetheless to have me scuttling back to Molehill immediately after breakfast the next day. I think Primrose was slightly put out that I had not tarried to mow the grass and dig the flower beds. But pleading a bad back and a mountain of parish duties, I gathered the animals, and slipping thankfully into the Singer pointed the bonnet firmly in the direction of Surrey and the vicarage.

For three blissful days peace reigned uninterrupted. Mavis Briggs was apparently taking a late holiday in Bexhill and, unless her hostess was desperate enough to develop some rare and sudden malaise requiring immediate isolation, would not be returning for at least a week. The Mothers' Union, in an access of rare wisdom, had mercifully decided to cancel their autumn play-reading – a woeful business in which both Shakespeare and Terence Rattigan were annually mangled in lugubrious monotone. And even more mercifully, my locum had shown himself to be a wizard with paperwork and had actually seemed to revel in challenging the labyrinth of my chaotic filing system. 'Not too good on psalms and such,' he had confided shyly, 'but give me a shamble of desk stuff and I'm as happy as Larry. It beats jigsaws any time. All to do with the tarts,' he added thoughtfully.

'*Tarts*? What tarts?'

'The jam tarts. Our mother used to bribe us with those to keep the playroom tidy. I had the neatest toy-box on the block. And do you know – I could put my hand on a king marble or special Dinky car within five seconds. None of this business of rummaging behind the bookcase or in the school satchel. Oh no, all lined up and ready to go, they were. Never lost a lead soldier in my life!' He spoke with nostalgic pride.

I regarded him respectfully – fat, neat and spruce – and thanked him warmly for his generous attention, observing that I would do my best to retain such pristine order. He beamed amiably. 'They all say that. But you'll only muck it up, they always do. Another week and it'll be like Armageddon again. Still, enjoy it while you can.'

I assured him I was bound to, and apologizing for not having any jam tarts to hand wondered whether walnut cake and whisky might do instead. He said that on the whole he thought perhaps they would.

It was Miss Dalrymple who broke the idyll. I encountered her marching stoutly through the tombs to the east door, hotfoot no doubt on her perennial mission of spying out the chewing gum stuck under the choir stalls. I braced myself for the usual complaints. Surprisingly none came. Instead she greeted me cordially, enquired after my holiday, and then pulling a newspaper from beneath the library books in her basket, said, 'Very odd, that French thing in the Massif Central. Turned out to be one of those missing warders from Broadmoor; though really, what he was doing wandering about in those parts I cannot imagine. Should have taken his holidays in Bournemouth like anyone else – much more appropriate. Shot between the eyes, horrid! Mind you, the French seem to go in for that sort of thing . . . I remember there was that recent business with the poor Drummond family – all very bizarre. Still, at least *you* seem to have survived unscathed, Canon. They tell me it happened quite near where you were staying. Is that so?'

I hesitated, not sure whether to admit a passing knowledge or to plead ignorance of the whole affair. I opted for the latter, saying that my time in France had been mercifully very quiet and uneventful, and since I always confused French place-names I would have to check the map when I got home.

I had the impression that she felt my vagueness was no more than to be expected, and changing the subject she said, 'A nice little man, your locum. *Much* nicer than the awful one we had a couple of years ago – Rum or Rumble something. But I shall be glad when it's you in the pulpit again delivering one of your soothing homilies. This man sounded like Montgomery giving a military briefing: everything was listed and classified. Colonel Dawlish liked it of course, but I could see that some of the older ladies felt distinctly bemused – as if they were being hit by a hail of ping-pong balls! However, he was invaluable on the Ladies' Sewing Night – sorted out all their silks and ribbons quicker than you could say "thimble"; graded Mrs Higgins' needles for her, and even showed Edith Hopgarden the correct way to fold her embroidery cloths . . . being Edith, of course, she didn't like that, but the others took note all right.'

'Splendid,' I beamed, mentally seeing Climp on the high cliff with the bullet between his eyes, and wondering how long it would be before Mullion too was discovered. I also started to wonder how Crumpelmeyer was reacting to his minders' disappearance and what effect, if any, it would have on his lunacy – or indeed his loathing of me . . .

However, such thoughts were scattered by Miss Dalrymple's voice exclaiming, '. . . and then, if you please, the dear man ate all the special tarts – every one. Can you imagine!'

'Yes, yes,' I replied hurriedly, 'rather a sweet tooth, I believe, but worth his weight in jam. Most useful.'

'Indeed,' she agreed. 'We must have him again when next you go off on one of your little jaunts. He may be able to sort out the rubble in the vestry.' And tapping me lightly on the shoulder with the rolled-up newspaper, she took off in pursuit of the chewing gum.

Some 'jaunt', I thought moodily, as I wandered disconsolately back to the vicarage racking my brains as to what sort of 'soothing homily' I could devise for Sunday's sermon: the necessity and rewards of gritted teeth in the face of remorseless adversity, perhaps ... I mused. Rewards? Not a hope!

At the gate I was met by Bouncer who, now fully recovered from his enforced 'bed-rest', seemed in particularly matey mood. He belted over, pawed my knees and shook the shaggy tail in frenzied salute. His expression I could not see, shrouded as it was by cascading fringe and beard, but I assumed it was one of riotous welcome. I also caught sight of Maurice lurking behind the water butt and eyeing me intently – though rather surprisingly with a demeanour bordering on the benign. I guessed their recent experiences must have made them thankful for small mercies and that, like myself, they had discovered life in the vicarage could be a lot worse. Together we went into the house, where after gin, pilchards and Bonios we settled down for the evening: they to their snoozes, me to the emollient sermon. If Miss Dalrymple et al. would feel better after such comforts who was I to cast a cloud?

Clouds rolled in thick and fast the following day. First there was the postcard from Bexhill: Mavis Briggs extolling the charms of that resort and trusting that I was feeling as 'braced' as she after my time in the Auvergne. A postscript made the proposal that she should display her holiday snaps on the church noticeboard, or better still, give a lantern lecture. The prospect of this, let alone the looming poetry recitals, made me feel distinctly unbraced. However, the postcard was merely the prelude to far worse: the arrival of the telegraph boy. This could mean only one thing: Primrose with an edict.

GOT HIM PINNED, the message announced, PAINTINGS IN THE BAG STOP MEETING LONDON NEXT WEEK STOP WANT YOU THERE STOP SHOULD I BUY NEW HAT QUESTION MARK

I pondered the millinery query for some time, for it was a convenient means of stalling thought about the telegram's essential point, namely that Rupert Turnbull would be in London, and that thanks to my dear sister's addiction to money I was to be dragged yet again into his disquieting orbit. My own dastardly act was undeniable, but that did not necessarily fit me for hobnobbing with those of similar ilk. Besides, assuming that Turnbull really had committed the double murder and the blackmailing of the students (and it seemed likely), it put him in a class much above my own blundering capability and which I did not care to join. And in short (to quote the diffident Mr Prufrock) I was afraid . . .

'Fully deserves both fear *and* hanging!', the retort might be. Doubtless. But in the meantime I had Primrose's hat to consider and how best to avoid Mavis Briggs's holiday slides.

39

The Cat's Memoir

He lay sprawled on the terrace in his favourite spot, facing south under F.O.'s study window, the grimy rubber ring two inches from his muzzle. Having important things to say, I approached briskly. And ignoring the snores (suspecting them bogus), I was about to open my mouth, when he growled sleepily, 'Go away, Maurice, you are blotting out the sun – there's not much left of it.'

'I most certainly will not go away,' I replied with asperity, 'there are certain matters which I wish to discuss. So kindly listen.'

He opened an eye, rolled it and shut it again. 'Attend!' I mewed irritably, and gave him a light prod with my unsheathed claw. This produced a histrionic yelp, but it did the trick for he scrambled to his haunches and reluctantly cocked both ears.

'Now look here, Bouncer,' I said, 'you may think that the all clear has sounded, but I can assure you it hasn't. There is more to come.'

'What?'

'I said that there is –'

'What *matters*?'

I paused, surprised at the swift response. 'Matters to do with France and one of the unsavoury characters we encountered there.'

'Which one? Do you mean that porker in the yard who kept winking at me? Or that stupid cat with cross-eyes, or those half-baked ducks by the pond? If you ask me –'

'I am not asking you, I am trying to tell you, so be quiet!' I took a deep breath and continued quickly. 'No, the unsavoury one is not of the animal species but the human. And I think he is about to cause trouble.'

'What's he called?'

'His name is Turnip.'

'Oh, *that* one – the one that did in the corpse by the pool, where I got your Special Eye from. You know, Maurice, that was a jolly good bit of retrieving I did that day … I bet even O'Shaughnessy couldn't have –'

'Yes, yes,' I exclaimed hurriedly, 'utterly brilliant. One is most grateful. Now the point is …' And I proceeded to relate what I had heard F.O. telling his sister on the telephone after the boy with the yellow envelope had called. 'He told her most emphatically,' I explained, 'that she should indeed buy a new hat and that in his opinion it should be at an angle with a short veil.'

The dog stared blankly, sniffed his rubber ring and then said, 'What's hats got to do with the price of fish?'

I sighed. 'Nothing to do with fish but all to do with what to wear when having a social engagement with an assassin in a fashionable part of London. These things have to be carefully thought out.'

'If you say so, Maurice. But supposing he doesn't like the hat? What then – monkey business at the crossroads?' He gave a sinister chuckle. 'And besides, why's the vicar bothering?'

'Because the vicar is going *with* her. And you know what that means – bedlam all round!'

The dog fell silent for a while, and then said in a faraway voice, 'Hmm, no wonder I couldn't settle in the crypt the other day. Kept scratching and feeling odd. Thought it was the ghosts and spiders ganging up on me, but I can see now it was the old sixth sense getting into gear.'

'Oh yes,' I said sceptically, 'and what does it have to say this time?'

He pondered, and then said slowly, 'It says that there is trouble ahead.'

'Well, of course there is trouble ahead,' I cried impatiently. 'Haven't I just said so!'

'Ah, but you didn't mention the bulldog.'

'*What*?' I said sharply.

'Gunga Din of course, the large lady's dog. I tried to tell you – he was in one of my dreams when they gave me the pills. I dreamed F.O. had bumped into Mrs T. P. on the boat coming back and that she was dead keen to see him again … That's it, I remember now, they were drinking at the bar and she was going on about her "sweet little poppet". Funny the way dreams work, isn't it, Maurice?'

'Hilarious.'

'Yes,' the dog snuffled thoughtfully, 'in fact, now I put my nose to it, I can sniff old Gunga in the wind. Won't be long now, I shouldn't wonder.'

I stared at him in dismay. 'You don't mean to say that we are to be involved with Mrs Tubbly Pole and her gin-toping stooge *again*? And this on top of the Turnip fellow and after all I have gone through abroad!'

'Looks like it,' the dog said cheerfully.

'My nerves,' I hissed, 'my mangled nerves!'

'If I were you,' said Bouncer, 'I'd go and have a quick round with your Special Eye. Give it a good drubbing. You'll feel much better afterwards.'

I did as he suggested, but the effects were negligible. And I curled up that evening in a mood of considerable pique, wondering not for the first time why a cat of my singular charms should be plagued by so much human and canine lunacy.